D0393296

Alana Marshall-H... .... hey're Prada, Tiffany, and Gucci. The African-American princess has never met a pricey retailer that didn't practically cry with joy the minute she pranced in. But now that her credit-card bills have exceeded the price of her college tuition, her parents have cut her off. They even want her to get a (gasp) job! Alana's not going down without a fight. After all, she gets credit-card applications in the mail every day, and where there's a will to shop, there's a way . . . right?

Tall, blond Hailey Starrett grew up on a farm, making jams with her hippie parents. Now, she's making up for lost time by shopping till she drops. Hailey's determined to make it as an actress in NYC, and she just might succeed . . . if she can keep herself from spending all her money on shoes, clothes, and accessories. The blond beauty's just been given the chance of a lifetime—starring on a soap opposite daytime's hottest hunk . . . and nastiest diva. But being in the spotlight means even more pressure to look good, and looking good doesn't come cheap. Or does it?

Witty, wicked, and laugh-out-loud funny, *Retail Therapy* is a nonstop romp through New York's dressing rooms, green rooms, VIP rooms, and rooms-for-improvement—proof positive that with a little ingenuity, a lot of moxie, and true friends, any girl can live the high life without breaking the bank.

"If readers thought Becky Bloomwood of *Shopaholic* fame was bad, wait until they meet Alana Marshall-Hughes . . . The author of *Party Girls* and *Girls' Night Out* again delivers a lighthearted, entertaining comedy."—*Booklist*

Books by Roz Bailey

PARTY GIRLS

GIRLS' NIGHT OUT

RETAIL THERAPY

POSTCARDS FROM LAST SUMMER

Published by Kensington Publishing Corporation

Retail Therapy

ROZ BAILEY

KENSINGTON PUBLISHING CORP.
http://www.kensingtonbooks.com

Part One

LONDON LEDGER

**Page Six—Fab New Designer Linked
to Aztec Princess**

**Are They Playing "Hide the Bangers,"
Or Simply Playing to the Crowd?**

1

Alana

There is nothing quite as sweet as the taste of success. At this particular event, the accolades were being showered upon my friend Pierre, a young couture designer who was showing his line in Europe for the first time; however, since I had been linked to him in the press, I felt that my fashionable presence elevated his turnout here in London. The fact that they'd called me an Aztec princess had made me laugh, though I knew that if my father, the descendant of slaves from the Underground Railroad, ever saw the piece, veins would pop in his forehead. Poor Daddy took these things way too seriously.

Now cameras flashed around me as Pierre dashed onto the stage and took a dramatic bow. I was already on my feet in the first row, clapping as loudly as my gold lame gloves would allow. Not that my applause would be noticed amid the audience roar. London's celebrity crowd adored Pierre's fashions almost as much as they adored the skinny, self-effacing brother who now blew kisses to the audience. Let me tell you, he'd come a long way from his days as Pete Brown, the ambiguous genius at Harvard who was afraid to tell his parents that he was minoring in design. My boy Petey had hit the big-time, and I was happy to be counted among Pete-turned-Pierre's supporters.

"You go, Pierre!" I called, lifting my chin slowly so as not to tumble the gorgeous gold Aztec-princess headdress he'd designed for me. It was the perfect centerpiece of my Pierre original—a black sheath trimmed in gold, gold gloves, strappy black Manolo Blahniks.

Just then Pierre turned toward me and extended a hand, and the spotlight turned my way. In a gush of exhilaration, I moved sleekly toward the stairs, stepped up to the stage, struck a sultry pose that showed off Pierre's couture and my well-toned curves to advantage.

Let me tell you, there is a sensual thrill that hits when you are the object of so much admiration. Not the personal rush of the big O, but a real power rush. Yes, success is sweet.

We rode that sweet river of honey backstage, hugging each other and doing air kisses with the bony models.

"You are the ultimado!" Pierre told me.

"No, *you* are!" I insisted, nudging the shoulder of his dapper silk brocade jacket. He staggered back, the little twig. "Did you see who was out there?"

"Someone mentioned Uma. And Sir Ian. Sarah Jessica. And Ms. Hilton straight from the farm. Could it be true? Here in London?" He clasped his hands to his face. "How did I ever pull this off? I am so unworthy."

"Get out!" I linked my arm through his, tempted to remind him of the way his parents had disowned him, the catcalls he'd elicited on the streets of Cambridge when trying out his own designs, the pervasive misery he'd been mired in at the math department. "Sweetie-Petey, you endured a lot to get here. Own it and enjoy it."

His boyish, cutie-pie face dimpled with joy as he squeezed my arm. "Thanks, Alana. You're the best . . ."

His words faded as the stage manager let loose a swarm of reporters who thronged around Pierre, looking for quotes and off-color remarks for the London tabloids. Someone insinuated that I was Pierre's mistress, and I managed to keep myself from laughing, wondering how they could look at my dear friend and see a heterosexual bone in his body. Not that I really cared if they started rumors about us. Neither of us was involved with anyone at the moment, and if a little posing could land Pierre in the scandal sheets, more publicity to him.

Someone tapped the shoulder of my silk gown—Darla, one of Pierre's "people." "We got two calls during the show from a Judge Marshall-Hughs," she said. "Says he's your father. He's trying to reach you."

He'd left a message earlier at the hotel, but since it didn't sound frantic, I'd tucked him into the back of my mind until the show ended. "Thanks, Darla," I said, moving away from the reporters. Perhaps now would be a good time to deal with Daddy, who didn't abide having his calls dodged. I told Darla that I'd meet the group down the block at Taman Gang, the restaurant we'd booked for the after-show celebration. Then I retrieved my tiny little beaded black bag and headed out.

Contrary to London's reputation, it was not raining but cool and sunny—early May. I turned on my cell and retrieved Daddy's progressively agitated messages. Lord, give that man some patience! As I strolled toward the restaurant, quite aware I was turning heads in my Aztec-princess garb, I came upon a shop I couldn't resist called Solid Foundations. It was a tiny little place that featured men's underwear in endless varieties:

briefs, boxers, and bikinis in cotton, silk, and various blends. I found myself drawn in by the frank presentation of underwear on plastic mannequins with rather appealing bulges. Did I mention that it had been a while since I'd had a boyfriend? Maybe too long . . .

In any case, I couldn't resist acquiring a few "foundations." Not sure what Daddy preferred, I got him three pairs of Dolce & Gabbana ribbed boxer briefs—a conservative design befitting an elder statesman, judge, and father. For Pierre, I found black jersey trunks with the sweetest little heart buttons closing the fly—so precious I was tempted to snag a pair for myself, though I knew these tapered shorts would lack the capaciousness my little butt required. Did I say capaciousness? I would have to tell Daddy those two years of Harvard tuition were paying off.

I was waiting for the clerk to wrap my purchases when my beaded bag began to vibrate—my cell. I flipped it open, not bothering to look at the caller ID. "Daddy! I was just about to call you."

"Alana!" he barked, clear as a bell. Hard to believe he was across the pond in New York City. "Where the hell are you? Yesterday I got a call from the credit card company about approving an over-the-limit charge from Paris. What in God's name are you doing in Paris?"

"Paris was yesterday! Today I'm in London." The Foundations clerk, a gangly young man in an ill-fitting tie, shot me a look of awe. I smiled back; maybe that would just make his day.

"London! What are you doing in London?"

"At the moment, I'm buying you some underwear."

The clerk smirked, and I rolled my eyes as Daddy began to sputter. "Why would you do that? I don't need underwear!"

I held the phone away for a second. "No need to shout," I said. "I can hear you just fine. I'm here to support Pierre in his fashion debut. He's been doing shows in all the key cities. A little off-season, I know, but people seem hungry for some new designs. Milan is next, and then—"

"I don't want to hear about Milan! I want you to tell me why I'm supposed to pay a two-thousand-dollar restaurant tab from Paris."

"Did it come to that much?" I sighed. "I wasn't sure about the conversion rate."

"You need to come home."

"Next week." I gathered up my purchases and mouthed a "thank you" to the clerk. "I'll be back next Sunday. Didn't Mama tell you? I'm taking her shopping for new furniture for the Hamptons house. I've already done the sitting room, but—"

"Apparently there are many things your mama has not seen fit to illuminate."

Uh-oh. A big uh-oh. Daddy had discovered a breach—possible budget violation.

"What's that supposed to mean?" I asked in a teasing voice.

"Your charges have come up on my American Express account. How did you get a card on my account?"

Mama, of course, but I wasn't about to give her up. "Is that what's bothering you? No problem. I'll stop using it."

"Come. Home. Now." His voice was packed with a powdery anger.

"Daddy, is everything OK?"

"Everything will be fine when you get yourself home and sit down with me and set the record straight." His voice boomed, imperious, commanding. Can't you just imagine the scales of justice upon his shoulders? Judge Daddy sometimes acted as if the world were his courtroom.

"Can it wait till after Milan?" I asked sweetly.

"No, it cannot wait. I want you home. Tonight."

"But the Concorde doesn't fly anymore . . ."

"That . . . what the . . . ?" he blustered. "I wouldn't want you spending that kind of money even if it flew you to the moon and back! Get yourself on the next flight home, Alana. If not, punitive measures will be taken." Ever the judge, but the man was serious.

Disappointment seeped cold into my veins as I stepped out onto the trendy London street. "Would tomorrow be OK? Remember, we're a few hours ahead of you."

"Today," he barked, and I imagined his gavel falling in the background.

Case closed. Defendant to return home.

As I strolled past a shop window filled with tempting lotions and perfumes and waited to connect to the airlines, I couldn't shake a pang of worry over the tone in Daddy's voice. He sounded angry, frustrated, impatient. Typical Daddy, ruining my little junket with Petey. But that curvy, lavender bottle of lotion looked so delicate in the window. I could picture it on the console in the guest bathroom of the Hamptons house, right beside a bowl of floating sterling roses and that blue mosaic sculpture I'd had shipped home from Paris.

I plugged the earpiece into my cell and pushed into the boutique. I had to have that lavender bottle. Daddy would understand, once he saw the way it all came together at the beach house.

In the end, he always mellowed with me, realizing I wasn't some icky lawbreaker yammering away in his court. I was his baby, his little pork chop. I tried to keep that endearment under wraps, but in tense moments the recollection seemed to soothe my father. Yes, a tender hug from the little pork chop was good for ten grand on the Visa bill. Ha! Maybe even twenty!

NEW YORK SOAP SCOOP

Will Daytime's Undersea Maiden
Be Sent Swimming?

2

Hailey

First, let me tell you how I was dressed that day on the set, because I'm the kind of person whose confidence hinges on the right attire. I was wearing my favorite pair of jeans—worn soft on the thighs and knees, the blue washed out to a powdery shade, the pockets jutting hard over my hipbones to reveal just a hint of tight tummy. I have always been thin with the long legs of a dancer (though I don't have the moves to survive Simon on *American Idol*) and jeans suit me well. Denim can be so flattering on beanpole legs, and I think blue jeans are reminiscent of the good things about America, like baseball and apple pie. With my golden blond hair—not from Bergdorf's, I swear!—and my wiry, athletic legs, I think the jean thing sort of rings midwestern for me, which should give me a squeaky edge when I'm competing for a part against scores of cold, semi-goth beauties and sultry brunettes with a blue henna sheen on their hair that makes your eyes fritz.

Of course, I dressed up the jeans with a fabulous shell pink tank and off-the-shoulder three-quarter sleeve T from Nine West, with matching pink sandals that tied around my ankles. The sandals and the tank had tiny pink and black polka dots—maybe you saw them recently in *Vogue?*—and the two-inch heel in the back made my legs look impossibly long, combining denim cool with flirty spring fashion.

Not that I think I'm all that or anything, but I figure that if I want to be a major player in daytime television, it's time that I started dressing like a star. Two years ago, I landed the part of Ariel on *All Our Tomorrows.* I'm the girl found swimming in the river under Indigo Falls—the one who may or may not be a mermaid, may or may not be the sneaky heir to the fortune of Preston Scott, may or may not be the child of Meredith Van Allen, the megadiva of daytime played by Deanna Childs. Ten or so years ago Deanna's baby was snatched from her crib by a pack of wolves and reportedly carried off into the hills where she was raised by toothless mountain men. By my math, that would make me about ten years old; fortunately, soap-opera time can be conveniently warped.

Need the *Soap Opera Digest* version? Suffice it to say that I'm a young actress from the Midwest who got a thirteen-week contract to play a mysterious character in the show that stars the Hope diamond of daytime— Deanna. The show's producers have re-signed me a few times, but so far, reception to my character seems to be a little lukewarm, which really hurts me. Even if I don't write the story, it's me that's stepping out there. That's me, Hailey Starrett, on your TV screen, and although I played it cool and even on the set, inside I was crumbling.

"I'm not sure if people like me," I'd worried to my friend Alana one day over a skim decaf cappuccino. I'd been suffering a self-confidence freak prompted by a phone call from my agent during which she'd relayed that the show's executive producer wasn't sure she wanted to sign me on for another thirteen weeks. My agent, whom I'd nicknamed Cruella, for obvious reasons, never minced words when delivering bad news. "I don't know what to do," I whimpered as I tore at the cardboard sleeve around my coffee cup. "What if they don't like me?"

"Of course they like you," Alana had insisted. "Don't be getting all misty-eyed over the whims of a bunch of producers who talk up their asses. You're a talented actress, and you know it."

"But I want to keep this part. I need this part."

"Honey, you don't need them." Alana tapped powdered cocoa onto the foam of our cappuccinos and handed me a spoon. It was a ritual of ours—savoring the foam of our skim cappuccinos as if they were ice cream sundaes. She lapped up the foam and stared off into the distance, calculating and dreaming as if a vision were playing out like an MTV video. "You know what you really need?" she said, her eyes alight like a clever cat. "You need some retail therapy. A shopping trip."

While I knew my budget wasn't ready for Alana's whim, there was no denying the therapeutic charms of an inspired purchase. Although Alana and I had been roommates for a year at that time, the moment had forged a bond like no other. We'd decided that an aspiring star needed to dress like a real star. Before our lattes could cool, we'd hopped a cab up to Bloomingdale's, where I'd found a fabulous Marc Jacobs skirt with a flounced ruffle at the bottom and matching sleeveless top. After that it was Saks Fifth Avenue for new jeans, which is where Alana decided that denim was to be my trademark.

"You wear jeans so well, and with your blond hair, it just speaks of fields of daisies and cornflowers," Alana said from her throne in the dressing room. She leaned over her brown legs to wipe a speck of soot from her Prada mules, then smiled in inspiration. "You're the leggy, midwestern girl-next-door, the girl every mama wants her son to date, the girl every boy wants to marry."

"Do ya think?" A ball of insecurity, I modeled the jeans in the mirror.

"Absolutely. Jeans will be your trademark."

From that day on, I worked to fulfill the image of myself as the young actress spotted around Manhattan in her casual jeans and designer tops. Alana's decree had reassured me, but it was the shopping process that provided the real breakthrough. Shopping eased the pain. Shopping washed away my insecurities. Shopping was something I could do pretty darned well.

And now, shopping was something I could do to advance my career.

That revelation had brought on a flurry of retail excursions with Alana, a girl with a fashion sensibility so powerful it should be bottled and sold in the boutique section at Henri Bendel's. Nurturing, generous, stylish Alana . . . thank God for her! A store crawl with Alana made up for all the thrills I never had as a kid, the child of two latent hippies who fled their Wall Street investment careers to put up jams on a farm in Wisconsin. While girls in my class were stocking up on the latest "it" jeans and boots and sweater sets from Neiman Marcus, I was stuck wearing caftans made from weird fabrics hand-woven by alpaca ranchers in the Peruvian mountains. Rule to live by: never wear clothes designed by alpaca ranchers.

Anyway, it was Alana who had insisted that I spring for these amazing pink-and-black polka-dotted shoes, which I now admired. I sat in a director's chair on the set of *All Our Tomorrows*, flexing my ankles, worrying over a smudge of gray near the pinkie toe of my left foot. Had I stepped in chewing gum on the subway, or was it just one of those indeterminate spooge stains that plagued shoes that walked the streets of New York? Let me tell you, contrary to the mythology of *Sex and the City*, it is quite difficult to maintain the pristine condition of your favorite shoes in New York City; one misstep in the park and your favorite mules are history. Pigeons, pollution, and urinating men be damned!

As I admired my retro Nine West shoes, the set began to perk up, with assistant directors summoning staff, the props guy wheeling out his cart, the cameramen taking their places and chatting with each other on their headsets. It was early in the morning and none of the actors were in makeup yet, since we would do a quick run-through to figure out blocking and camera angles. My friend Rory Kendricks stumbled over, coffee cup in hand, mimicking a zombie.

"Rough night?" I asked.

He checked his watch. "I closed the Rum Room about, oh, three hours ago." In real life, Rory was a snappy piano player—a blast at parties—and at the moment, he was filling in for Karen, the regular late-night performer in the bar of the Hotel Edison. My closest friend on the cast of *All Our Tomorrows*, Rory played Stone, an aspiring songwriter who earned a living banging out tunes at the local inn. If you're filling in family trees, Stone was also the bastard son of Preston Scott, but that old story had run out of steam a few years ago.

He yawned. "Really, why do I let myself get into these situations? I need my beauty sleep."

"You can sleep when you get old." I crossed my legs so he'd spy the shoes.

"Hellooo? This may be the face of an angel, but the party days are over for me." In truth, Rory does have a gorgeous face. He was just a teenager when he got his start as a print model for Northland, a shopping center outside Detroit. With stunning blue eyes and cheekbones Michelangelo would have liked to sculpt, he would have had a long future in modeling if he'd continued growing. But since it was not to be, Rory had moved to New York and worked as a lounge lizard between acting gigs.

"Don't try the hermit act on me," I said. "Every time we go out, you're the one who stays to close the bar."

"That's because I'm looking for love, darling." He began singing, "Looking for love in all the wrong places . . ."

I winced. "Please! It's too early for country and western, and I think your voice is a little strained from all that rum-running."

He smacked my knee lightly, then stood back. "And what have we here? A new purchase, I take it?"

"You like?"

"I *love*." He lifted one foot for inspection, then gasped. "Tell me these aren't the ones in this month's *Vogue*!"

I nodded like a bobblehead. "With the matching top."

"Oh, you bad, bad girl. I thought you were on a new budget crunch?"

"Well, I am, but I figure Gabrielle is bound to give me another contract here, don't you think?"

His gaze darted back and forth across the set. "Ix-nay on the op-shay alk-tay."

"What? I never did get that code."

He lowered his voice. "Our esteemed EP might be on the set this morning."

I scanned the dark shadows at the edge of the set in

search of the EP—the executive producer, Gabrielle Kazanjian—who is the show runner for *All Our Tomorrows*. She's the big boss, the figurehead at the top of the pecking order, though sometimes network people and stars like Deanna Childs try to elbow her to the side.

There is a very well-defined pecking order on the set of any soap opera, something I learned with chagrin the first day I showed up with my short scene in my sweaty little hands. One of the cameramen had slid his camera beside me, with an enthusiastic "Hey, how's it going?"

I spun around full of warm, fuzzy feeling. I was making a friend my first day on the set! "I'm fine!" I chirped.

But he had already gone on to something else, talking into his headset. "Yeah, he's on vacation this week. Taking time off to renovate the house."

"Excuse me?" I said, not getting the fact that he was not talking to me. Since then I'd learned that his name was Les, but he's never spoken to me since the day I mistook his greeting and he responded with an awkward look. I had breached the cultural barrier, trying to engage someone from another social class, another union—Camera Operators Local 385. Unbelievable. A few more friendly words and the snob police would storm the set and rip up my Screen Actors Guild card.

Two years later, I had learned a few valuable lessons. Never mess with the props or the furniture on the set, as most of it is flimsy junk. Knock on a door too hard and it will pop off its hinges. Bang on a wall and the whole flat might fall to the ground.

Another rule of our show: Diva Deanna reigns supreme.

"Are we ready to rehearse?" one of the assistant directors, Sean Ryder, shouted, holding up his clipboard.

Sean Ryder's booming voice usually quieted things down, and today was no exception.

I slid out of my chair, ready to work, but the crowd seemed to turn inward, parting for a tiny figure dwarfed by cascading red curls. Deanna Childs.

Rory lowered his head to my ear and muttered, "All hail, the queen."

"I'm still waiting on a rewrite," Deanna said sweetly, her lips gleaming with supergloss. "I'll be across the street at Chez Jacques."

As she marched off in a dignified exit, Rory sighed. "The bitch has left the building."

Sean waved him off and tuned into headsets—panic mode. Deanna was refusing to do the scene as written. Nothing new, as she'd pulled this stunt a few times before.

"Can someone contact the writers?" Sean Ryder spoke urgently into the mouthpiece of his headset. "Do the writers even know that Deanna wants a rewrite?"

I crossed my arms and took a deep breath, wishing that one of the overhead lights would fall on her bobbing head and send her into a soap-opera coma that lasted until February 2006 sweeps. From the bored faces of the cameramen to the nervous flurry of the AD's clipboard, I knew I was not alone. Despite her impenetrably strong fan base—a bevy of viewers who assumed Deanna was as sweet, good-natured, and hardworking as her character Meredith Van Allen—Deanna was difficult to work with. She'd gotten a handful of people fired for minor gaffs, had once jabbed a befuddled wardrobe assistant with a straight pin, and was once written up in the tabloids for throwing a tantrum while waiting in line at a local banking institution.

Was I obsessing again? Sounding like an ingrate when I was lucky to have a recurring role? The truth was that Deanna's smug attitude only emphasized that

I was one of the little people—the short-contract players who waited for that call week to week. OK, I was jealous, had just a little professional envy. Given half her success—or just give me a contract!—I would pop out of my limo with a smile and perform the scene as written. I'm a very accommodating person, maybe too accommodating. That's my problem.

"Well, at least this time she came into the building," one of the cameramen muttered. In the past, on days when she didn't like the script, Deanna had refused to leave her limo outside the studio, but phoned the executive producer from her cell that she was stalled on Fifty-seventh Street. "I'm waiting for the rewrite," she'd call to the assistant director through the sliver of open window. When the AD, who had been sent to get her told her that the writers were not revising, she would simply shake her head, say, "Oh, yes, they are," and ease the window shut.

The cameraman's gaffer moved a fat cable and straightened with a grin. "Yeah, so it can't be that bad. Maybe she just wants to buy a little time, have some breakfast." He tucked his thumbs into his belt loops. "Let's get to the craft services table before all the muffins are gone."

Rory yawned. "I'll be napping in my dressing room. Wake me up when hell unfreezes over."

I tinkled my fingers good-bye and flopped back into one of the director's chairs. Should I go over my lines again, or would that make my performance too stale? Memorizing was not a problem for me, but sometimes the lines were so pat that I felt as if I were reciting a nonsensical children's poem.

Wiggling my toes in my beautiful shoes, I hoped that wardrobe would give me something halfway decent to wear today. Since my character had been discovered swimming in Indigo Falls, I'd been stuck in weird turquoise bodysuits and spangly green gowns that made me look like a carp doing the Charleston. Much as I begged for something different, our wardrobe designer simply shook her head. "This is what Gabrielle wants," Jodi kept telling me, with that uncomfortable glint in her eye indicating it was all beyond her control. Translation: Gabrielle had put the kibosh on wardrobe changes in deference to Diva Deanna, whose exclusive size-two wardrobe needed to far outclass any other attire on the show. Deanna shimmered in Chanel. She dined in Dior. She cruised in Calvin and waxed opulent in Oscar. Yes, our wardrobe designer, Jodi Chen, has a fine eye for costuming, and she's been rewarded with two daytime Emmys. But it's always Deanna who wears New York's most spectacular designs soon after they strut down the runways of Seventh Avenue. As for the rest of us, Jodi has to dress us on the down low so that Deanna can reign supreme in fashion splendor.

Did I mention there was a pecking order?

In theory, the executive producer is at the top of the pyramid, and in fact, when Gabrielle is on the set, everyone gives a little nervous smile, knowing that this is the woman who calls to let you know you're off the show. She's very pert and polite, sort of the antithesis of most casual production people with her shiny pantyhose, cashmere sweater sets, and home-blown hair. While the crew usually resembles the leftovers from a collegiate beer blast, Gabrielle comes off like a schoolteacher from an old Disney movie.

So at the top of the pyramid are the executive producer—our very own Mary Poppins—as well as a bevy of network executives who dabble with casting, fuss with the writers on story issues, and attend all the parties.

Then there's the team of writers, whom the actors either love or hate, depending on whether they pass down scripts with lots of dramatic close-ups or meaningless drivel to be recited over cold mugs of coffee. As the writers work in another building, we almost never see them, though when we do have a chance to engage, I notice them eyeing the actors with the wariness of an allergy patient at a petting zoo. Are they confusing us with the characters we play? The indigent, lying, conniving, serial-killing, merry folk of Indigo Hills? I do wonder.

The director has a certain amount of clout: the director is king or queen for the day, with limited power, since various pros trade off in directing each episode. Our directors are fairly easy to work with, as long as they get along with you-know-who.

Today's director, Stella Feinberg, was one of my personal favorites, a no-nonsense woman whose oversize sweaters and nurturing concern made you want to initiate a group hug.

"Ok, ladies and gents," Stella called some thirty minutes after Deanna's dramatic exit. "We have a revised script to work from. Sean and Iris are giving out copies. Read over your lines quickly and we'll do a run-through."

"That was fast," someone commented as I flipped through the revised script in search of my only scene of the day. There it was—a scene with Deanna, not cut, thank God, but significantly changed. In the previous version, my character, Ariel, who was trying to figure out her past (like whether or not she was a mermaid) had approached Meredith (Deanna's character) and accused her of locking Ariel in the pickle barrel and pushing her over Indigo Falls.

No more.

Now Ariel was threatening suicide, confessing that she'd locked herself in the pickle barrel, telling Meredith that she had nothing to live for. The scene ends with Meredith demanding that Ariel pull herself together.

When Ariel curses her for caring, Meredith slaps my character across the face.

Smack! Wham!

"How's that for ending with a punch?" I said aloud. The abrupt violence surprised me, but then again, what did I expect when the writers had squeezed this one out in a matter of minutes?

"Hailey?" Stella glanced at me over her reading glasses. "A word?"

"Sure!" I followed her over to one of the darkened sets, a graveyard scene with a stained statue of a fierce angel in the foreground. Creepy. "What's up?" I asked cheerfully, ever hopeful that she had something to say about my recent performance or Q ratings or a new contract. Directors didn't usually deal with personnel issues, but hey, I could hope.

"It's about the rewrite." Stella threw an arm around my bare shoulders and pulled me into her cable-knit sweater. For a second, I got a mouthful of fuzz and soapy smell.

"My new scene with Meredith?" I lifted my head and wiped a bit of fluff from my lips. "You're not cutting it, are you?"

"No, of course not. But tread carefully, sweetie. The rewrite? The suicide intentions? The slap?" Her brown eyes held a doleful expression. "They were all Deanna's ideas."

"Oh." I tried to absorb the meaning of it as Stella nodded knowingly. "But what does it mean? I mean . . . is Deanna trying to get rid of me? Doesn't she like me?"

Every once in a blue moon, the writers and network took it upon themselves to explore an "issue"—sort of a public service announcement. For the actors, it meant weeks of anorexia, infertility, alcoholism, or Alzheimer's. Recently, there had been some buzz about exploring youth suicide, which could be compelling, yes, but I didn't want my poor Ariel to be the victim of the issue of the month!

"Please, tell me the truth, Stella," I said. "Is Ariel going to kill herself on the show?"

"Honey, for all I know, Ariel could turn into the Easter Bunny and hop off to China. Actually, that would be more interesting than some of the stuff that's come from the writers lately."

"Oh, no." My heart began to pound in my chest, the beginning of a minor panic attack. This couldn't be happening to me, and on the heels of a minor heartbreak. My boyfriend, Walker, had just ended our relationship in a totally rotten way, not calling me back for three weeks. Three weeks of torture ended when I showed up at his office at lunchtime to confront him and he acted like he didn't even owe me an explanation. "Sometimes, things just don't work out," he'd said with an awkward shrug.

A shrug! After three months of intimacy, I had to stalk the guy to get a shrug. I have to admit, it weakened my spirit. I went on a bender with Diet Cokes, fatfree chips, and an armful of magazines, which didn't really help because no one really reports on nonrelationships with irresponsible men who don't even care enough to break up with you. I tell you this not to gain your sympathy; I only want to explain why I was feeling a few chinks in my armor when Stella hit me with the weird advice.

"Don't take it personally, Hailey." Stella squeezed my hand, rubbing my wrist vigorously with that motherly vibe. "It doesn't mean anything. Consider the source—Deanna. It's a quick script fix to whomp up the drama for her, not necessarily a turn in the story line."

But I couldn't let it go. "How can they cut me from the show? Did you see the guest spot I did on *Soap Central* two weeks ago?"

"Not a worry," Stella insisted. "It's a quicky rewrite done to get today's script past Deanna. Chances are, you'll never hear the word 'suicide' again."

The pounding in my chest slowed. "Right." I swallowed hard. "Unless they don't renew my contract."

"Oh, you!" Stella patted my shoulder as she escorted me back toward the living-room set. "Just wanted to give you the heads-up, so you don't step on any toes."

"Thanks for that," I said. With the new panic beating inside my chest, I felt totally unprepared to do the show today, a little skittish about facing Deanna, but there was no way out of it. Sucking in a breath, I tried an old yoga trick I'd learned—energy in, tension out.

Energy in, tension out . . .

The breathing exercise helped, as did the mental exercise of focusing on pleasant thoughts: the fragrant cosmetics counter at Bloomie's, the splendid museum-lit jewelry cases at Tiffany's, the racks of gourmet gadgets in Macy's Cellar, the plush, brown-and-white-striped bathrooms at Henri Bendel's with stalls bigger than most Upper West Side studios . . .

"People, I need you to focus here," the director called, holding up her hands like a flight attendant flagging in a jumbo jet. "We're going to rehearse before we send the cast off to makeup and wardrobe."

Oh, but I didn't want to focus on the awful scene that might spell the death of my soap-opera career! I wanted to think of the retail territory Alana and I would conquer when she returned from Europe. My mind floated off to the fountain in the Trump Tower, its water flowing steadily like a zen poem . . .

"Oh, goody," Ian Horwitz said in his crisp British accent. A handsome, white-haired chain-smoker, Ian plays a doctor who mistakenly killed his evil twin last season. He put an unlit cigarette into his mouth and opened his script. "Let's get this party started."

Reluctantly, I released my euphoric department store reveries and tried to memorize my new lines as Deanna and her entourage appeared on the set. This time she had brought her dog, a loud little Yorkie with thin gray fur and a pinched face that reminded me of a bat's. The dog was always a show in itself, as everyone was obliged to fuss over it, and someone had to be there to hold and entertain the beast while Deanna ran lines.

"And how is Muffin doing today?" Stella said, nuzzling the pooch adoringly.

"Not too well, poor pookie." Deanna handed him off to Sean. "I'm afraid it's . . ." she lowered her voice to whisper, "diarrhea."

I could see Sean wincing behind Deanna, nearly dropping the Yorkie, and it took all my acting ability to keep a straight face as Deanna turned to me. "Hey, you!" she smiled, showering me with fake affection. "Something is different about you today. A new hair color?"

I didn't tell her that the golden blond hue of my hair belonged to me; news like that might make a person like Deanna shrivel up and croak like the wicked witch in a downpour. I blinked shyly. "No, same hair."

She tapped her chin, looking me over from head to toe. "That's it! The shoes."

I modeled my Nine West polka dots demurely, trying not to show off. "You're right. They are new."

"Hmm. Very nice shoes, but really . . ."

"Really, what?"

"Oh, just the combination."

I glanced down my body. "This shirt came with the shoes."

"Yes, of course, dear. But the shoes and the jeans?"

An uncomfortable quiet wrapped around us as people shuffled and pretended to consult their scripts.

"It might sound silly to you, but jeans are sort of my

trademark. You know, that I mix and match jeans with formal tops and casual Ts?"

Deanna gave a little laugh. "You and a few thousand other aspiring actresses."

I wanted to wipe the smirk from her Botoxed lips, but I forced myself to veer away from career suicide. "Anyway." I bent back one corner of my script. "The shoes are new. Nine West."

"And they're lovely," she said effusively, "though the combination is a bit gauche. Didn't anyone ever tell you not to wear ankle-strap shoes with pants?" She pronounced it as "paahnts," so haughtily you'd think she was starring in a British comedy.

"But the jeans are my trademark," I said, feeling mousy.

She sighed. "Of course they are, but not with shoes like that, dear."

I lifted the fabric of my pants and glanced down at my beloved shoes. Was she right? Could it be that both Alana and I had missed a fashion mistake that would put me in the x-files of *Glamour* or *Cosmo*?

"All right, then," Deanna said, taking charge. "Shall we rehearse our new scene?"

The crew came alive, hopping into place as Stella looked up over her reading glasses. "Yes, of course. This one takes place in the parlor of the Childs mansion. Let's do a run-through, without the slap, of course."

"Of course!" Deanna chimed in, reaching over to touch my cheek with cold affection.

I tried to smile, but it was hard to get past the wounded feeling inside.

I was wearing ankle-strap shoes with pants.

I had committed a fashion faux pas.

My life was over.

Part Two

Part Two

**ARRIBA! IT'S CINCO DE MAYO
SALE DAY!**

3

Alana

Damned cathedrals! Why couldn't they keep their chimes to themselves?

I was climbing the tedious stone stairs of the bell tower, trying to get to the top to put a sock on the clapper, but the higher I rose, the darker the stairwell became.

"Who's doing that?" I called. "Stop!"

I flailed in the darkness, then realized I was writhing in my own bed.

I tore off the mask and looked at my digital clock. Twelve noon. Ugh.

With a tap of my fingertips, I hit the snooze button to cut off the cathedral chime alarm and fell back against the pillows. Sleeping till noon and still exhausted . . . I was in very bad shape. Jet lag was one thing, but this was a weariness more pervasive than a small time difference.

Spring ennui.

Yawning, I sat up in bed and reached for my peignoir,

the lacy pink one that was an accessory to this pink neg-
ligee. What a find! The fabric was amazing, and it draped
so gracefully, I felt like one of those heavenly bodies
Reverend Tyson preaches about at Aunt Nessie's church.
The only snag with the gown was the pink color, a poor
match for my smooth mocha skin. Hmm. That's a problem with many designers' attire. Some of those creative
geniuses just don't choose colors that go well with
African-American skin tones. I swished the gown around
my legs, letting the skirt fall open on the air. Pink didn't
work for me. I would have to find one in a better color.

But that was a chore for later. At the moment, I had
to get moving if I was ever going to make my one-
thirty facial at Armage, followed by a much-needed
mani-pedi. If I had time, I would squeeze in a hot-stone
massage with Chantelle, but it was going to be tight if
I was going to make my date with Hailey. We were on
for high tea at the Plaza—a much needed pick-me-up
for Hailey, who was suffering some sort of career crisis. I don't know . . . something about ankle-strap shoes?
I was going to treat her to tea, then lure her off for some
retail therapy. Both of us were in need of some serious
shopping to cure the ills in our lives.

Myself? I was simmering mad at Daddy. During the
flight back from London the night before, I'd had time
to ponder the lunacy, the sheer ludicrousness of his cross-
Atlantic summons. Really! I had ventured to Europe for
a very worthy cause—the support of my good friend
Petey—and to be scolded and ordered home like an
errant puppy! The indignity of it all had my blood boiling, and it didn't help that the air was humid and hot
when I stepped out of the Manchester lobby.

"Good Lord, is it summer already?" I shielded my
eyes from the sun and smiled at the doorman, Mr.
Barnes.

"It's still May, but we have summer weather." Mr.

Barnes squinted at me, the laugh lines deep around his eyes. He was one of the few African-Americans on staff at the Manchester Apartments, and his presence made my father uncomfortable. Daddy always frowned and fumbled for some dollar bills and felt incredibly guilty that a brother was opening the door for him when he was perfectly capable of doing it himself. I guess that's one of those notions you're stuck with when you start out in the middle class—wanting to do things for yourself, feeling guilty when other people provide services for you. As one of five children growing up in Great Neck, New York, my father was forced to learn so many tedious tasks. Cooking, washing, sewing, vacuuming, dishwashing. How many times had I heard of the Sunday dinners after which he and his sisters spent three solid hours scrubbing pots and pans and buffing the kitchen till it shone? Please. If the Lord had meant us to spend our lives scrubbing, He would have given us scouring pads on our fingertips instead of nails. And that is enough about that.

Still, it's a shame that my father will probably never be able to shed his guilt. Here he is, a successful federal judge, and he can't take a vacation in the Caribbean or hire a limo or live in a doorman building without having his guilt button pushed. Poor Daddy; poor Mama. She has no qualms about being pampered, but she's stuck with the Mother Teresa of the service industry.

Me? I think it's great to see a black man in a well-paying job that suits him, and since Mr. Barnes is a fine conversationalist and a bit of a flirt, I'm happy to let him open my door any day.

"Do you need a cab today, Ms. Marshall-Hughs?"

"Yes, I would appreciate that, Mr. Barnes. And let's pray you can find one with air conditioning."

As he leaned toward the curb and whistled for a cab, I felt a familiar tug of longing for this city I loved.

Could I manage a stop at Fifth Avenue and see if the summer handbags had arrived at Bergdorf's, where I had an Alessandro Dell' Acqua embroidered clutch on order? I checked my slim diamond Rolex. No, no time. When would I fit Bergdorf's into my schedule?

Facial.

Manicure/pedicure.

High tea.

Ah . . . afternoon shopping! There would be time before the obligatory dinner with the 'rents. And to think I wanted a man in my life! It would be nice to have someone special for evening occasions, but honestly, there wasn't a minute of free time in my schedule.

Really. For a girl in her twenties, I was way overbooked.

Someone hand me a cappuccino, please. The ennui is killing me.

4

Hailey

I need more work.

Why aren't they signing me on for another thirteen weeks?

Why hasn't anyone mentioned a new contract?

Why hasn't my agent called?

Do I have coffee breath?

Insecurities shuddered through me as I held my mark on the set of *All Our Tomorrows*, waiting to finish up for the day. I would be finished by one o'clock—a sad summary of my life.

Finished.

We had already taped the two scenes that were Dullsville for my character. In today's episode, Ariel was hanging out in the restaurant of the Indigo Hills Inn, sipping a Cherry Coke and listening attentively while other characters unloaded their problems. I had to nod and ooze sympathy while Bella worried that her parents would notice she'd been skipping school all semester to noodle with her boyfriend. Then there was old man Gellers, lamenting how much he missed his wife, Trixie, who had passed away last year. It was the one-year anniversary of Trixie's death—the actress having gone on to play a grandmother in a sitcom—and in today's episode the writers were flashing back to scenes of Trixie's life, mostly to capitalize on the actress's new-found popularity.

Across the set, my friend Rory banged out a rendition of "Surrey With the Fringe on Top" on the piano. Today Rory/Stone was performing at the Indigo Inn, tickling the ivories in the background while the characters lamented their problems.

I leaned on the simulated oak bar of the restaurant and yawned. We were between takes, and today's director, Percy Blake, didn't want any of us to leave our positions. Group scenes are tricky to tape, orchestrating the moves of a dozen or so players; if the actors are allowed to leave the set, chances are someone will return with an altered hairstyle, a new shade of lipstick, a donut crumb on their collar—some telltale change that will stick out when the editors try to cut the scenes together.

"Ok, then, ladies and gentlemen." Percy paused, pressing his fingertips against his lips. He's one of those gorgeous black men who exude charm and creativity, always a pleasure to work with. When it comes to containing Deanna, Percy is a pro. Fortunately, she wasn't in any of my scenes today, so I didn't have to face her and follow up on the nasty shoe comment. Percy came out of his trance. "I think we're ready to move on to our Act Six scenes."

"Act Six, Scene Two!" Sean announced. "We have Bella approach the piano and confide in Stone. Lizzie Slate meeting Doc Willoughby at the door."

"Ah, yes!" Ian Horwitz waggled his eyebrows at Susan Lazlo, who plays Lizzie. "I believe this is the scene in which I diagnose you with a debilitating disease based on the dry condition of your cuticles."

Susan folded her hands and took her place without comment. She's a short-term contract player, like me, and you never hear her complain (though I can imagine what she's thinking!).

"And . . ." Sean continued, "we have Ariel crossing to Kostas in the corner booth."

At last! The scene I'd been waiting for: my first significant exchange with the lean, dark, mysterious Kostas, played by daytime heartthrob Antonio Lopez. His beautiful face lit up the covers of the soap opera weeklies, his wide, white smile and smokey eyes tucking into your soul and giving a joyous little squeeze. I had to agree with the viewers—Antonio was magnifico, despite the fact that he had never paid much attention to me, perhaps due to the fact that he had spent most of the last year sucking up to Deanna. Smart man. From his first day on the set, he buttered her up like a Thanksgiving turkey, and she lapped up the attention. Gobble, gobble.

And I must begrudgingly admit, the heat was rising from their scenes together. Although Deanna is probably a good ten years older than Antonio, they were a hot soap opera couple until her character learned that he had once killed a man in a Salvadoran prison . . . and that man just happened to be her brother. Or maybe it was her father? I wasn't paying close attention. Who could focus when Antonio's tan, rippled muscles were flexing against the satin bedsheets?

"Excuse me, Percy?" Rory called to the director, stretching his hands over the keyboard. "Sorry to interrupt, but can I take five? I need to"—he lowered his voice to a stage whisper—"use the facilities."

"Good God, man! You took the words from my mouth!" Horwitz exclaimed, shoving a cigarette into his mouth and striding toward the door. "I shall return!"

"Don't go far!" Percy called, pressing his hands to his jowls. He took the clipboard from Sean's hands and checked the schedule. "Next time I agree to tape an episode with a group scene, please, just shoot me."

Amused, Sean scratched the soul patch on his chin. "Whatever you say, boss."

I stood up and began to stretch and do some yoga twists. I was sucking in energy air when someone jabbed me in the ribs.

Rory flashed me a sneaky grin and chanted, "Nanny, nanny, foo-foo, you get to kiss Antoonioo."

I grabbed his shoulders. "Would you put a cork in it?" Fortunately, Antonio had left the set for the moment. "Lucky he's gone, or I'd have to kill you on the spot."

"I think he likes you," Rory teased, his blue eyes flashing.

"Don't be silly. He's more your type."

"No, no, no! I have it from a reliable source that Mr. Lopez is quite hetero. Score one for your team." Rory is sort of a daytime TV pioneer, having revealed his sexual orientation eight years ago at a time when it could have cost him future roles, but fortunately, viewers responded with approval. Since then, he's become a fixture on the show.

"You are such a troublemaker," I told him.

"I'm not kidding, Hailey. Antonio is hot for you. I hear he's got a poster of you taped up in his dressing room."

"Would you stop it now?" I smoothed down the ugly ruffled teal shirt of my costume and dabbed at my forehead with the back of my hand. "How do I look? Got any Altoids?"

He reached behind the bar and produced a tin of cinnamon-flavored, my favorite.

"Why, thank you!"

"Shh! I stole them from props. And you look glam, despite the unfortunate costume choice. When is Jodi going to stop dressing you like a moray eel?"

"As soon as the diva realizes I'm not a threat." I popped a breath mint and smiled. "Curiously strong."

"Are you nervous?" he prodded, leaning across the bar. "I think he likes you."

"Get out!"

"I'm serious." He cocked an eyebrow. "For once in my life."

"Really?" I stole a glance back at the booth where Antonio had been sitting. Still empty. "Do you mean 'like'? Or 'like-like'?"

"Honey, I'm talking throw you down and—"

"OK, OK, you don't have to draw a diagram." I could feel my face heating up, and it ticked me off that Rory was so good at embarrassing me.

Rory folded his arms, clearly on a roll. "So on a scale of one to ten, one being you'd let him peek at your panties and ten being you'd swing naked on his chandelier, what would you say—"

"OK, people, we're ready to continue!" Sean shouted. "Places everyone."

There was a flurry of movement as the actors and crew returned to work.

Rory winked. "Good luck, doll."

I scowled at him, but he ignored me. He sauntered back to the piano and started playing "Do Ya Think I'm Sexy?"

Taking my place at the bar, I tried to suppress the flurry of nerves Rory had elicited.

This isn't your first stage kiss. It's acting. It means nothing, said the professional actress.

But you get to kiss Antonio Lopez! squealed the yearning girl.

As the hairstylist fluffed up my hair, I let the yearning girl win me over. A little excitement wasn't going to hurt my performance, and since the kiss was in the script, what was the harm in enjoying it?

Sean called for everyone to settle down, and Joanne counted off to begin the scene. I started my cross to Antonio, pretending not to notice him at first, then agreeing to join him for a second as he—I mean, as Kostas—spilled his troubles to Ariel.

I sat beside him, folding a napkin tentatively, even shyly. The lines fell from my lips as if we were in normal conversation. I wasn't sure I was sticking to the script, but I felt confident I was turning in one of the finest performances of my life.

"No one understands," Kostas said. "But you . . . ?" He turned my hand and ran a finger along my palm, eliciting a tiny stir inside me. "You seem to know. It's as if you've come from another world."

I lifted my chin to him, tears in my eyes. "I can't tell you of my past," I said. "I wish I knew. But I do understand. I can't help but see how you feel, deep in your soul. Somehow, I know."

He tilted his head toward mine, so close I could feel his breath stirring my hair.

"Yes," he whispered, his gorgeous face closing in on me. "I believe you do."

I stopped breathing as his lips pressed against mine for the kiss. Most actors sort of maul you with a closed mouth, but Antonio opened his lips to mine and gently teased my upper lip with his tongue. With a moan, I opened my mouth and let my tongue edge along the smooth surface of his even teeth.

Heaven . . . the man was sweet heaven.

"And . . . cut!"

5

Alana

"He really kissed you?" I asked Hailey as she popped the end of a watercress sandwich into her mouth. She looked cuter than ever in her low-waisted jeans, purple T and Jimmy Choo stiletto boots, her blond hair loose and shiny on her shoulders. "You were just kissed by Antonio Lopez?"

"Mm-hmm!" She nodded enthusiastically, her eyes round with amazement as she chewed on the dainty little sandwich from the elegant platter served in the lobby dining area of the Plaza Hotel.

I leaned forward, lowering my voice. "Tongue and all?" Just the idea of being within inches of Antonio Lopez was provocative, but to receive a hot, juicy kiss . . .

"Tongue and teeth! I've never had that happen while performing. I mean, whew! We were on fire." Hailey waggled her hands, air-quenching the imaginary flames.

"Good for you, honey!" I toasted her with my china cup, so glad to be back in my city, sharing high tea with my good friend. "So . . . then what? What happened next? Tell me everything!"

"There's nothing else to tell! He nailed me with the kiss, I melted inside, and then, when the director yelled cut, he dropped me like a sack of potatoes. I'm telling you, that man can turn the heat on and off like a faucet."

"She said with a sigh of longing," I teased.

"I guess I'm just flabbergasted. One, I never thought he was my type, and two, I didn't think he had that much acting ability."

"Well, he was either acting or sending you a message. I'll bet Antonio is into you."

Hailey pressed a hand to her mouth. "That's what Rory said, but I thought he was just ragging on me." She shook her head.

One of Hailey's more endearing qualities is her total unawareness of her own beauty. My theory is that her granola parents kept her so well hidden under those stupid hippie caftans that she missed the fact that she's a knockout. Or maybe it was that three-year period that the Starrett family spent in a Buddhist ashram. Imagine missing your prom because you're living in a commune of meditating longhairs! It's appalling, what some people do to their children.

"This is an exciting new development," I said. "So you're feeling better about Deanna's public assault on your wardrobe?"

"A little." Hailey picked up a wafer cookie. "I don't know why I let her get to me, but I do."

"Don't be so hard on yourself," I said, "but what pair of shoes did she pick on, anyway?"

"The Nine West," she said indignantly.

"Not the Nine West? Pink with polka dots? And dots are so hot!" The nerve of that woman! As Hailey gave me a play-by-play description of the exchange, I felt anger rising on my friend's behalf. Deanna Childs was a walking menace, a bully who picked on weak and vulnerable people around her, like Hailey. When Hailey finished her story, I reached across the table and squeezed her hand. "Listen to me, honey. You looked gorgeous in that outfit—I saw it! Denim will never go out of style. Did Deanna miss Demi Moore in her jeans and Gucci shell at that premiere last month? How about Naomi Campbell? Jessica Simpson? Linda Evangelista? Please! Deanna Childs wouldn't know fashion if Christian LaCroix hijacked her limo and airlifted her to Paris."

She brushed a crumb off the tablecloth. "Even if that's true, she's got an awful lot of clout on the show."

"Yes, and you're smart to defer to her. But don't ever *believe* her act. Deanna is out to promote Deanna, and she doesn't care who she has to climb over on the way." I poured some more tea for her, and she spooned some clotted cream onto a scone. Hailey has an amazing metabolism that burns just about anything she eats like an industrial furnace. Personally, I've tended to wear desserts on my ass, but most of the guys I've gone out with had no complaints. "You just hold tight," I said. "Things will work out."

"I'm just glad to have you back, Alana. With a new French manicure, I see."

"Salon Armage." I held out my hands—petite, with buttery-smooth chocolate-hued skin and the barest hint of knuckles. "They do fabulous work."

"But your hands are perfect to begin with," Hailey said. "Now I want to hear all about Europe, but first, you never told me why you came back early."

"That's my father's doing—the pain in the butt. Can you believe he called me over in London and told me to come home for a family council?"

Hailey stopped chewing, powdered sugar on her lower lip. "Something wrong?"

"He's just harping on the money thing again, and

really, I'm getting sick and tired of fighting with my parents over the budget. Don't they understand what things cost these days? They know I don't settle when I shop—they know I have an exquisite sense of style and fashion, an uncompromising eye for quality."

She shook her head. "Sometimes parents can be so dense. I see my parents sitting on old sofas with slip-covers, wearing clothes they've had since the first George Bush was president, and I don't get it. What happened to that generation? They can't seem to grasp the joy in spending money."

"Exactly!" What a relief to talk to someone on the same track! Hailey totally got it. "So I've decided to take this situation in hand. If they insist on this ridiculous budget restriction, the least they can do is double it."

"Really. What do they give you now? If you don't mind my asking."

"Not a worry. It's something lame like three thousand a month, not counting the co-op payment."

"With the way you spend money, that must disappear fast."

"Please! Three thousand is a pittance in Eurodollars. Three thousand will barely buy you a Prada gown or an afternoon of shoe shopping. And it's not like it's all about me. I'm constantly buying little gifties for my parents. I do all their Christmas shopping for them, and now Mama and I have plans to redecorate the house in the Hamptons. I'm excellent at what I do, but I can't function within these ridiculous parameters." Ever since Daddy's brusque phone call I had been dreading the family council, but it helped to run my argument by Hailey, who got it.

"So where are you meeting them?" she asked. "How are you going to play the scene?"

"Like the most professional daughter in the world."

I had thought about it on the plane ride from Heathrow. "First, I'm going to put the numbers in front of them. That my budget, at three thousand dollars a month, is a mere thirty-six thousand a year. Most people can't survive in Manhattan on a salary like that, and with their two salaries and trust funds and investments, I'm costing them a minuscule amount."

"I like it." Hailey passed me the tray, and I took a butter cookie dipped in bittersweet chocolate. "Then I'm going to give them a bit of proof—an example to prove my point. I figure Daddy will be particularly impressed by that."

"Bravo."

"Which I could use your help on. I'd like to head out now and pick up a few things for the Hamptons house. This way I can demonstrate how silly Daddy's budget rules are. He's going to be so happy to see the place redone. I was thinking of everything in shades of white—vanilla walls, snowy wicker, bleached pine."

"Yes, I've seen that done, and it's so elegant yet casual." Hailey looped her Fendi bag over her shoulder and scooted forward in the chair. "Where should we start?"

"Bloomie's and Bon Nuit are having Cinco de Mayo sales." Hailey and I cannot resist sales—the unbelievable deal of getting something at twenty percent off makes our pulses accelerate like seasoned runners'. I handed the waiter one of my shiny hologram credit cards and waved Hailey's cash away. "My treat, honey. You need some coddling after those rotten things Deanna said to you." I tucked my card into my Kate Spade bag. "Should we start at Henri Bendel's?"

"They don't sell furniture at Bendel's, do they?"

"No, but I hear M.A.C. is coming out with new shades of lipstick this month, and the sales clerk told me she expected them in today."

"Ooh! That's right." She checked the lipstick on her napkin. "I'm feeling a little washed out. Let's stop in the rest room and primp."

"I was just going to say that!" That's the thing about Hailey and me: if we didn't look so different, I would swear we were twins separated at birth. It's hard to believe two people could love the same things, like Caribbean martinis and Prada gowns, and hate the same things, like sticky cinema floors and men who talk to women's breasts. I swear, we have the same cravings, laugh at the same jokes, even have the same pee schedule. If I have a soul sister in the world, it's Hailey Starrett.

6

Hailey

It started at Bendel's, where the spring shades of lip-stick weren't in yet, so we ventured upstairs and came upon an unusual set of coasters—white enamel with the tiniest wildflowers along the edges. Each coaster was different, hand-painted. "Like tiny works of art," Alana said. "I have to get them for the summer house."

"No, let me." I snatched them out of her arm and turned toward the sales clerk. "I've been wanting to give your parents a little something for all the times they've hosted me there, and now that I know you like these, they'll make the perfect gift."

"Well, thank you! That's so sweet."

I grinned all the way to the counter, wondering if the clerk recognized me from the show or simply liked the way I carried myself. She was so deferential, nearly bowing to me as she rang up the purchase.

It was easy to bestow a smile on her . . . until I signed the charge receipt and noticed the price. *Two hundred forty dollars*—six disks that kept the condensation off your table?

Oh, well . . . it was a gift, well deserved, and it would be the last time I used my card until that new contract came in. It would have to be the last time, as I recalled that my balance was hovering dangerously near my credit limit.

Maybe they'd raise my salary on the show . . . maybe double it? Or triple!

I checked the tag on a summer scarf and pretended not to be shocked at the five-hundred-dollar price. Yes, a raise was due. I would call my agent Cruella in the morning.

At Saks, Alana and I got lost in a huge circular rack of summer dresses just out from Marc Jacobs. Alana freaked over the abundance of size sixes, and we hustled armloads off to the dressing rooms. Now, there is something about a summer dress that doesn't quite suit Manhattan. Maybe it's that so many people in this city still wear black year round, giving many a function a funereal pall. Or maybe it's just that, in the canyons between the tall buildings in midtown, we don't see a lot of sun. In any case, try wearing a sundress down a busy street in Manhattan and you'll see what I mean; it just feels out of place.

That said, the exception to any rule is Alana, who was modeling the ruby and white tropical print in front of the mirror. "Perfect!" She clicked it onto the "buy" rack and slipped into a crisp white dress straight out of *The Great Gatsby*. "Oh, Mr. Marc Jacobs, I love you!"

I whirled around in a peach gingham print, feeling like a barefoot sprite in a field of wildflowers.

"Don't you dare tell me you're not getting that," Alana said. "I won't let you put it back."

Twisting my hair into a knot, I tried to hate the dress. I failed. "Where would I even wear it?"

"Trust me. When it's a gazillion degrees out, you'll be wearing it everywhere."

I looked at the price. Ouch! Amazing that a cotton blend dress could be $499. I mean, really. It was way too expensive, and there were no Cinco de Mayo discounts here. And my credit card balance was edging into the danger zone.

No. Absolutely not.

"Remember what we said about dressing like a star?" Alana backed toward me so that I could zip up a smart black-and-white-striped dress for her. "You have to invest in yourself, invest in your dream."

I hung my head down and faced my reflection, a weak smile evident through my silky hair. She was right of course. The dress made me feel special. Pretty.

And every so often a girl needs to feel pretty.

Click! I added my peach gingham to the "buy" rack.

By the time we reached Bon Nuit, our petite fingers grasped shopping bags of telltale colors and emblems— the handsome brown-and-white stripes of Bendel's, the bold S of Saks, the pale teal of Tiffany's, where Alana had purchased a sterling tie clip for her father and a pair of amber earrings that we both agreed screamed Rose Marshall-Hughs. Alana led the way up to the balcony, where we checked our bags and coats, then we took the elevator up to the furniture department so that Alana could get serious about a summerhouse purchase.

I felt like Goldilocks, flinging myself onto leather couches, striped ottomans, white divans. Too hard, too soft, too ugly for words. We quickly decided that nothing was "just right."

"I can see I have furniture research in my future,"

Alana said, eyeing the love seats as she strolled down the aisle in her smart Dolce & Gabbana heels.

Downstairs we moved through accessories, trying on hats, which always worries me. What if a previous shopper had dandruff or head lice? Wasn't that all highly contagious? It was a gross-out possibility; however, I couldn't resist plunking a few hats on my head.

"I'm not sure how I feel about Burberry plaids," Alana said as she tried on a sporty plaid hat. "Sometimes I love them, other times I hate them. I'm just so conflicted about Burberry."

"It's a classic." I folded my arms, assessing the hat. "Some people love Burberry. The color is good on you, great with your skin tone."

She frowned in the mirror. "I know, but I'm just so torn."

"Madonna made plaid cool again."

"Yes, but Madonna is so Madonna, and I'm so not. Do you know what I mean?"

I did. "I would wait on that purchase. Buy the Burberry when you're in a Burberry mood."

She dropped the hat back on the rack and wagged a finger at me. "You, Ms. Starrett, have a knack for this!"

Our energy was winding down as we meandered past the cosmetics counter, disappointed that the new M.A.C. lipstick wasn't out yet. We browsed for a while, then came upon a brand of cosmetics called Trenda.

"Have you tried Trenda? I love it." I marveled at the glass display case. "Summer makeup kits, massage-therapy beads. Oh, and their lipstick. It's the best!"

"I think I tried Trenda years ago," she said. "Great blush, flaky eyeshadow, right?"

"I wish I could remember my color." The cabinet was across the aisle and there wasn't a sales rep in sight.

But I could see the boxes. "Pleasantly Plum. Iridescent Moon. Plush Cherry . . ." So far nothing rang a bell.

I squinted, peering into the cabinet. "That's it! The last row on the bottom. Carnation Kiss. That's my shade." I straightened and flicked my hair back over one shoulder. "Oh, this is so great! I haven't been able to find this shade forever."

The sales clerk slid the little carton out of the cupboard and routed through the other stacks. "That's funny. It's the last Carnation Kiss."

"Let her try it," Alana said.

"I can't. It's the last one. If I let her try it, then it becomes a sample. And if it's a sample, I can't sell it to her."

"Well, that's stupid," Alana said.

The sales clerk tossed off a careless shrug. "It's the policy. For your protection."

"Can we just see it?" Alana was getting impatient. "Take it out of the box."

"I cannot do that."

Alana's eyes went wide. "You have got to be kidding . . ."

"I want it." I put my purse on the counter and dug for my card. "Just ring it up, OK?"

The sales clerk stared at the box, her mouth puckering. "I know this shade. I've sold this line for years. This color is not good for you. Carnation Kiss is gonna make you looked jaundiced." She pronounced it "jyawndist."

I put my card on the glass counter with a click. "That's OK. I'll take it."

She shook her head, her red hair bobbing. "I don't think so. I'm trying to do you a favor here and save you from looking like a poky yellow chicken with its lips on fire. Do yourself a favor, honey, and pick out another color."

Can you believe this woman? I checked her name tag. "Listen, Marcella, I used to wear Carnation Kiss. I loved it. For years."

"So for years you were jaundiced." Another little shrug. "Who knew?"

"Oh, this is ridiculous." Alana extracted a credit card from her Kate Spade bag and slapped it on the counter. "I'll take the lipstick. I want it. Give it to me. Or does it make me look jaundiced, too?"

The redhead assessed her. "Actually, it would be very flattering for your skin tone. But I know what you're up to. So put your charge cards away, ladies."

"Listen, Marcy . . ." Alana growled.

The clerk pointed two fingers an inch from Alana's face. "That's Marcella."

Alana shrugged. "Who knew? Now sell me the lipstick. Carnation Fucking Kiss."

Marcella drew a deep breath through her nostrils, as if it was all too tedious to bear.

"Give me the lipstick," Alana went on, "plus two summer makeup kits. And throw in one of those pedicure pooch pillows. My niece will get a kick out of it."

I expected another rebuttal from the clerk, but instead she picked up Alana's card and turned to the register. "I am selling you this under a lot of duress," she said as she scanned the card, then moved the wand over the purchases. "So don't think you can come back here and complain that this lipstick makes you look jaundiced, because I'm warning you."

Alana rolled her eyes dramatically. "Consider us warned."

"Ha!" Marcella scanned the card a second time, then pushed a button on the register. "Is this your Bank of Freedom card?" She turned back to us. "Are you Alana Marshall-Hughs? Got some ID?"

"Who wants to know?" Alana demanded.

"The credit card company." The clerk grinned as she tapped the card on the counter. "Bouncy-bouncy!"

"Oh, that's ridiculous." Alana cut around the side of

the counter and lunged toward the clerk. "Give it to me. Give me my card. I'll ring it up myself."

"You can't be back here!" The redhead lowered her head bullishly. "That's it!" She gestured to a clerk at a nearby counter. "Courtney! Call security."

"Yes, call them!" Alana said, closing in on the shorter clerk. "I'll need them here to carry you off after I rip that lipstick out of your hands."

"I was selling you the damned lipstick! It's not my fault your card is cancelled."

Paralyzed by a mixture of shock and amazement, I stood at the counter watching the two women. I'd never seen Alana act this way, but then, I'd never seen her credit denied.

"Give me that lipstick," Alana growled.

"I'll give it to you." The clerk held it back, back, back. "Just as soon as you pull that stick out of your ass!"

Alana reached over for it, but suddenly Marcella ducked and dove under Alana's arm, lunging forward. I think she was trying to race ahead but she tripped and dove into the floor.

My friend couldn't stop her momentum in time and fell right on top of her. Together they were a squealing pile of designer shoes, fine fabrics, and manicured hands.

"Where is it?" Alana lifted her head enough to grope the floor. "Give it to me!"

"Ladies? What's happening here?" A heavyset guard trotted up, his belt jingling. He paused when he saw the puddle of feline fury. "Someone hurt here?"

Alana sat up. "She won't sell my friend her lipstick!"

The clerk pushed herself up from the floor and smoothed her hair back. "She has no credit," she said, pointing at Alana. "And she"—Marcella pointed at me—"looks jaundiced!"

Another guard appeared, a female, who seemed equally confused. The heavyset guard shook his head.

"We didn't do anything wrong," I told them. "It all started over a tube of lipstick."

"Yes, ma'am," the female guard said. "Sometimes it happens that way."

Really? Did they often have altercations over lipstick? Fistfights over exfoliants?

The female guard moved behind the counter. "Nobody hurt, right?"

No answer.

"Marcella?" The guard helped her up. "Back upstairs. They'll be expecting you in Human Resources."

The other guard motioned to Alana. "And you'll need to come with me, miss."

"Where are you taking her?" I asked, feeling a little worried. I'd never been involved in a department store infraction before.

"Just escorting her to the door." The wide man with the rather large walkie-talkie on his belt seemed to have a slight lisp. "This way, ma'am."

"My coat and packages are in the coat check," Alana stood her ground. "I'm not leaving without them."

"Of course." He gestured toward the balcony. "After you."

She turned her pointy-toed Dolce & Gabbana shoes toward the broad stone steps and walked with dignity. I have to hand it to Alana: even in a cat fight, she had class.

A shriek came from the rising escalator, and I turned to see the redhead looking back at us. "I never forget a face!" she shouted. "I will *never* sell you that lipstick."

Alana turned toward the escalator and cocked an eyebrow. "We'll see about that," she said. "We shall see."

7

Alana

The Collington is a social club, one of my parents' favorite places to dine. While Daddy is uncomfortable flaunting his social status, he's quite at ease with the envelope tip system at the Collington, and equally pleased that the club was founded by families of diverse ethnic backgrounds. On any given night, you're bound to run into local arts patrons, doctors from India, businessmen from Asia, scientists from all over the world, and a handful of city politicians. That's the boring part.

The good news is that the food in the dining room is decent, the family members of the aforementioned prestigious men usually can hold their own at the bar, and the club has built one of the better swimming pools in New York City. Not that I've used it much, but Hailey and I keep promising ourselves we're going to start.

I left the little gifties for Mama and Daddy in the coat-check room, then straightened my Chanel suit. As

I crossed the rose-patch pattern of the dining room I could see that my parents were already ensconced at their favorite table, Daddy with his Chivas and soda, Mama with her vodka martini. Of course, Mama noticed my new plum suit immediately, commenting on it even as she pulled me into a hug.

"Is that Chanel?"

I kissed her cheek and nodded, touching the fake fur on the lapel.

"Of course it is. And it's perfect for you, Lanny." Her eyes glimmered with pride as she patted my shoulder.

"Thanks, Mama."

"Chanel?" my father rumbled. "How much did that cost me?"

I tilted my head slightly, letting the long ponytail of baby dreads fall to one shoulder. I wanted to chastise him because he hadn't paid for it at all since he'd let the credit card bill lapse, but I held my tongue, having learned long ago that, above all else, my father valued and demanded respect.

Instead, I played Daddy's little girl. "Oh, Daddy, you have a one-track mind," I said, reaching over to hug him. "Did you miss me?"

One side of his mouth twitched up like an angry bulldog's. "How can I miss you when I'm bombarded by credit card bills suggesting a widespread path of decadence?"

"Ernest . . ." My mother's voice held a warning.

"Yes, yes, I missed you, but we must go over the rules, Alana. Certain rules of order we all must abide by in civilized society."

I sat down and shook the linen napkin open. "May I order a drink first?"

That took the wind out of his sails—at least for the moment.

"Yes, yes, of course. Sit." He summoned the waiter and I ordered a greyhound—grapefruit juice and vodka. While Daddy fished out his reading glasses to study the evening's menu, I motioned for the waiter to make it a double. The man smiled at my gesture of desperation, then hurried off.

Mama reached across the table and tapped my hand. "I'm dying to hear, how was Europe?"

"Spectacular. I was there to help Pierre launch his new line of gowns." When Mama squinted, I added, "You remember Petey from Harvard? Pete Brown?"

"Skinny little thing?"

We giggled together, recalling some of Petey's antics one summer at my parents' house in the Hamptons. We had decided to throw an impromptu luau, and for the occasion, Petey quickly fashioned mumus out of shower curtains, grass skirts from a broken wicker chair, gaudy necklaces from large plastic shower curtain rings. Mama had laughed heartily over his creations, but my father had been thoroughly unsettled to discover the shower curtain missing from the master bath.

The waiter took our order then disappeared, and the light conversation continued. As Mama and I caught up on news, I began to relax. Maybe this dinner with the 'rents would actually be enjoyable. After all, my mother totally got what I was about, and she adored the way that I held up my friends, providing an occasional lift for Hailey, endless support for Petey, fabulous neckties for Rory, and streams of baby gifts for Carla, Joyce, and Nayasia, my college friends who now had little droolers of their own. Now that I thought of it, I was pretty darned benevolent. Maybe I should incorporate myself—the Alana Foundation. Yes, I liked the sound of that, and wouldn't Daddy be proud?

"Oh, look, Ernest, the Schnabels are here," my

mother said as she cast her gaze over her martini glass. "I wonder how their show went? And I think that's Dr. and Mrs. Chin in the corner. I hear they returned from the conference in Stockholm. Sadie Williams says they stayed in an ice hotel in northern Sweden. Wouldn't that be fascinating, Ernest?" Mama's brown eyes were dreamy, full of adventure and wonder.

I guess I'm my mama's daughter.

My father squinted as if the concept of a hotel made of frozen water did not compute. "But, Rose, what about your sabbatical?"

"Oh, I meant down the road," my mother said, but my radar was on the word "sabbatical." "Mama? You're taking a vacation from NYU?"

"Actually, I'm taking off next year to do a research project on reading comprehension of urban youth. An unpaid sabbatical, and I'm quite excited about it."

"That's great, Mama. Where will you travel for your research?"

"Lots of exotic places," she said. "Rosedale, Flushing, Murray Hill, the Grand Concourse."

I blinked, liking the wispy feel of my new mascara. "Aren't those neighborhoods in New York City? Oh, right! I get it." Had she said something about not getting paid? That sounded dumb, but I didn't want to be the one to point out the downside, since Mama seemed so enthused. "I'm really excited for you, Mama."

My father cleared his throat. "Which leads me to my agenda issue this evening. With your mother's lack of income next year, I've asked the accountant to take a look over our family budget and the results, I must say, were quite shocking."

"Now Ernest," Mama warned, "you promised not to be dramatic."

Dread hit me as I sat back in the velvet chair, feeling like a character in a movie scene. "Oh, God! This isn't the part where you tell me the family fortune is gone! That you've lost it all to gambling or bad investments or identity theft or something." I pressed a manicured hand to the faux-fur trim of my suit. A financial crisis . . . this was the worst kind of news.

"Of course we haven't lost it all!" my father snapped. "You've been watching far too much of Hailey's soap opera if you think I would be so foolish with our financial stability."

"What your father means to say," Mama went on, "is that we all need to do our part to cut down unnecessary expenses. And Lanny, your spending has increased quite a bit."

Cut down? Cut *down!* I needed more—an increase! These people were insane. They couldn't be my parents . . . it was all a bad dream.

8

Alana

Somewhere during the veal chop and broccoli rabe, I managed to soak up the information that our family was not going bankrupt—except in Daddy's mind. That knowledge calmed me a little, though I must admit my parents' surprise strike had unnerved me. For the moment, I decided to hide in my baked potato and let them ramble on while I prepared a counterstrike.

"Don't you ever miss your friends from Harvard?" Mama asked me. "Do you think of returning there?"

"Sorry to disappoint you, but no, Mama. I see my Boston friends all the time. Love Beantown. But Harvard wasn't my thing."

Daddy had been the first to recognize the huge mistake he'd made in sending me off to Harvard, a university set in a lively cosmopolitan area with thousands of merrymaking college students and twice as many shops and boutiques. In the spring of my sophomore year, when my credit card bills surpassed the hefty price of Ivy League tuition, I was yanked back to New York. Despite a tearful breakup with my Harvard man, I'd been relieved to come home, realizing that Manhattan had all the nightlife of Boston, without the term papers.

"I just wondered," Mama went on. "We'd love to see you finish school, Lanny. I was thinking that if you had more to do, you wouldn't spend so much time shopping."

"Lord knows, I'm trying to save money here. I don't want you returning to Harvard," Daddy started.

A good thing, because that's not going to happen, I thought as I added a dollop of sour cream to my baked potato. My friend Rory had told me that potatoes are disaster food on the Zone, which I find astounding. This innocent root vegetable that comes from the earth, its skin loaded with minerals? What kind of rhetoric is that?

"However, isn't it about time that you consider completing your degree?" Daddy continued, prodding.

"Most of your credits would transfer," my mother added. "You could attend NYU or Columbia."

"Or City College," my father said with emphasis. It was his alma mater, the college that had launched him into law school, and if I had to hear one more time how he rose from humble beginnings to preside over a federal courtroom, I was going to fling my baked potato over to the Schnabels' table. "It's time, Alana. Enough dillydallying. You need to complete your education."

Education? Conventional school was the furthest thing from my mind. I figured Mama had that area all sewn up with her doctorate and her niche teaching students to write at NYU. No reason to tread on her field of expertise when mine was so different. The city was my playground. Retail stores were my classroom. Shoe displays, jewelry cases, and clothes racks were my learning tools. "I don't think so," I demurred. "Conventional schooling was never my thing."

"Perhaps you need to make an adjustment, then," the Honorable Ernest Marshall-Hughs ruled in a surly voice. "In today's world, you'll never get ahead without a college degree."

Never get ahead? Didn't he realize that I was miles ahead of the pack? Half the girls I went to high school with now toiled in boring office jobs dressed in off-the-rack sportswear from crummy little chain stores. You know that brigade—the girls who wear sneakers to work, eat a yogurt out of a bag for lunch, and spend their weekends house hunting in the suburbs with their husbands-to-be. Please! How could my own father not realize I was destined for finer things?

"If it makes you happy, I'll think about going back to school," I said. "Somewhere down the road. Right now, I'm so busy, I barely have a minute to squeeze in a hot-stone massage."

"Busy doing what, pray tell?" Daddy's jowls roiled with anger. "I ran into Cravitz last week and he told me that you were no longer employed at their firm."

Mama shot me a strained look, a desperate "don't tell him that I already knew you quit!" plea. I glanced back down at the remains of my baked potato as Daddy rumbled on about the work ethic he'd learned growing up as one of five children in a three-bedroom house in Great Neck. "When was the last time you worked a full day?" he asked. "An honest day of labor?" I wanted to tell him of the late nights I'd spent helping Pierre prepare for his Paris show, but apparently the question was rhetorical, as he was deep into a "value of hard work" lecture.

His disapproval made me feel small, which was completely unfair because the law firm of Cravitz and Rutter had been a very poor match for my skills. First, they expected me to sit at a desk all day, a very cheap desk made of pressboard that snagged my skirts, ruining a Missoni dress and a navy Chanel suit. Then there was the phone, which never stopped ringing and inevitably delivered the annoyed, harried voice of someone who wanted to yell at me because they could. After two weeks, those angry people had me twitching and shifting at my desk, which made me snag my skirt even more.

"I'm sorry you're disappointed, Daddy," I said respectfully. "But honestly, I hated every day at Cravitz and Rutter. I spent the whole day looking for Mr. Cravitz's reading glasses! They refused to bring in a cappuccino maker. I got blamed for every little thing, and the days stretched on like blackstrap molasses."

"I see." He folded his hands on the table and eyed me as if I were a criminal. "In that case, why don't you tell me what you're planning to do with your life, Alana."

Let me tell you, as I stared down at my cold broccoli rabe and heard the imperious tone in my father's voice, I realized that I could not verbalize an answer he would find acceptable. Forget about the Alana Foundation, or my skills at shopping for the perfect gift, or my endless support of friends and family.

"You don't understand what I do, Daddy," I said quietly. "My life is dedicated to making people happy. I work hard at that. I'm an independent woman, and I think I do a pretty good job of taking care of myself."

"You're right, I don't understand you," he admitted. "What . . . what is it that you do all day?"

I reached for my water glass, my hand slipping over the condensation. "I am all over town." I took a sip. He was waiting for more. "I have appointments."

"For job interviews?" Daddy pushed.

"Salon appointments," I clarified. "A girl's got to get her hair done." Across the table Mama was nodding, thank God. "And I shop. It's sort of a ritual for me, finding the perfect gift. In fact, I got you both a little something this afternoon. Oh, and Daddy, I found the best Dolce & Gabbana briefs for you at a funky little store in London called Foundations. It was so cute!"

"Underwear!" my father gasped, turning to my mother. "She's spending my money on *underwear!*"

"You don't have to be snarky about it," I said, a little hurt. "I'm an excellent shopper, not just good—excellent. I get a charge out of snatching up a new design before anyone else has even heard of it. And then there are the sales. You have to be one of the first ones into the store if you want your pick of discounted merchandise, and I'm vigilant about that."

Across the table, my father snatched off his reading glasses to stare at me. "You're joking. Tell me you're pulling my leg."

"Daddy . . . it's what I do."

"Shopping!" he said explosively. "Good God, Alana! You've got to get your life under control!"

"Ernest . . ." Mama shot a nervous glance over her shoulder at the Schnabels' table. "No need to raise your voice."

"Really," I muttered. "And you don't need to have conniptions. Shopping isn't a crime, Daddy."

"When will you take responsibility for your life?" he demanded.

"You want to talk about responsibility?" I felt the thread of anger unraveling, and I couldn't stop it. "How about the person responsible for paying the Bank of Freedom bill? Were you aware that you're behind on the credit-card payment?" *Try that on for size, Daddy dear.*

"Quite the contrary," he said. "The account is up-to-date. I simply cancelled your card when the accountant informed me that you had charged more than ten thousand dollars on that card alone in a single month. Ten thousand dollars. Do you realize that is more than three times your budget?"

"I can do the math," I said, though multiplication facts had always bored me. "What you don't realize is that many of those expenses were for the Hampton house. I bought two brand-new bedroom sets that will be delivered next month. Some fabulous Tiffany-shade lamps. Bed linens, quilts with matching wallpaper, statuary, and the most elegant antique secretary."

"Sounds lovely," Mama said.

I told her, "I'm working on furniture for the sitting rooms, but you may want to give me some input on what you'd like to see in the master bedroom."

"Don't encourage her, Rose," my father snapped. "We are going to put an end to this spending madness." His last words sent saliva spraying onto the table.

I pushed my plate away and folded my hands. "Daddy, when you calm down, I think you'll realize that it costs money to redesign a summerhouse. It may seem expensive, but I promise you'll be delighted with the end results."

"No, I won't. I want it stopped—the orders cancelled, the sheets and statues and lamps returned. I like the old lamps. I can sleep on the old sheets another season or two. In fact, I don't care if they carry me out on those old sheets. I want it stopped!"

His voice carried well. At the table beside us, the conversation stopped while faces turned our way. My father was making a scene—my father the conservative, low-profile judge. This moment was history.

The waiter stepped up to our table tentatively. "Everyone OK here, ladies? Judge Marshall-Hughs?"

The silence burned my ears; my father didn't even answer but slapped his hands to his face.

"We're fine, thanks," Mama told the waiter.

But I knew it was a big lie. We were not fine. My father and I were on the verge of declaring war.

"I want it to stop," Daddy said from behind his hands. He rubbed his eyes, then dropped his hands to the table, the strain evident on his face. "I'll cancel the rest of your credit cards tomorrow. Your monthly allowance will end as of now. I will pay off your previous debts, and I'll continue to pay the fees on your co-op, so you'll at least have a roof over your head."

Panic rose in my chest, booming there like an oversize heart. He wasn't bluffing. This was for real. The man was trying to kill me.

I turned to Mama, who merely shrugged, her eyes rueful. "He does have a point, Lanny."

His point eluded me, but I wasn't going to stick around and ask for clarification. I picked up my Gucci bag and, head held high, I marched from the table.

In the coat-check room I spied the two tiny shopping bags containing my parents' gifties and felt a wave of sickness. I hadn't had a chance to give them the things I had brought for them, the items I had chosen so lovingly.

After I tipped the coat-check person, I thought of taking the gifts inside, chasing the bad feelings away and putting an end to my father's brutal edict.

I turned toward the dining room, then paused.

This was not a breach that would be healed by a few small gifts.

I slipped into my cashmere coat and headed toward the door, calculating the cash refund from my Tiffany purchases.

Many unhappy returns.

9

Hailey

Maybe I'm too blindly optimistic, but when the phone rang, I crossed my fingers, hoping it was my agent. I had left a message for her that afternoon, and thought maybe, just maybe, she was calling to let me know that one of the producers from *All Our Tomorrows* had called to renew my contract.

Did I mention that my thirteen-week contract was about to expire?

Did I mention that I can be a ball of insecurities at times? As in most of the time.

I grabbed the phone hopefully, but the caller ID flashed WISCONSIN. My parents—probably calling from the nearest dairy store, where they would be stocking up on tofu, sprouts, and fresh veggies. Sunflower seeds and nuts and vitamins came in ten-pound packs through the mail. Otherwise, my mother, Teddie, made her own yogurt and bartered for eggs from a nearby farmer. Dad was the canning expert, and whenever I was home I tried to stay out of the garage for fear I would touch something that had been sterilized or leave the wax out in the sun to melt or snitch a berry, which was a big no-no when Dad was ready to make jam.

"Hey, Mom," I answered, wishing that they'd waited another few days for their weekly call. My folks didn't have a phone at the house—Dad had gone there determined to escape the invasive pressures of society, of which telephones topped the list—and consequently, they called me once a week, when they ventured into one of the local stores for supplies.

"Hey, Bright Star! How's it going?" It was Mom's nickname for me, a play on the fact that I was named for the comet. Yes, Halley's Comet. Part of that latent-hippie thing, but I always figured it could have been worse, and I might be trying to shed a name like Sunshine or Moonbeam.

"I'm fine," I said.

There was a muffled sound, after which Mom said, "Your father wants to know if they called you about a new contract yet?"

That was the pattern of the weekly call. Mom took the lead, with Dad in the background, feeding her questions.

I bent one leg and stretched into the warrior pose. "Not yet. But I had a pretty hot scene with Antonio Lopez today, and I think someone at a store recognized me."

"That's so exciting!" Mom said.

She probably didn't even know who Antonio Lopez was. How could she? My parents didn't have a television in their home, another post–Wall Street career measure to cut off the stress of civilization. At the homes of relatives, they had seen videotapes of me playing Ariel in *All Our Tomorrows,* a phenomenon that probably reinforces their resolve to avoid televisions.

"How's everything there?" I asked.

"Oh, fine. We got a new delivery of firewood, which will probably last us well into next winter. And before I forget, Sally Wallace's daughter may call you. She's headed off to New York to try the acting thing, so I gave her your number and told her you would show her the ropes. Her name is Jennifer."

Great news: another aspiring actress named Jen who can screw up my latte order at Starbucks.

Mom went on about Jennifer's family. Didn't I remember the family with the four girls who used to canoe together on the lake? Dark hair, all of them, and their mom had moved to Wisconsin from Chicago?

Not a clue, but I pretended to recollect the Wallaces to move the conversation along. Which was a mistake, since she boomeranged back to the crucial questions: "When do you think you'll hear about more work? How are you paying your bills?"

Beep! I was saved by call-waiting, flashing Alana's cell number.

"Mom, I've got another call. Do you want to hold?"

"Oh, no, that's OK. I'll phone you again next week."

After a quick good-bye, I clicked to Alana.

"Thank God you picked up," she said, an oddly high pitch in her voice. "I need you now. Can you come?"

"What happened? Where are you?"

"I'm just outside Bon Nuit. Can you meet me here right away?"

"Sure." I grabbed my Nine West heels. "But what are you doing there?" Wild thoughts flashed through my head: that Alana had returned to the store after I left an hour ago, that she'd decked the redheaded Marcella, that she'd been handcuffed by security and arrested . . .

"I'll explain when you get here. Meet me in cosmetics, at the Trenda counter."

I grabbed a leather jacket, one ankle wobbling in its high heel as I snatched up my keys. Flying out the door, I tried to speculate about what could have happened to Alana.

With my imagination, that was dangerous territory.

10

Alana

What's that notion that a thief returns to the scene of her crime?

I admit, it felt tacky to be back in the cosmetics department of Bon Nuit on the very same night I'd had the altercation with the sales clerk. What was her name? Martha? Marley? Marchesa?

Oh, it didn't matter as long as I never laid eyes on her again. The only thing I cared about was buying Hailey's favorite shade of Trenda lipstick and leaving the scene before the sales clerk from hell tried another round of thumb wrestling. I never did get my credit card back, but it was OK, since that one was cancelled and Daddy wouldn't get to the rest of them until tomorrow morning.

It was already after seven. I had approximately twelve more hours of financial freedom . . . and less than two hours until most of the stores closed. One last night of shopping before the bottom fell out of my life, and I was determined to make the most of it. Somehow

I knew I had to start my last hurrah by purchasing Hailey's lipstick; if I could just right that one wrong, maybe it would set some positive karma in motion for me.

I retraced my steps to the Trenda counter, disappointed to find that no one was there. What is with these clerks? Either they hover over you like they own the cosmetics factory, or else there's no one in sight.

By contrast, there were three clerks over at Estee Lauder, two at Ralph Lauren—and one of them was that red-haired clerk. I felt my shiny talons emerge. My nemesis. What was she sounding off about now?

Had she been fired for her transgression? Slowly, I moved closer. She was still wearing a mint green cosmetics-counter smock, and from the way she was prattling on to her coworker, she seemed in need of some therapy. I sidled within earshot, planting myself behind a watermelon-size bottle of purple eau de toilette.

"You know, when they took me upstairs to HR, I thought, 'That bitch! She could've lost me my job.' "

I froze. She was talking about me!

"But it didn't turn out that way at all," Marcella—I finally remembered her name—went on. "I thought Mr. Pomerantz was going to yell at me, even fire me, but no! Instead, they are going to transfer me to the buyers' division. Can you believe that dumb luck? A buyer, all because they think I have real potential, but maybe not so good at working directly with the customers. So I get to go to buyers' school and channel my aggressions toward those idiots from the wholesalers. Can you believe it? So I should thank that hipster monster."

"Yes." I stepped out from behind the giant perfume bottle, my hands balling into fists. "You really should thank me."

Red's eyes flashed with fury, and for a minute I

thought she would spring onto me with claws and teeth bared.

But no . . . a subtle shift, a steely resolve. And what was that in her eyes. Respect? Or maybe a flash of humor.

"The hipster monster returns," she said. "That's good, 'cause I have something for you." She took a box from the pocket of her smock, a small box with the Trenda foil seal on it. "I saved this for you."

I stared at the lipstick as if it would brand my palm. "Carnation Kiss?"

She shrugged. "It's all wrong for your friend. But don't listen to me. Let her walk around like a hideous buffoon in clown makeup. Sometimes you gotta look the other way and let people be happy with themselves. Anyway, that's what Mr. Pomerantz said."

The surge of delight over my victory was slightly offset by Marcella's surrender and the fact that she had reserved a tube of lipstick for me . . . well, it just wasn't done.

This woman was the rare exception, though I wasn't yet sure if that was a good thing or not.

"Everything OK here?" Hailey came onto the scene, moving tentatively. Her hair swung back as she looked over her shoulder. "No one called security yet?"

I passed her the tube of Carnation Kiss. "Try this on."

"My shade." She brightened a little, then turned to the mirror on the counter. I think every clerk in cosmetics watched with bated breath as she slid the shiny marbelized tube out of the box, uncapped it, unrolled, applied.

The bright red glistened orange on her lips. A clownish shade.

Gorgeous Hailey looked hideous.

"It's awful," I delivered the verdict quietly. "It does make her look jaundiced."

Hailey smiled into the mirror, then shuddered. "Yucky." She took two tissues from a box offered by a nearby clerk. "I can't believe I ever wore that shade."

"You were right," I told Marcella, gracefully conceding. Like my father, I fight my arguments to the finish, but when proven wrong I defer to the truth. "Those were your words exactly."

Marcella straightened the lapels of her mint smock with pursed lips. "Uh-huh."

"I was so wrong," I admitted, addressing the cluster of clerks. "This woman knows her colors. I will always buy cosmetics from Marcella."

The women chimed in with "Oh, sure!" and "She's the best!" and "I thought they were doing a makeover." The tension dissolved as people returned to their stations, shoppers went back to their shopping, and Marcella stepped up to the counter and picked up the controversial lipstick.

"You try it," she told me. "It's your color."

I rolled it on and blotted. Let me tell you, it looked like spicy red joy on my lips. "Hallelujah," I sang.

Marcella cracked her gum. The woman chewed gum. Unbelievable. "Told ya," she said.

"Look, I feel like an idiot," I said.

"Well, at least you don't look like one." Having removed the last of Carnation Kiss, Hailey was applying a cinnamon shade from her bag. "I just had big, orange clown lips in front of a dozen cosmetics experts. Do you think anyone recognized me?"

"I apologize, Marcella. Hey, do you work on commission? Would it help if we bought tons of makeup tonight?" I asked.

She tugged on a dangly earring. "Sure, but, did you bring cash?"

Cash? Oh . . . the credit thing. I felt my face warm with embarrassment. "I do have a purse full of charge cards, one of which is bound to be valid, and Hailey and I are dying to stock up on cosmetics. Anything you can show us in the spring colors?"

"Plenty!" Marcella motioned us over to the Trenda counter. "We can start by establishing your personal palettes, since you know firsthand that every color doesn't suit every person. Over here. Let's start with you, blondie . . ."

The woman had an eye for color, but she definitely didn't belong in sales. Maybe I'd done her a favor by getting her bumped up to buyers' school. As Marcella began explaining about hues and skin tones and seasons, I checked my watch. Already past seven-thirty.

"You'll have to step up the pace, Marcella," I said. "We're already converted, so no use preaching to the choir. Just load us up with the goodies. We've got a lot of shopping to do before the doors close on us."

A whole lot of shopping.

11

Hailey

"So let me get this straight," I said as Alana and I watched that smiling, petite granny-type at Zarela's carve up an avocado to prepare our fresh guacamole right at our table. "All that stuff you bought tonight? You don't really want it?"

"Exactly." Alana dipped a chip in salsa. "Except maybe for the Burberry. As I said, I'm conflicted about that plaid."

The Burberry hat had been a "what the hell!" purchase. Otherwise, Alana had chosen her items mostly by price tag, the more expensive the better. We'd quickly cut over to Tiffany's because she realized that jewelry was compact and easy to carry with the added bonus of being outrageously expensive. As the bell rang to close the store, Alana paid a porter to transport our purchases back to the apartment, leaving us free to cab it over to Zarela's and join the Cinco de Mayo celebration.

"So you bought the closetful of stuff to return it . . ."

"And get cash back. Let me tell you, it's going to

take me a few days to return all that merchandise, but at least it will give me a little liquid cash to get myself going. I tell you, I don't believe my father. He's never pulled a power trip like this before."

"Do you want to talk about it?" I offered. She'd given me just a few salient details as we shopped.

"Honey, I couldn't bear to give you a play-by-play. Let me just say that he's going to cover the co-op expenses, so at least I won't be homeless."

We won't be homeless, I thought, recalling that I was a few months behind on the rent I owed Alana. I really, really needed that new contract from *All Our Tomorrows*.

"But beyond the roof over my head and an occasional salad smuggled in by Mama, when Daddy cuts me off, I'm going to be penniless. No spending money whatsoever. And you know I can't live that way."

I shook my head. "I am so sorry. What will you do?"

"Find a job, I guess," she said airily. I don't think the real trauma had sunk in yet.

Poor Alana. The question remained, what would she do? "What kind of work were you thinking of?" I asked, recalling that she did not possess any so-called marketable skills.

"I had a tiny epiphany while we were having that lovefest with Marcella back at the cosmetics department. I've always marveled at the easy job those perfume sprayers have. Don't you think I could wax that? How hard could it be to say, 'Endeavor? Endeavor? Endeavor?' like, twenty-five times a day?"

She had a point.

"And now that we've bonded with Marcella, I figure I've got an in at Bon Nuit," Alana went on. "I'm going to call her in the morning, first thing tomorrow. Or maybe the next day. I've got an appointment for a hot-stone massage, and then there's all that merchandise to return. But eventually, I am going to get myself a new job spritzing elegant ladies."

"Been there, done that. It was kind of fun, too, but after the Christmas season they let all of us go." Talk of my spritzing experience reminded me of the lean days before I had gotten acting work. No health insurance, no spending money. I lived in a creepy basement apartment with two roommates who eventually became a couple. I waited tables in a diner, which didn't help when I sneaked out to auditions smelling of grease. I saved up my change for a cup of designer coffee in the morning, going to Starbucks a little later so I could read someone else's leftover newspaper. It was not a pretty life.

Those were the days before I'd been adopted by Alana, who let me move into her spare bedroom for a fraction of the Madison Avenue rent. Before I could afford to have my hair set and cut by a stylist. Before I could afford manicures and facials and fabuloso dinners at places like Zarela's where the little granny makes you guacamole.

If you've even been to Zarela's, you know the woman. It's her job to go to each incoming party and offer up her fine avocado-smashing services. I have watched her do her thing over businessmen trying to best each other, over the argument of a couple, over a rather lurid conversation I once had with my girlfriends about the hazards of giving blow jobs to uncircumcised men. And no matter what's going on at the table, the little granny smiles and smashes away. I love the little granny.

"Thank you," I told her as she finished up. I handed her a few singles and Alana slipped her a twenty-dollar bill. Granny bowed as if we'd both handed her gold bullion, then moved to another table.

"Did I just hand that lady twenty dollars?" Alana

asked me. When I nodded she smacked her forehead. "What an idiot I am! I'm poor myself and I'm giving away hefty tips. I wish I could call her back."

"Consider it a parting gift. Besides, you're not poor until tomorrow, Cinderella, and the night is young."

"Exactly what I was thinking, Hailey. Dinner is on me, then after that let's go bar hopping or out to a club or something. You've got your contract coming up and I've got my parental problems and I say we deserve a little treat. If this is our last chance for a while, let's go for it!"

"That sounds more like the Alana I know." I lifted my margarita glass in a toast, knowing this was a bonding moment. Not that we hadn't bonded a million times over shopping, but to date, we had not been down and out and broke at the same time. "And thank you. For everything. You're such a giver, Alana. I don't know where I'd be without you."

"Don't start! You're going to get me choked up." She waved a petite hand, rapidly fanning her eyes. "And you're too sweet to be living without a fairy godmother in New York. Just remember me when you're up on stage at Radio City, accepting your Emmy Award."

"Remember you? You'd better be there." We clinked glasses and some slopped over my hand. We both sipped, then I dabbed at the spill with a napkin.

But Alana, having latched onto something transpiring behind me, slammed her hand on the table. "Damn them!"

"What happened? Who?" I looked over my shoulder but didn't see anything out of the ordinary.

"It's just so typical," she said, snapping a corn chip in half. "I think my father called in his spies."

12

Alana

When I saw them walk in, I was so annoyed that I considered slipping out the back door of the restaurant. Please! To send them here to watch me now—it was all so controlling, I wanted to barrel through the crowd at the door and pummel Trevor on his chest.

However, I have always been conscious of the image I cut in society, and my impeccable reputation does not come from sneaking out of establishments—save for the one time when I was aiding the escape of a well-known rock star who shall remain nameless. But I was only twenty then, and he was incredibly gorgeous, and sometimes you have to compromise a little and know that you're on a roller coaster ride that's going to end, but not without a thrill of satisfaction.

"Where are the spies?" Hailey hissed as she studied the people waiting in the reception area.

"Just my cousin Trevor and his friends. I'm sure my father sent him to keep an eye on me and report back."

I gritted my teeth. "I'm going to scream. Can I scream here?" The restaurant was crowded now, every table filled, and with the festive acoustic guitar music playing over the sound system, I wasn't sure anyone would notice an isolated shout of anguish.

"I remember Trevor," Hailey said. "He's the party animal, right?"

"Big coke hound. Partied his way into rehab a few times. His mama, my Aunt Nessie, even sprang for the Betty Ford Clinic, but it didn't stick: he fell into the cocaine again and nearly got himself a year in jail." I had to admit, he didn't look the druggy type tonight, his face a little more filled out, his dark eyes mellow instead of that hopped-up, nervous, glassy appearance. He wore a fine gray suit with a darker gray shirt that complemented his dark brown skin. Trevor is tall and lean, with the mile-high stature of a pro basketball player without that stretched-out look.

At the moment, he was flirting with the hostess, who seemed charmed by Trevor and his right-hand man, Xavier Goodman. Let me tell you something about Xavier; if you give him an inch, that brother wants a yard. He is a pushy, smooth-talking piece of work who makes it his daily mission to charm the panties off sweet young things. Consider X a living example of the damage a pretty face can do: give a man perfect teeth, dimples, and sympathetic eyes, and he will never bother to use the brain in his head.

"Do you recognize his friends?" Hailey asked.

"That caramel cool brother with the killer smile is Xavier Goodman. He calls himself a comedian, but I beg to differ."

"I think I've seen him on HBO," Hailey said.

"Oh, he'd love to hear that. And the third dude is a sweetheart. I adore Kyle. He's always polite and witty and dressed to kill. I don't get why he hangs out with those two losers, but he sticks around for some reason."

As we talked, Trevor spotted us at our table. He made a motion to join us, but I shook my head and swiped my hand over my neck in a cutting gesture.

But did Trevor listen?

He was already pushing past the hostess, borrowing a chair from a nearby table, and tucking into the head of our four-seat table. "I should have known you'd be out doing the party thing on Cinco de Mayo!"

"Right." I gave him a cold look as he kissed me on the cheek. "Pretend it's a coincidence."

Bulldozing over my comment, he turned to Hailey and extended his hand. "Hi, I'm Trevor Marshall-Hughs, Alana's cousin. Haven't we met before? You do look familiar, sweet pea. These are my friends, Kyle Dexter and Xavier Goodman. Like to call him X-man, if you know what I mean. I hope you don't mind if we join you, but as you can see, the joint is jumping and packed to the gills, and we've got three hungry brothers here with places to go."

As he spoke, Kyle and Xavier slid into the two empty chairs and started fussing over Hailey and me as if we were offering them water in the desert. It's just so typical of Trevor and Xavier, buttering up and sucking up to get exactly what they wanted.

The waitress came over and I sulked as she took our order. If my frantic night of spending was taking an unwanted detour, why couldn't it be with an eligible bachelor I was interested in? Kyle was nice enough, but not my type, my cousin was like an annoying brother, and Xavier was the antithesis of my perfect man. And now that these brothers had hooked up with us, they were a toxic mix of manicide, guaranteed to chase away any healthy, well-adjusted possibilities.

Please. OK, dinner was a write-off. But at least Kyle had the seat next to me.

"Hey, pretty lady," he said almost shyly. "That is one fine suit you're wearing." He tilted his head over the table for a better look. "Damn if it isn't Chanel. And that ring . . ." He lifted my hand onto the table to study my amethyst-and-diamond cocktail ring. "Now that is exquisite. It looks like a Gerrard. Did you get it in Europe?"

I squeezed his arm, my fingertips falling into the buttery texture of his sleeve. "You know your designers, Kyle. Actually, Gerrard just opened a boutique here, in a Soho loft. Haven't you heard? Jade Jagger is their creative director."

"I did read about that, but it's by appointment only. I can't believe you got in already. I'm so jealous."

"When are you going to get out of that horrendous insurance company and get a job that uses your talents?"

"And starve?" Kyle lamented. "No, thank you, girl. I'm happy in my little cubicle, going over actuarial tables and bringing home the bacon every two weeks. Some of us need a steady paycheck."

Our attention shifted across the table where Xavier and Trevor were making a huge fuss over Hailey, having recalled that she appeared on a soap opera.

"A real, live actress!" Trevor shouted for the tenth time, causing heads to turn toward our table, where Hailey, God love her, was flushing strawberry pink.

"I can't believe I'm sitting beside the fish-girl on *All Our Tomorrows*," X said.

Trevor flung a hand at him. "She ain't no fish-girl! She's a mermaid. Get it right, bro."

"Excuse me!" I cut in. "Her past is a mystery. She doesn't remember where she came from, but was found floating in Indigo Falls. You know, if you guys can't watch, at least buy yourself a copy of *Soap Opera Digest.*"

"So, Hailey, you're a woman of mystery," Kyle said. "I confess, I've never seen your show, but if you're an example of the new cast of daytime, I just might tune in."

"Thank you!" she said sincerely. "Honestly, it's been a roller coaster ride since they signed me on. And New York became a much friendlier place once I could afford a cab ride. I'm not from around here."

"How did I know that?" Trevor asked.

"Maybe it's the fact that she hasn't solicited you or lifted your wallet yet?" Xavier added.

"Not to pester you," Trevor went on. "But can you answer me one question about the show? Are you really a mermaid? Or is that just some lame-o twist the writers threw in to make us tune in tomorrow?"

"I really couldn't say," Hailey answered.

"Aaaww!" the guys moaned in unison.

"No, really! The truth is, I don't even know what's going to happen next week! I'm not sure the writers know yet. And forget about figuring out who my parents were and if I'm really entitled to part of Preston Scott's vast fortune. The writers seem to change their minds on those details every month."

"That must be a challenge for you," Kyle said politely. "Playing a scene without knowing your full character drive and motivation."

Hailey was nodding. "Well, yeah, it is. Do you work in the business?"

Xavier laughed. "Naw, he's just in the boring business."

"Insurance," Kyle said apologetically.

"Well, let me give you one word of advice there, Ariel," Trevor said. "Whatever you do, don't be getting into bed with Preston Scott, 'cause if he turns out to be your father, that is downright skelly."

Hailey nearly choked on her margarita. "I promise, I'll do my best. Oh, that would be so *Chinatown,* wouldn't it? I hope the writers don't go that way."

"I never did like that Preston Scott," X said. "Man walks around like someone shoved a stick up his tuxedo tail."

"Enough of the Q and A," I said, turning to my cousin. "You might as well fess up now before I poison your salsa. Tell us the real reason you're dogging me tonight."

"Dogging you?" Trevor's face crumpled in a comic smirk. "I don't think so, but let me check my calendar. Oh, right, Thursday night. It's dog-the-cousin day."

The three guys laughed as if this were the funniest thing they'd ever heard.

I smoothed the fake-fur lapel of my plum Chanel suit, waiting for them to settle down. "Did you, or did you not receive a phone call from my father instructing you to keep an eye on me?"

"Uncle Ernest?" His eyes narrowed. "You serious about this? What's going on?"

"Just answer the question."

"Spoken like a true judge's daughter," he said. "Look, I swear, your father didn't sic me on you, though I'm liking the sound of this little situation."

"Intriguing," Kyle said.

"Almost better than *All Our Tomorrows,*" Xavier said, and Trevor shot him a scowl. "Almost."

"So tell us, Alana. What's happening with Uncle E?"

"Nothing, really," I lied. "Just a little cold war."

"It's worse than that," Hailey said ruefully. "They had a fight and Judge Marshall-Hughs cut off Alana's budget. Cut her off completely, without warning. Isn't it awful?"

She'd blurted out the whole thing before I had a chance to wince, scowl, wave frantically, or shove a corn chip in her mouth. I was left to face a table of confused, disquieted men who probably didn't have a clue about the sacred relationship between a single girl and her wardrobe budget.

"Get out!" Trevor said. "The judge has a big, soft spot for you, Alana. What you do to make him so mad?"

"Nothing," Hailey said. "It's just so unfair."

"Have you tried to talk with him?" Kyle asked. "It's always best to keep the lines of communication open."

"I think it's a little soon for that," I said. "He's still boiling over. But you know what? This is all a flash in the pan, and—hey, look at that. Our food is here! Who ordered the tamales?"

As we ate, Trevor entertained us with stories of my Aunt Nessie, how he was trying to help her computerize her business records, but she continued to back everything up with her old ledgers and notepads and clipboards.

"I come in, and everything's input on the computer and I'm like—great! But then I see Mama working on her little charts and clipboards, and she tells me she needs to have her records on paper in case the electricity goes out. Can you believe her?"

"Woman's got a point," Kyle said. "After that big blackout in 2003? New York shut down, but Ms. Nessie still delivered her dinners to her customers, didn't she?"

X dug into his rice. "That's the beauty of cooking with gas."

Before I was even born, my Aunt Nessie started cooking meals for the neighbors who worked too late to make dinner, and within two years she had her own homemade dinner catering business, serving Great

Neck, Manhasset, Little Neck, and Douglaston. There are two hospitals in the area and lots of doctors and technicians were willing to pay good money for some home-fried chicken, meat loaf, ribs or fried flounder, with comforting sides like mashed potatoes, black-eyed peas, buttered greens, and sweet corn.

These days, she has a million-dollar business, still cooking in Maw-maw's old, though renovated, kitchen, in the house where my Daddy grew up. My other aunts, Faunia and Coral, also live in Great Neck. Faunia works in a doctor's office, but Coral helps Nessie cook, with desserts being her specialty. For them the business is a labor of love. Trevor doesn't cook but wants to take over the management, and there's some speculation among the family members that he might not "do the right thing," though so far, my parents have not intervened.

It all makes me a little crazy, since Trevor, God love him, has gone down the tubes three times but somehow maintained his hero status. Me, I go to a charity ball where Courtney Love pops out of her bra and my father thinks my reputation is tarnished for life.

Don't you hate that double standard?

The talk segmented into different groups. I stabbed a section of lobster enchilada and turned to Kyle, who seemed to want to say something.

"I can tell this thing with your father has got you down."

I reached for my margarita. "I'm trying not to think about it."

"Don't feel bad. I used to fight with my dad all the time."

"That's the weird thing, Kyle. We usually don't argue. Daddy used to want to take care of me . . . daddy's little girl. He used to enjoy paying my bills, looking after me."

"Well, I gave up fighting with my dad," Kyle went on. "The last time we argued, hip-huggers were in style." He shot a glance at the waitress, who wore low-slung jeans beneath her white apron, then frowned. "OK, then. Maybe that was yesterday."

I smiled. Kyle always worked hard to make everyone in the group feel at ease. I wondered why a good, solid woman hadn't snatched up this sweetheart long ago.

Somehow the talk turned to the almighty X—no surprise—and Hailey believed him when he told her he'd been pitching a sitcom to a cable network. How many times had I heard that story?

"We're in development now," he said. "If we get a green light, I'll have to relocate to the West Coast, at least for a while."

"That is so exciting!" Hailey enthused.

You have to feel for the girl; two years in Manhattan and still not a scratch in her trusting soul.

"Maybe you can find a part for Hailey," I pressed X. "Something funny for a gorgeous, fashionable, wholesome girl from Wisconsin?"

Xavier flashed his killer smile. "Maybe. You know, we could write something in."

"That would be so great!" Hailey waved her fists in the air like a runner doing a bony victory dance. Cute as a button, but the girl doesn't have a lick of soul.

"Yeah, X is getting hot here on the comedy circuit. In fact, he's got a gig at Stone Cold Comedy tonight." Trevor checked his watch. "That's why we were so pressed to get a table; the man's got commitments. In fact, we should get going."

"You ladies like to come along?" Kyle offered. "We could share a cab."

Hailey turned to me, her eyes wide with that "please-please-please!" look.

"I don't think so." A night of forced laughter and Trevor's friends did not fit into my spending plans.

"You have to come," Xavier said. "If you don't come, I'll think you don't like me. I'll be destroyed. Devastated. And all that nasty stuff."

"Do you have an early call tomorrow?" Kyle asked Hailey.

"Actually, I have the day off." Her eyes were on me, begging.

"Come on, Alana," Trevor scolded me, "snap out of your funk and tell your friend you'll make it a party."

I sighed. "Fine. Excuse me while I go put on my comedy face."

Leaving my cousin Trevor to take care of the bill, I slipped off to the ladies' room to take the sheen off my face. Afterward, I popped out the door to find Xavier waiting for me, dangling my coat.

"We were getting ready to deploy a SWAM team for you," he said.

"You mean a SWAT team," I said, turning to ease my arms into the sleeve.

"Nope. Mine stands for Stop Wearing Allthat Make-up."

I rolled my eyes. "Xavier, I wish I could laugh, really I do. I'm afraid I'm just a little too smart for your humor."

"You calling my humor dumb?" He reached around and pulled my jacket closed, letting his hands linger there, a warm weight over my breasts. It felt good, I admit that. I'll also admit that those hands have been there before in a much more intimate setting, skin on skin. But that was long ago, before I knew the perving, prowling X. Since then, I had learned that those warm hands led to a path of destruction.

I stepped away and turned around, hands on my hips. "Can I ask you a question? When are you going to get the message? When are you going to stop trying to get up my skirt?"

He feigned innocence. "Did I do anything?"

"Don't start with the act. I don't know how many ways I can spell it out for you, Xavier. I'm not interested. The kitchen is closed. Alana has left the building."

He gave a slight smile. "Left the building? I like that one."

I turned toward the door. "Just as long as you believe it."

13

Hailey

"This is so exciting," I said as we stood in the back of the club, waiting to be shown a table. Xavier was hanging back in the bar, along with the other comedians waiting to go on, while we went in to enjoy the show, and the atmosphere at the smoky bar reminded me of backstage in the few small productions I'd been in. Tense. Hilarious. Morose. Manic.

I loved it. I wanted to stay in that electrified jungle, but Trevor ushered us through to the club, promising that Xavier would join us after he performed.

"Who cares about Xavier," I shot to Alana, feeling giddy.

"Damn right." She tilted her head at me. "Honey, you are looped."

"Hey, it's Cinco de Mayo!" I giggled and snapped my fingers, feeling more festive than I'd felt in a long, long time. It didn't hurt that I'd lost count of margaritas after Trevor had ordered a few pitchers. The alcohol had rushed right to my insecurities, putting a bandage on my problems. When I stopped into the restroom and caught myself in the mirror, I considered myself a very attractive person—really!—and in the full-length mirror there, I saw that my Nine West polka dot ankle-strap shoes did look fine with jeans. Actually, they weren't fine, they looked fucking great.

I looked fu— well, I think I looked pretty darned good.

"I can't believe we're at a comedy club with one of the performers," I said. "This is just so exciting for me."

"Hello?" Alana squinted at me. "Honey, you are Ariel on *All Our Tomorrows.* You are leagues ahead of low-life comics like Xavier Goodman. Believe me, this is no big deal. I think they pay him cab fare for his fifteen minutes on stage."

"But he's getting a cable show soon. Alana, I know you're not a fan, but the guy is talented."

She sucked in a breath. "You'll see."

"Either way, I'm at a comedy club for the first time ever, staying up late, and I don't even have to work tomorrow. Even if I don't get paid for the day, I'm going to stay up late and I'm going to own it." Enough of whining and worrying about getting my contract renewed. That was so dumb. Nobody wanted to hear that. I shouted over the applauding audience, *"I own this night!"*

"You do that, girl. Take control and enjoy the ride. Somebody's got to be in the pilot's seat."

Our eyes were adjusting to the dimly lit rows of tables surrounding a stage of white light where a dark-haired woman in a black leather jacket talked about how she worried over her daughter wanting only blond Barbies, blond brownies, and vanilla ice cream. We zigzagged through crowded tables and chairs to our spot. As we went to sit down, someone squealed behind us.

"Girls! Get out! What are you doing here?"

Alana and I turned together. Marcella sat at a long table with a crowd of women; from the density of their foundation and eye liner, I guessed they sold cosmetics at Bon Nuit.

Alana gasped politely. "We were dragged here screaming against our will."

"We're friends with the talent," I said in that insider's voice. "How about you?"

"It's girls' night out. We do this every month or so, a bunch of us." She gestured to her friends, then leaned closer to my ear. "Let me warn you, there's a two-drink minimum, and don't let them talk you into the frozen drinks. They cost twice as much. Not worth it."

"Thanks for the tip," Alana said, taking a seat on the other side of the table.

My seat ended up backing up to Marcella's, and she turned her chair around so that we could talk. At first I was a little nervous with her. I wasn't quite as good as Alana at making instant best friends. While other people ask a million questions and try to plumb the details of your life, I'm sort of stuck on small talk, worried about whether it's too invasive to ask the other person a string of personal questions. "If I want someone to know about my life, I'll write a book," my father used to say when people barraged him with questions about where he grew up, where he used to live, what he did for a living.

But not to worry—Marcella had the conversation covered. She clearly wanted to give me her opinion about the woman on stage, the price of appetizers here, the condition of the ladies' room, the poor choice of floor tile. Listening to her, I was amazed at the total flip in the situation. Here this woman who had been wrestling with my friend was now giving me advice and telling the waitress I wanted my drink with ice on the side "so's they don't skimp on the booze," she said.

It was all so warm and fuzzy—my new friend Marcella, my big night out, the lady at the next table who told me I was great on *All Our Tomorrows*. I felt the urge to hug somebody, but I figured that was probably the tequila kicking in.

"Oh, this next guy is good," Marcella said when she spotted the tall Hispanic man waiting at the edge of the stage. "You are gonna laugh so hard, honey. He's a total pisser."

She was right. I started letting my buzz take over, letting my mind follow the images the comics conjured, letting myself laugh.

At the break, Alana introduced Marcella to Kyle and Trevor, who insisted that she join our table.

"I would love to!" Marcella responded. "But first let me pay up for my gin and tonics." She turned back to the table and opened her purse—a smart little beaded bag. Fendi, I think.

"Don't worry about it." Trevor leaned over to the next table, and snatched up the running tab. "We'll take care of it. Drink up and enjoy, my friends. My man X is coming on soon, and we want you all to be ready to laugh."

"Oh, Jesus, did you see that?" Marcella said to me. "Does he mean that?" She spoke up. "What's the matter with you, Trevor? You can't pay that bill! My friends are prepared to pay for their own drinks."

"Relax! I've got it covered, short stuff."

"Let him do it," Alana told Marcella. "It's all part of the Trevor show."

When the lights went down, Marcella settled in beside me and set her focus on Alana, Trevor, and Kyle, who sat across the table.

"That was awfully nice of him, picking up my tab and all the girls from work, too," she said. "Either he's totally insane or the man is loaded. And since he doesn't seem too crazy . . . what, is the guy rich?"

"Their family is fairly well-off . . . the Marshall-Hughs," I said, keeping my voice low, as I didn't think Alana would appreciate me sharing her life story. "Trevor's mother owns a catering business—a big deal out on Long Island. And Alana's parents are sort of prestigious. Her mother teaches at NYU, and her father is a federal judge. There's some talk that he might be appointed to the Supreme Court one day."

"Really." She sucked it all in, savoring.

A few minutes later, she tapped my shoulder and asked: "But is Alana happy?"

I shrugged.

Marcella answered, "No."

"I'm not so sure."

"Trust me, honey. Your friend Alana is miserable. Do you know that story about the poor little rich girl? The one where her family's got all the money, but they get separated, and she has to live in poverty at an orphanage with all that money. Then her father comes along but she doesn't recognize him, and since he got blinded in the war he doesn't recognize her either."

And critics claim daytime dramas are far-fetched?

"It's so sad," Marcella went on, though I wasn't sure if she was referring to Alana or the story of the little rich girl. "Do you see how those guys tried to talk to her during the break? How they tried to get a rap going, but she turned them down flat? I'm telling you, she is more concerned with the right color lip gloss than with letting a relationship happen. And the whole point of getting the right color lip gloss is to make that relationship happen."

Hard to follow, I know, but I sensed an odd thread of logic in Marcella's proclamation.

"I'm going to help her," Marcella said, folding her arms. "I am going to make our beautiful African-American princess my personal mission."

I lifted my cosmo glass and hid behind it. Alana was staring at us, probably because we were talking through the comic's performance. "How would you do that?" I asked Marcella.

"Simple. I'll fix whatever is wrong with her life."

I shook my head. That would take a lot of fixing. Any life requires major repair work.

I hoped that Marcella wouldn't get stuck in a pothole.

14

Alana

When Xavier stepped on stage, introduced as X-man, I admit I was struck by his fine, real fine appearance. The lights gave a vibrant sheen to his chocolate brown skin, and when he smiled, those dimples softened the killer grin, making him a study in contradictions: bad boy meets dream date. If Hollywood is really the land of illusions, maybe X did have a shot out there.

As Xavier warmed up the audience, I remembered that he wasn't so bad in the looks department. If only the brother weren't so obnoxious.

"Let me ask you, we got any royalty here tonight?" He held a hand up to shield his eyes from the stage lights. "Every guy has at least one princess in his life. You know what I'm talking about, right, guys?"

I reached for my cosmo. Slow start there, X.

"I don't care if she's a midwestern princess, a Jewish-American princess, an Asian princess, or an African-American princess . . . every culture has them. And the United States, this country is a magnet for princesses.

Hell, in England they've got one or two, maybe a handful in Liechtenstein. Liechtenstein, I love to say that. Sounds like you're soliciting a prostitute in Bavaria. Lick-ten-stein? Ya, ya! Good!"

Of course, he would go for the sex joke. So predictable.

"But every culture has its princesses. Hell, I think every guy has at least one princess in his life, that unattainable, smoking sister who wavers between spoiled bitch and sultry vixen. And she always thinks you're coming on to her. You do something innocent, like help her on with her coat and she says, 'X! X? Now we'll have none of that!' like a little old librarian. She'll say, 'Ain't never gonna happen.' Or, 'The kitchen is closed.' Or, 'My coco has left the building.'"

I bolted up in my chair. The bastard! He was using our conversation as part of his routine.

"Sometimes you think, is it me? Am I doing something wrong? But the thing is, the princess doesn't date anyone, and that's because her standards are so high. Only the perfect man for the princess."

All around me people were laughing, and I didn't get it. Why was that so funny? Why shouldn't a girl find herself a perfect man? Didn't these people read *Glamour* and *Cosmo* and *Vogue*?

These people were weird.

"Now you might wonder how to recognize a princess? Well, the manicured nails are a dead giveaway. We're not talking about a little polish. They're encrusted with gems, with little flowers and hearts painted on, and tiny tattoos.

"These nails are sacred. Ain't no boogy flickin' going on with these little gems. No doors get opened, no typin' on a keyboard. No peeling, scrubbing, slicing, or dicing. The princess gives these nails the royal treatment.

"I'm waiting for these chicks to start embedding microchips in their nails. Know what I mean? Microchips. So they wouldn't even have to hold a cell phone anymore. Just flip one finger up and talk to the hand."

He flipped up his index finger and recited in a high voice, "Speed dial Tiffany's!"

The audience started to roar as he then stuck his finger in his ear and squeaked on. "Hello? Quick question: can I get a solitaire diamond ring with three diamonds? Only one? But my friend Muffy has three!

"Microchips. Yeah! I'm gonna patent that idea—don't you steal it! I'd like to patent it, but I do see one potential problem. See, if a brother's really lucky, his princess knows how to use her hands. Know what I mean? That's right. The princess whose daddy spent all that money on music lessons. The princess who plays the flute. Every guy wants to go out with a princess who knows her way around a mouth pipe. That's right."

He pointed to a man in the audience. "You'd rather have tulips on your organ than flowers on your piano, right? Right?"

I snatched my bag from the table, ready to spring. I didn't have to take this abuse.

"The princess and the flute. Problem is, if she's got a cell phone in her fingers, you don't know what kind of calls she'll be making during sex. I mean, she'd be moving her hand along down there, at a nice, steady rhythm, and suddenly she's speed-dialed her hair stylist. And you're there screaming, 'I'm coming! I'm coming!' And someone from the salon is on the other end shouting back, 'Not today! Not today! We're totally booked!' "

Enough! I stood up so abruptly my chair fell back, but I didn't care. My movements were muffled by the applause and laughter of the audience. No one cared. No one even noticed as I pushed out into the lobby bar, the heels of my shoes striking the tiled floor with a satisfying thunk.

That bastard. He could talk to the hand, all right!

15

Hailey

She had flown out of the comedy club so quickly, I thought she'd gotten sick. Instead, she was bolting for the street exit.

"Alana! Wait!" She turned at the curb, but didn't lower the hand flagging a cab.

"You coming along?" she asked.

"Where are we going?" came a voice behind me. Marcella.

"We'll figure something out." A yellow taxi pulled up and Alana opened the door.

Marcella marched past me and scooted across the backseat.

"You coming?" Alana asked me.

Of course I was, but things were moving just a little too fast for my slightly buzzed head. Inside the cab, tucked in the middle, I started feeling sick and asked to have a window rolled down. Alana gave instructions to the driver, and I gripped the back divider and tried to keep my eyes on the street outside.

"What a useless waste of humanity," Alana said. "Xavier Goodman. He should change his name to Badman."

"He was totally out of line, using you for material that way," Marcella said. "What are you gonna do now?"

"I'd love to string him up . . . by his short and curlies."

It took a while for me to catch on to that. "Ouch." My teeth slammed over a pothole, but that felt good. Solid felt OK; it was the fluffy, loopy turns that made my stomach shriek.

"And then there's Trevor, who might as well have been spying on me for the way he just about ruined my night. He's my cousin, family, but I don't buy his straight act for a minute. That brother can't be trusted."

"I thought he was nice," Marcella said. "He picked up the tab for me and my whole table. That's a real gentleman for you."

Alana swung her baby dreads toward the door and faced us. "If you could buy gentility, my cousin would be Sir Trevor, the way he throws money around."

Wait . . . I thought throwing money around was good? Didn't we like people who threw money at us? Wasn't that what Alana's family war was about? It was so hard to keep score after a pitcher of margaritas and . . . and lots of other things.

Suddenly the cab wrenched to a stop and Alana handed him some bills and Marcella was pushing me toward the door. I clambered out, suddenly feeling tall in my polka dot heels and tapered jeans.

"Where are we?" I asked.

"Le Bar."

"Le Bar?" Marcella squeaked. "I have always wanted to go here. What, are you a member? If this isn't a night for firsts! Un-fucking-believable. Wait till I tell my sister I went to Le Bar."

"Hailey?" Alana touched the sleeve of my jacket. "Don't you remember? I've brought you here before."

Ah, yes. The members only bar with the dance floor, the pick-up palace that was supposed to be safe since you had to be a millionaire to join. Alana was addicted to this place, though I didn't understand its allure.

"You OK, honey?" Alana asked.

"Perfect!" I straightened and took a deep breath. "Let's go."

"Watch your step on the stairs," Alana told me. "And maybe you'd better pull over to the slow lane. Try a few Christian cosmos until the world stops spinning in your head."

We descended into the basement club, where the bass beat was thrumming like an approaching subway train. Wait a second, maybe that *was* an approaching subway train . . . Alana led the way, her shoulders back, her chin held high as she passed the crowded tables like a princess reigning over her subjects.

Not that Alana was a snob, but maybe Xavier was on to something with that princess thing.

We meandered through rows of tables with leopard-print upholstered chairs whose dots danced before my eyes. Alana cut toward the back of the club, and there, lighting up a large table at a tiger-print banquette was Rory. My Rory! Fresh and crisp as if he'd just hopped out of the shower—and maybe he had. It was known that he often napped through the evening and started his partying late at night.

I tripped on the step leading up to his table and nearly fell into his arms, interrupting his conversation with some generic-looking man—probably a fan.

"Hailey!" He saved my dignity and gave me a big hug before tipping me back onto my feet. "Glad you could drop by!"

"Rory, what are you doing out on a school night?" Alana asked.

He bowed and kissed her hand. "Lovely ring. A Gerrard, I see. And who's this vision of cosmopolitan chic?"

While Alana introduced Marcella, and the Rory wannabe disappeared, I slid into the booth and took a steadying breath. "Great table."

From here you could see most of the club and the dance floor, and the soft lighting in this area eased my queasiness.

"Can I get personal with you?" Marcella asked Rory.

His eyebrows shot up, but there was no stopping her.

" 'Cause I just gotta tell you, that is a kick-ass suit you're wearing. I saw it in the Brooks Brothers catalog, and I know it cost a fortune, but seeing it on you, it's probably worth it. It's a really classy suit."

"And you have a classy name . . . Marchhhellla," he said with relish. "Are you Italian?"

She waved him off. "Puerto Rican."

He said something in Spanish that I didn't catch—not that I'd understand it, anyway—and she nearly melted at his feet.

I leaned back against the tiger-print cushion and sighed. "This is much better."

"Don't be shy," Rory told me as I pushed the flower vase aside for a better view. "Make yourself at home."

"Sarcasm doesn't work on me," I said, motioning for everyone to sit. "Besides, we know you've been pining away here, all alone."

"Were you expecting friends?" Alana asked.

"If he was, his plans have changed," I said, feeling a bit more steady. "Rory, you have to help us. We're trying to spend Alana's inheritance in one night, and the stores have all closed. Marcella here helped us out at Bon Nuit, but now we're running out of steam."

"What a pity you can't buy a penthouse in Trump Tower at this hour," he said. "Though we can order a pricey bottle of Dom Perignon. Any takers?"

Marcella raised her hand eagerly, and Rory called the waiter over to order some ridiculously expensive drinks. I ordered a ginger ale so I could pretend to be imbibing, and the talk turned, as usual with Rory, to *All Our Tomorrows*. First, Marcella gushed about how she wanted to start watching the show now that she'd met Rory (note that she did not mention me, not that I took offense). Then Rory launched into complaints about the ineptitude of the writers who kept tossing him lackluster story lines.

"I just got my sides for the next week of taping," he said, folding his arms defensively, "and the minute I saw the first line, I smelled a rat. I could see exactly where they were going with Stone's story line." He reached across the table and squeezed my wrist. "Want to take a guess? It's to be the new disease of the year; they want Stone to test HIV positive."

"No!" I gasped. "But Stone isn't gay."

He nodded, his blue eyes glistening with anger. "And he's not an IV drug user, and he didn't have surgery in the years before they began testing the blood supply. So I ask you, how was Stone exposed to HIV? Through the mints at a diner? On a toilet seat? Through the mail? I am livid at the irresponsible behavior of these writers. If they want a character who is HIV positive, the least they can do is portray an accurate depiction of the disease in the story line. These writers! Why don't they do their jobs?"

"It's a problem everywhere." Alana lifted her champagne glass, her slender fingers delicately gripping the narrow flute. "People just don't do their jobs, and when they do, there seems to be a real lack of follow-through and commitment. I see it all around me—incompetence. It's sad."

"Not everyone is a loser," Marcella objected. "But in this case, I agree that the writers are wrong. Especially with you and your character. I mean, what are they doing? Are they trying to kill you?"

Rory shot me a look of panic. "I think my head is going to explode!"

"They can't be planning to kill you off," I said, though I had been thinking the same thing. It's so frustrating to be on the receiving end of the writers' whims, not knowing what tragic twists of fate were in store for your character from one week to the next, but it was a hazard of acting in daytime television. "Hey, maybe they're planning to fake your death! Those are great stories!"

"The empty coffin trick." Alana wagged a finger at him. "I love that, when the coffin is empty. Or the body disappears and then comes stomping into the room, scaring the bejesus out of everyone."

"Or the coma device!" I piped in, on a roll. "You get to play sick in a hospital bed while the cast members cry over you, confess their evil deeds, vow revenge . . . You have to admit, that is one great story line."

Rory cocked one eyebrow. "I would like *that*. Maybe I'll mention it to the writers. God knows, they've stolen worse plots."

I bit my lower lip, worried about the long-term prospect of losing Rory from the show. "So what are you going to do? Have you called your agent?"

"Immediately! She was trapped in a deadlock negotiation and couldn't take my call. Such timing! I decided to take the bull by the horns; I rushed right down to the production office and demanded a meeting."

"You did?" I admired his gumption. Not everyone could barge in on the producers and live to tell the tale, but Rory was fairly well-liked on the show.

"When Janet the receptionist told me the producers

weren't available, I threw myself across the door, barring their exit." He flung his arms out dramatically, clearing the top of the champagne bottle, much to my relief.

"You did?" Even Marcella was impressed.

"Why, they interrupted their closed-door session and finally gave me a moment. They listened, heard me out. Gabrielle suggested that perhaps this is just an HIV scare—faulty testing, or else some evil vixen has switched the test results."

"The big switch! Yes, yes, people love that," I agreed, feeling my perky self returning.

"Of course, she and Dirk made no promises."

"Well, you can't expect much out of Dirk," I said. Known as Dirk the Jerk, Dirk the Dick, and Dirk the Money-Grubbing Suck-Up, he was the money man on the show.

"Dirk is a waste of time, but Gabrielle is usually true to her word, and we all parted as the best of friends." Rory sighed. "They're going to talk to the writers on my behalf, and I'm going to send them all Cartier cufflinks."

"Oh, no, get them from Tiffany's," Alana cut in, touching Rory's sleeve. "I know just the ones! With black jet and mother of pearl."

"Sweet mother of pearl!" Rory rolled his beautiful eyes. "Sounds just like SpongeBob!" Rory did the voice-over for a character who appeared on that cartoon occasionally, and he never let anyone forget it.

"Call me tomorrow and I'll set it up for you with my sales associate there," Alana said. "They're so lovely, you'll want a set for yourself."

"Not that I have any shirts with French cuffs," Rory said.

"Oh, please!" Alana shook her head. "Like that matters!"

16

Alana

"Alana! How are you?" asked Zackary Nieder-man, an old friend from high school. He leaned over our table to kiss each of my cheeks, and I did the introductions. Zack was followed by a string of men, young and old, who were old friends, family acquaintances, and Le Bar regulars. A few asked Hailey and Rory for their autographs, but mostly they wanted to dance with me.

Of course.

I don't know what it is, but once inside Le Bar, men are quite susceptible to my charms.

Within minutes, I was on the dance floor, doing the moves in a circle with Rory, Marcella, and Hailey. Men kept dancing up to us, trying to push in, but once they got near me I just turned and butt-bumped them away.

That cracked Marcella up. "You're a pisser! How do you stand it?"

"You get used to it," I said, shimmying in the shoulders.

"No, really!" Marcella shouted over the music. "How do you fend off these leeches? It's like they want to do you right here on the dance floor."

"When they're really persistent?" I smiled. "I just tell them I'm a lesbian. Works like a charm."

Back at the table, Marcella expressed her amazement at my guy-magnet ability. "You are like chum in a shark tank, honey! They gather around you for the feeding frenzy."

And why did that surprise her? This was my territory, my place. At Le Bar, I rocked.

"Our Alana is a true princess," Rory said, "our very own African-American princess."

I felt myself tense at the comment, but Hailey took care of things, nudging Rory with her elbow. "Don't ever say that again."

"What? What did I say? Alana rules! Every straight man wants to hook up with her. Some gay men, too," he said, blowing a kiss across the table.

"That's better." I wasn't usually so caught up in what people thought of me; Xavier had shot a few holes in my ego, and it took time to repair that sort of damage. Time, champagne, and a few strolls through the tables full of socialites at Le Bar.

"You know," Marcella began, "I have always been dying to get in here, but now that my curiosity is resolved, I must admit I don't see the allure. I mean, these people are so fake, and these men are so obvious. What's the satisfaction in strutting for a pack of leering old men?"

I felt my jaw drop. "They're all prospects, you know. No one can join here unless they're financially qualified."

"They're not prospects," Marcella scoffed. "Honey, for all your passion about the dating scene, you don't have a clue how to really do it."

Rory's mouth formed a round O.

"And I'm not talking about sex," Marcella snapped. "Any baboon can manage that function. I'm talking about meeting a partner, finding a mate. Don't you girls know you're not going to find him in a bar?"

"That's news to me," Rory said.

I agreed, but I didn't want to admit that there might be a guide to dating that I'd missed in girl training.

Hailey scratched her head. "OK, then, where do we find Mr. Right?"

"If you're looking for a partying boozehound, this would be the place," Marcella said.

Rory winced. "Ouch."

"Otherwise, get yourself in the environment of Mr. Right. If you want someone in big business, go to a really nice office building and ride the elevator up and down. You'd be surprised who'll talk with you on an elevator. If you want a doctor, volunteer at a hospital. Want someone who does investments? Get your butt down to Wall Street for lunch. I'm telling you, the men you want don't have time to go out and wiggle their fannies on dance floors at three A.M. They're working hard, living their lives, and you have to find a way to put yourself in their faces, insert yourself in their lives. You step into his path." She folded her arms. "That's how you do it."

"Marcella has spoken," Rory said, holding his hands out. "And it was good. So, when do we start riding elevators?"

"When it's right," I said. "I like the way you think, girl."

"No big deal," Marcella said. "It's just common sense."

"Do ya think?" Hailey asked. "It's a very direct approach. So obvious and yet, elusive."

The only part I didn't like about it was the way it

discounted all the men here at Le Bar. Not that I was interested in any of them, but it undercut all the networking I'd done in the past three years, all the late nights I'd remained at the bar, hoping someone new and interesting would appear. Was it possible that my work had been in vain?

Only one way to find out.

I lifted my champagne glass and took a sip. "Who wants to have lunch on Wall Street tomorrow?"

17

Hailey

"Love your shoes, darling," Rory told Marcella as she returned from another spin on the dance floor.

Marcella kicked up one heel behind her in a sassy pose. "Thanks, sweetie. They're Liz Claiborne. I got them at an outlet in Jersey for a fraction of retail price."

"Really?" Rory gushed. "They make you look like you're dancing on a cloud."

The lovefest between Rory and Marcella tickled me.

"You do the outlets?" Alana grabbed Marcella's arm. "You have to come with me to do the Hamptons outlets. I drive by them all the time, but they're so lacking in charm, I just can't muster the enthusiasm."

"Not even for a bargain?" Marcella seemed appalled. "Fifty percent off retail. Do you realize what you're saying?"

"I love a sale!" Alana said. "Oh, don't tell me I've been missing out all this time. We have to do this together. Why don't you all come out with me? We'll go during the week when the traffic is light and do the out-let thing. The weather has warmed up, and there's plenty of room at my parents' summerhouse. Though it's in the throes of redecoration."

"I would love to do the Hamptons," I said, "but with my schedule on the show, it's so hard to get away."

"In that case, there's definitely a shopping trip in your future. I've gone through the thumbnail story lines for the next two weeks and none of them mention Ariel. Looks like you're going to have some time off," Rory told me.

"Oh, then I can go," I said lightly as a wicked, sick feeling began to seep in. "Wait a sec, is Ariel even mentioned? Two weeks of shooting and I don't appear in any of the scenes? Not even one day?"

Rory pressed a finger to his chin. "No, I definitely didn't see your character mentioned. It's like . . ." His eyes flickered with realization of the grim reality. "You've disappeared without a trace."

"No wonder I haven't heard about a new contract!" My queasiness turned to a full-burning panic. "And they promised me more appearances. Gabrielle said so. Or at least that's what my agent said." No wonder Cruella hadn't called; probably too busy chasing pup-pies on her broomstick.

"Now, don't have a freak-out," Alana said, pinning me with her dark stare. "Look at the facts, honey. Ariel is too popular to be cut from the show."

"That doesn't mean anything," I lamented. "Maybe they're going to recast my part, give it to someone else. Oh, this feels very bad to me."

"Let's not jump to conclusions, Hailey," Rory said reassuringly. "You know the ever-changing world of daytime! As soon as you get used to having things one way, they go and change things on you!"

"Yeah, like axing your character," I said sadly.

"Excuse me, but I'm going to go leave a message for my agent." I tucked my bag under my arm and headed off to the ladies' room, where I left a call-me-or-you're-fired message on Cruella's voice mail.

Afterward, I flipped my phone shut, feeling a pang of remorse.

Was I overreacting?

Having an artistic tantrum?

Somehow it didn't feel very creative, and if my agent couldn't return my call after a week of pleading, well, maybe it was time to move on.

On my way back to the table, someone called my name. I turned to find a familiar face—a middle-aged, bald man, grayish and pinched around the eyes, but familiar.

"Daryl," he offered his name. "Malkowitz and Malkowitz Theatricals. Remember? We met at the Emmy celebration."

"Oh, right!" An agent. Well, maybe that was good timing. Fire an agent, hire an agent.

He was sharing a booth with two Middle Eastern men, who smiled. "Come, sit. I want you to meet my friends."

Daryl introduced the men, men with heavy accents who shook my hand, never taking their eyes off me. Since the others didn't seem too quick with English, Daryl bulldozed through the conversation, telling me about the people he had once represented.

"Halle Berry, before she got her big break. Vic Taylor, country and western singer . . ." As he spoke, his hand went to the nape of my neck, stroking gently. I thought about what Marcella had said about worthwhile men not partying all night. Did that make Daryl worthless? I tried to be objective, but the neck massage was nice. Ordinarily, I would have flicked him away, but I was feeling low, my defenses down, and when he turned to me and leaned in for a kiss, I just let him.

His breath was minty—apparently he'd popped a few in preparation—and his tongue wasn't as goopy as you'd expect. Mostly, he molded my lips with his and rubbed my back, which did feel comforting.

When one of his hands moved along my side to stroke a breast, I gasped a little. I didn't really want it, but the sensation ignited a flicker of longing. I decided to toss my reservations to the wind and go with it, letting myself kiss him and be stroked as the music and flashing lights poured over us.

We were making out like two kids behind the 7-Eleven, our breathing heavy, nerves heightened. Spicy, teasing sensations. I felt safe and seductive, knowing it wouldn't go any further in this time and place.

He closed a kiss and nibbled my earlobe. "You look so pretty tonight," he whispered, sliding a hand up to cup one of my breasts again. This time I pushed it away, slightly embarrassed over the two Middle Eastern men staring at us from across the table. "Very pretty. Tell me," Daryl asked, looking at my chest. "Are these real? They feel real."

The sweet longing that had tickled me now oozed into a slimy, slutty feeling. I pushed away from him completely and grabbed my bag. What was I thinking? Making out with a man who wanted the 411 on my boobs? "Gotta go."

18

Alana

It was my turn to save Hailey. Rory and I intercepted her on her way back from the rest room, via some balding guy who seemed to know her a little too well. I hadn't seen Hailey hook up with a man since the ex dumped her, and I was certainly not going to let Mr. Bald-and-Horny be her rebound.

Although she was already leaving the table, she shot me a desperate look as I hooked my arm through hers. "Look at you!" I told her. "A few drinks and you're looking for love in all the wrong places."

"This party is moving on to breakfast," Rory said, motioning us toward the exit. "I can't work on an empty stomach."

Marcella laughed. "You're going to work now? After partying all night?"

"A six A.M. call. But I had a little nap in the evening," Rory admitted.

"I don't believe you," Marcella said. "I don't believe

me. I've never stayed out this late in my life. Well, not since prom night at Our Lady of Snows."

We climbed to the street, where Rory gazed down the line of black limos. "There we go. My driver is waiting, third car up. We'll have him zip us directly to 24/7, then I must turn into a pumpkin and be off to work."

"I can't believe I'm riding in a limo." Marcella patted the shiny roof of the car and beamed at the driver.

I realized I liked having her around, though she was a study in contradictions. Full of practical advice, yet awed and wide-eyed as a little kid when it came to certain practices that were tired ritual in my life. She had a way of cracking things open and examining them with wonder.

Sometimes a new point of view is refreshing.

Over omelettes at 24/7, Marcella questioned Hailey and Rory about how things worked behind the scenes in daytime television. Although Hailey was still in a bit of a funk over her future as Ariel, she tried to answer politely. Marcella seemed genuinely interested in the "process," and I suspected that she was going to make a fabulous buyer for Bon Nuit. I was going to send the store CEO a fat, juicy e-mail about how fabulous she was, just as soon as I got some sleep and took care of the zillion other tasks on my list.

Which reminded me . . . one of those tasks was the pesky need for a job of my own.

"Oh, I almost forgot," I said, stabbing a mushroom from my omelette. "I need a teensy favor, Marcella. I was wondering if you could help me get a position as a mister. You know, the girls who spray perfume on the shoppers? Don't you think I'd be great at it?"

Rory nearly choked on his French toast. "Princess Alana, working? When was the last time that happened?"

I kicked him under the table.

"Ouch! Those shoes have pointy toes."

"I've had plenty of jobs before," I said. "Just none as interesting as working with *scents*." I fantasized about receiving my first paycheck, a long stream of dollar digits that I could wave under my father's nose.

"I don't know about those girls," Marcella said. "I don't think they work for the store. I never see them in the break room. I think they're paid by the cosmetics companies."

"Hmm. So how do I apply for a position?" I asked.

"I'll ask around and find out for you," she promised.

Ha! Wouldn't Daddy be surprised? I was going to be hugely successful without his checkbook behind me.

As chalky daylight began to illuminate the street, Rory and Marcella headed off in his limo. He promised her that the driver would take her to Brooklyn once he was dropped at the studio, and Marcella was determined to wake up her sister and brother-in-law so that they could see her pull up outside the apartment in style.

Hailey and I took a cab home, but as we pulled up on Madison Avenue, the CVS sign flashed in my view, and I realized I'd better stock up on a few necessities before I was running my own tab.

I filled a basket with various shades of nail polish, hot-oil treatment for my hair, top-of-the-line shampoo, and a few other bathroom unmentionables. We also found a few shades of nail polish that had to be tried, and two adorable matching ceramic vases for our bathroom.

Bearing new purchases in embarrassingly cheap plastic bags, we made one more stop—Starbucks—for lattes, newspapers, and low-fat muffins to go, because we were both so tired we were yawning in unison.

Up in the apartment, Hailey flopped on the couch, popped in a tape of her performances as Ariel, and cradled her coffee cup sadly. "I wonder if it was me," she said. "Is it me? Or my performance? Or maybe my agent. No one likes Cruella. God, I can't believe they're cutting me from the show!"

As she critiqued her performance with "So wimpy!" and "Talk about fake tears!" I washed up, slipped into my peignoir, and fired up my computer to check my e-mail. Nothing good, but InStyle.com was featuring fabulous summer ensembles, most of which could be ordered on-line.

I sat down at the computer and sighed in wonder.

Honeydew-colored zip handbags with perky pale green flowers.

Big round orange dots on a baguette, so jaunty and whimsical.

And those strappy metallic sandals with shell disks designed by Colin Stuart. "Colin Stuart!" I shrieked in delight.

"Tell him I'm not home," Hailey muttered from the living room. I shot her a look; her face was buried in the pillow, one arm dangling over the couch.

Sleep tugged at me, but I kept one eye open and clicked on the little shopping cart that indicated, yes, I would buy these bags, these sandals. And, yes, this sweet petite yellow silk-chiffon dress with a ruched waist. Yes, yes, yes!

I typed in the number of my American Express, my fingers bouncing over the keyboard like raindrops on the pavement. *Quick, quick! Quick, before Daddy can-*

cels the card! He's never up this early, but in a situation this dire, you can't be too careful.

With a few more victorious purchases taken care of, I bypassed my unconscious friend, turned off the television, moisturized with night cream, and slid into bed.

Sleep mask, ear plugs, and . . .

I still had one earplug out when the phone rang. Caller ID indicated it was . . . Daddy.

Daddy, calling at eight A.M.? This couldn't be good.

I sank back into my pillows. I didn't have the energy to talk to him now—this time I had summer ennui, and I was still mad at him for last night.

If he was calling to apologize, he could leave a message.

I scooched down in the bed and savored the coolness of the sheets against my bare feet, visions of strappy metallic sandals dancing in my head.

Part Three

**ALL PRICES SLASHED FOR OUR
MEMORIAL DAY SALE!**

19

Hailey

They say suicide can be a real killer.

Fortunately for me, my character, Ariel, didn't muster the courage (or cowardice, depending on how you look at it) to do herself in. After a two-week personal hiatus during which my shopping therapy helped me accumulate more articles of denim clothing than a tourist at a horse ranch, I was offered a new thirteen-week contract on *All Our Tomorrows*.

Big sigh.

With the new contract money, I could pay the two months' back rent I owed Alana. And the monthly minimum on my credit cards. It had gotten to the point where I didn't even check the list of purchases when the bills came in. Not that I regretted the items I'd bought, but it was a little depressing to be reminded how much everything cost these days. Manhattan boutiques were certainly a step up from ordering fleeces and granny underwear from a catalogue in Wisconsin, but believe me, that insurance of quality and style was more than reflected in the prices.

But, hey! I could pay the monthly minimum on my charge bills! I wouldn't have my credit cards confiscated and clipped in half by a clerk with a Mussolini mustache. Instead, those power-hungry sales clerks would be scanning my purchase with respect, because two of the banks were extending my credit limit to twenty thousand dollars! Now twenty thousand times two is forty thousand, which is just an astronomical, gluttonous amount to think of spending on strappy sandals, lattes, and Chardonnay with a hint of peach and almond, but I love the idea of having a few fat steamer trunks of cash at my disposal; somehow it's very Greta Garbo.

So I skipped merrily back to the studios where we tape *All Our Tomorrows*, happy to be employed as an actress again. I gave Sean a big hug, even said hello to the cameramen, and didn't object when Lucy in makeup wanted to try a new shade on my lips. I was upbeat and sunny until I read the daily schedule. Since the actor who plays Preston Scott was unavailable today, his scenes were being moved to tomorrow, and tomorrow's scenes between Meredith and Ariel were being shot today. Bumped up to today? My haute-drama scene with Deanna Childs.

Now I am an actress who welcomes the opportunity to work with any fellow actor. However, having heard (and read!) rumors that Deanna was the person responsible for my expensive layoff, I admit I harbored a little distrust. A smattering of anger. A quivering fear that she would try to get me axed again. So, I admit, the scheduling change threw me.

But then Jodi brought out my wardrobe for the day—a strapless dupioni silk dress with kicking polka-dotted Manolo mules—and my throat tightened with emotion.

"What's wrong, honey?" Jodi asked, pulling the curtain aside so that every gaffer in the studio wouldn't see me in my underwear.

"It's . . . it's so pretty." I held my hair back as she zipped up the dress, a high-waisted, shoulderless, sassy design in various shades of green stripe.

Jodi pinched at the bodice, pursing her lips. "We might bring it in a bit there—you're so skinny!—but otherwise it's a good fit."

"It's a dream! I feel like Julia Roberts after Richard Gere takes her shopping in *Pretty Woman*."

The usually deadpan Jodi actually cracked a quick smile. "I loved that scene. Now try the shoes. The script calls for you to kick them off when you go out on the ledge, so I didn't give you any straps or zippers."

I slipped my feet into the open-toed shoes, so glad I'd sprung for a pedicure yesterday. The shoes were silk heaven, with a pert band of lime ribbon trim around the toes and slender heels. And the polka dots! How I wanted to do a high kick in Deanna's face, proving that dots are hot. "Wonderful," I said. "Fabulous. Very comfortable."

"Now the key to making a dress like this work is the accessories, so don't forget the necklace and earrings. Some silvery droplets, since we need to break the horizontal line of the dress."

My attention was glued to the mirror, to the smart, new Ariel. "It's so nice to be out of droopy seaweed clothes, even if I am still wearing green."

Jodi wrinkled her nose, tugging on the tape measure back and forth around her neck. "It was time. Everyone knew it, but the network had a focus group and they really shoved the results down Gabrielle's throat. No one wants to tune in to see people dressed in rags. Time for Ariel to have some style."

"Thank you." I would have hugged her if I didn't

think it would freak her out. At a time when I needed a confidence boost to face Deanna, Jodi had come through. "Thank you, thank you!"

She ripped the curtain open, indicating that I was finished and should leave her space and let the next cast member step in. So I glided out of wardrobe on my dotty Manolo heels feeling dazed and beautiful, whacked by the wand of the costuming fairy.

20

Alana

"Esperanza!" I whispered, trying to sound exotic and mystical. "Esperanza!"

To be honest, Esperanza was giving me a sinus headache, maybe even an infection. At first sniff, the scent hinted at clove and floral. Breathtaking! Or so I thought when I hit the cosmetic floor ready to whap some sales butt.

But the smell began to wear me down, and when one teenage girl joked that it resembled tiger urine, I couldn't lose that connection. Now, one spray of Esperanza and my mind was immediately transported to the restrooms at the Central Park Zoo. And as scents go, that is not at the top of anyone's list.

"Ladies, try Esperanza! The scent of mystical proportions . . ." I didn't know what the hell that meant, but since it was the damn theme of this perfume, Greg, my boss, wanted it "out there."

"Gotta get it out there," Greg kept telling me over the phone. "If women don't try it, they'll never know

Roz Bailey

they love it. So that's your primary goal: get the scent out there."

To be honest, the only ones really "out there" were weirdo Greg and the even weirder singer, *the* Esperanza, who was rumored to live with two Siberian white tigers in a two-bedroom apartment somewhere uptown. It's hard to figure the math on that—two bedrooms with two tigers? I guess the cats had to share. Hey, that's New York real estate for you.

I had read in the *Post* that Esperanza tongued their fur like a mama tiger, that the co-op board wanted her out of the building because her place wreaked of tiger piss, that PETA reps were hiding in Central Park waiting to douse her with fake blood, that she dropped out of Brown and lied about it on her application for Miss Teen Goth America.

Everything I'd ever read about my new employer was outrageous, but one simple fact remained: she was a wealthy celebrity, while I was a deb in financial rehab, pounding the marble floors of Bon Nuit to get wealthy again. Where's the order in that universe?

So far, my wealth goal was a distant target and all that pounding was wreaking havoc on my D&G sandals, as well as my delicate feet. Just yesterday when Suki was giving me a pedicure at Salon Armage she found a crack on the heel of my left foot. "Ouchie!" she said, showing me the spot. I had to restrain my horror long enough to ask for the hot wax treatment. Suki was very understanding, but my spa time had been ruined. Cracked skin, like an old granny! Please.

"Esperanza!" I hissed, holding up the bottle as an older blond with blue eye shadow happened by. "Would you like to try Esperanza?" I asked her.

"I guess," she said without much confidence.

I sprayed her wrist from the tiger-shaped bottle. She

gave a delicate sniff, then glanced away and headed off.

"It's available in toilet water and cologne," I called after her. Maybe she'd double back after shopping. Maybe she'd come back and buy two, one for herself, one to give away as a gift.

"Esperanza," I hissed, thinking that I sounded like a snake. I stepped up to a passing girl, who quickened her pace to avoid me. Obviously in a hurry, I thought, but she would be back.

Back to dodge me again.

Back to try a sample of Passion or Eternity across the aisle.

Who was I kidding?

This job sucked and I knew it. My feet hurt, my first full week of work had brought me a mere three hundred and thirty dollars after taxes, and this whole spray and buy sales tactic was so ten years ago. Nowadays, any woman who was into scents applied her fave before she left the house, and we all know that you never, ever mix scents, unless you want that table by the men's room at Nobu. Conversely, the women who wanted a spritz were novices, tourists in the land of scent, happy to visit but eager to leave before their visas expired. And if a tourist can get something for free, why pay?

"Esperanza," I called out as I gracefully crossed the cosmetics floor to the Bare Shoulders counter. They made the best lotions, and my hands were feeling so dry right now. I figured I'd steal a dab of lotion from the display.

"Esperanza . . . it means hope." More like hopeless.

Just my luck—at the Bare Shoulders counter, the tester of Exotic Cucumber lotion was empty. I looked around and waved to Karo, one of the nicer sales assistants. "Hey, hi! Could you help me out, Karo? You're all out of Exotic Cucumber."

"Again? Let's see." She crossed to the counter and frowned. "It's our best-seller in the hand cream line."

"And I can see why. It feels so velvety, and how about that antiaging formula? What do you know about that?" I asked.

"They tell me it's laboratory tested, and I say if there's even a chance of it working, let's give it a go," Karo said. She slid open the cabinet and put a "tester" label on a new bottle. "There. Try that, sweet pea."

I squeezed a tiny aqua pool on my hand and rubbed it in. "Heaven!"

Karo giggled. "I keep telling my husband, it stops aging, honey. One of these days I'm bringing some home to put on his johnson. See how that works out for him."

"You wild woman!"

"And you with the hands. Honey, you don't need antiaging cream on those beauties." She held my right hand up by the pinkie and examined both sides. "Perfectly proportioned. Shiny nails, healthy cuticles. And your skin . . . mmmm-mmm."

"Excuse me, girls, but I'm looking for Exotic Cucumber," the woman said, getting right into our faces. Her husband followed behind on an invisible leash, an over-the-hill bald man who was obviously pussy-whipped.

"Esperanza?" I asked the bossy customer, bottle at the ready.

"God, no! Talk about overexposure," the woman yapped to her husband. "I've had enough of the tiger lady, and I'm allergic to some of the chemicals used in perfumes. But Exotic Cucumber is intriguing. Is that a tester?" She lifted the bottle, turning it around. "I don't know. You're wearing it, right? Do you mind if I smell your hand?"

The husband folded his arms, obviously bored.

"No problem." I pressed my hands together prayer-style and waved them under her nose. "It's a very subtle scent."

Bossy lady sniffed cautiously. "Nice. And look at your hands. Daryl, look at her hands, they're like butter."

Again with the hands. I let myself grin. They were one of my better assets.

"That's not from the cream, Muriel," Daryl piped in.

"Who cares?" his wife snapped. "Darling, you have lovely hands. Doesn't she, Daryl?"

"Beautiful," he said in a tone that begged "can we go?"

I smiled at them, wondering why Daryl looked so familiar. I could see him in my mind, in another time and place. "Wait a minute, aren't you the agent? Daryl Mousekowitz?"

"Malkowitz." He nodded.

"The theatrical agent," I said, recalling that Hailey knew him from the business.

As he nodded again and Mrs. Malkowitz tried on some lotion, a light bulb popped in my head. Maybe even exploded. This was a big-ass idea. "Your timing is perfect, because I need to engage an agent."

"You and every waitress in town." Daryl shoved his hands into his pants pockets. "Muriel? She needs an agent. Give the girl a card."

"You see, I'm going into the business of hand modeling." I brought a hand demurely to my cheek and batted my eyelashes.

Daryl grunted, but Muriel turned toward me, her eyes growing wide. "Yes, I see it."

"So call my office next week," Daryl said lethargically.

His wife slapped his arm. "Don't be an idiot! This girl has fabulous hands." She popped open her purse and handed me a business card. "Forget the screening, doll. Call tomorrow and give your information to Sherri. We'll have a contract out to you next week, and I'll look tomorrow to see what auditions we can line up." She squinted at my hands one more time, then smiled. "Exquisite. I'm sure we can set you up with something."

Can I tell you, I wanted to throw my hands up in the air and do a happy dance right in the center aisle of cosmetics!

But first thing's first. I had to hit the restroom and wash the tiger stink of Esperanza off my precious fingers.

Then, of course, back to Bare Shoulders for another round of Exotic Cucumber.

Take it from me, exquisite hands are no accident.

21

Hailey

I felt my way along the ledge, my pedicured feet gracefully padding along the fake stone, my fingers trembling over the fake-stucco surface.

"Where is she?" a voice called from beyond the French doors. It was a voice I despised. "Why, she was just here a moment ago . . ."

I dared a glance at the street below, then threw my head back as vertigo struck. My body teetered on the ledge, my soul immersed in an exquisite dichotomy of emotion: fall to my death and end the pain, or cling to the ledge and continue this arduous journey in a strange land, never knowing where I came from or where I truly belonged.

I felt tears sting my eyes as the camera moved closer, panning in for my close-up.

"And . . . cut!" Stella called. "Great! Wonderful! Let's move to the next scene."

Sean waddled over the mat in front of me—the street set that was supposed to be ten stories below—

and peered into the penthouse set through the open
French doors. This was for the benefit of Deanna, as
the diva refused to do much of anything unless she re-
ceived a personal invitation. "We're on the same set,"
Sean told her. "Direct pickup in the Van Allen penthouse, interior and exterior balcony. Ready, Ms. Childs?"

"Give me a minute, please," Deanna said calmly.

Oh, great. A diva minute was ten in real time.

Rory sneaked onto the street set below my feet, his
face level with my belly button. "You were great! You
really nailed it, kiddo! This is going to be a hot day.
Does it air on a Friday? It's real tune-in-tomorrow material."

"Thanks," I said, my eyes still brimming with tears
from the emotion of my scene. "Can you grab me a tissue from the prop cart?" I asked, determined to stay on
my mark. This scene was going well—I could feel it in
my heart—and I didn't want to jinx it or wreck a shot
by moving out of place.

He handed me a tissue and I dabbed carefully. "Did
I smudge?"

"Nope. You're good to go." He peered over toward
the open French doors. "I'll bet she's steaming that you
got the dramatic beats in the scene."

I smiled. "How'd that happen?"

"An accident, I'm sure. Heads will roll in the writers' room. But in the meantime, you're really cutting
your teeth on it, kiddo. Keep it coming."

"I don't want to lose the lovely momentum we have
going, so can we move on quickly?" Stella asked.

"Only if you say please," Deanna called out sweetly.
I was glad that, from my position on the ledge of the
building, I couldn't see her face.

Rory rolled his eyes and hurried to the edge of the
set.

"Please, pretty please!" Stella clasped her hands together in a gesture of prayer. *"S'il vous plait! Por favor! Bitte!"* She turned to the AD. "Okay, Seannie, let's roll tape."

Sean moved directly in front of camera one and shouted, "In five, four, three, two . . ."

And once again I was Ariel, the ethereal goddess of the water who defied definition, the girl with no past who happened upon Indigo Falls quite by accident and who, finally, found herself a decent dress.

"Ariel?" Meredith called.

"Should I check downstairs?" With his British accent, Horwitz made even the most mundane lines sound distinguished. "Perhaps she's retired for the evening."

"I'm afraid that would be too easy," Meredith said. "A con artist like Ariel doesn't just leave on her own. She has to be driven out of town."

I gasped, swallowing hard over the emotion rising in my throat, the camera panning toward me.

"What was that?" Meredith asked.

I flattened myself against the wall, but it was no use. Meredith's curly head popped out. "Oh, my goodness, Ariel! What are you doing out there?" Her mouth was a wide O as she leaned out—way out.

"Don't come out here!" I said. The line wasn't in the script, but Deanna was about to climb onto the ledge to get in my shot! "Stop right there. If you move any closer, I'll jump, I swear it."

The set was deathly quiet. She recoiled and retreated, thank God. But who had the next line?

"Ariel? Ariel, darling, it's Dr. Willoughby." Good old Ian to the rescue. "Why don't you come in now, young lady, and we'll sit down and work this out."

"I can't!" I choked out. "Not while she's in the room. Meredith Van Allen can't be trusted."

"Me!" Meredith exclaimed. "I would never, ever harm another soul. Why, I don't even swat flies. I simply open the window and shoo them out. How could you say such a thing about me?"

"Because I know the truth," I said, so quietly it was almost a whisper. "I know what you did . . . to Skip." The air was thick with tension. Even the normally chatty makeup gals and hair people were watching breathlessly. "I know what you did!" I shouted.

Meredith shook her head, wordlessly suggesting denial of all charges and surprise at my revelation. Nice touch.

"Skip?" Doc Willoughby played confusion.

"How do you know Skip?" Meredith asked. "He was long disappeared before you came to Indigo Hills."

"He was like a brother to me," I said. "And you destroyed him. He only wanted to make you happy, Meredith. He would have given you anything, anything, but you wanted it all. You wanted him dead!"

"No!" she shouted, reaching out toward me. "It wasn't that way."

"You killed him, Meredith. His death is on your conscience." I turned toward the street and sucked in a breath for courage. "After this, you'll be able to add another tally to your scorecard, Meredith."

"Ariel, listen to me," the doc said emphatically. "You must not jump!"

"Stop!" Meredith shrieked, sobbing that fake soap-opera sob. "Stop her!"

Ignoring them, I lifted my face to the pretend sky, fixing my eyes on a catwalk along the shadowy ceiling. "It's OK, Skippy," I whispered fervently. "You won't be alone too much longer."

And with that, I flung my arms wide and jumped to oblivion. . . .

I rose from the mat to applause—roaring applause on the set! Stella was whooping and whistling, Rory clapped to the side of his head like a flamenco dancer,

Sean tucked his clipboard under one arm so he could applaud. The people from hair and makeup and wardrobe were cheering. Even the cameramen had lifted their heads to join in. Deanna's assistants were applauding madly, including the Diet Coke holder, who had placed the drink on the floor to free her hands.

I straightened my shoulders and let myself smile just a little. We'd nailed that scene! Everything had felt in sync, but sometimes it feels just right and some little clunker line or audio glitch pops up on the tape and you have to do it over again.

Not today.

"Bravo and kudos!" Stella boomed, rushing into the scene with her arms spread wide. She folded me into her bulky sweater for a warm hug, then moved on to Deanna and Ian for more fuzzy hugs. "Was that not the most riveting, most dramatic scene in the history of daytime television?" the director exclaimed.

Sean turned toward me and bowed dramatically. "Awesome."

I turned to Rory, who was dabbing at his eyes, trying to compose himself. When I gave him a questioning look, he flung his hands in the air, a gesture of disbelief. "Didn't know you had it in you, kiddo."

"I smell Emmy in the air!" Stella exclaimed. "Two Emmys."

Deanna walked to the edge of the set and took a sip from the Diet Coke, which her assistant quickly fumbled off the floor. "Two Emmys." Deanna's eyes glazed as she lobbed that notion in the air, like a cat playing, batting at a mouse. "I do like the sound of that. But really, how could I win two awards?"

Rory and I shot the panic look at each other. Had Deanna already forgotten that I was in the scene with her?

"Oh, you're too funny." Stella passed the gaff off as

a joke. "I was just thinking that this year you might want to share one of those Emmys with Hailey. Let her win for supporting actress."

"Oh, that . . ." Deanna assessed me, as if she really had a choice. "Oh, OK!" she teased, reaching out to give my arm a pat. She missed me by at least a foot, but who's measuring?

"Thanks loads, Hailey." Stella summoned me back for one more hug. "You're done for the day. But we'll see you next week. When's your call?"

"Tuesday," Sean jumped in. "Bright and early. We've got to get you in swimsuit and waterproof makeup for your landing in the rooftop pool." Sean rolled his eyes. "Writers."

"Hey, it's a lot softer than the street." I was glad to have the weekend off with the promise of a scene to tape after the holiday. Ariel went off the ledge, but she would be discovered a few days later in some billionaire's penthouse pool. I guess that mermaid thing just kicked in when Ariel needed it most.

I thanked everyone and said my goodbyes, then headed off to the dressing room I shared with Susan Laslo, another part-time player. From the corner of my eye, I sensed an incipient movement on the set. Deanna was on the prowl, moving in on Jodi, the head of wardrobe.

Stopping at the craft services table, I dipped a baby carrot in humus and tried to listen in. Mmm . . . the humus had extra garlic. The gossip was spicy, too.

"Who picked out Ariel's wardrobe today?" Deanna asked. I couldn't hear Jodi's answer, but apparently it didn't suit Deanna. "Would you talk to Gabrielle about it? Because, frankly, off-the-shoulder dresses have really been my trademark on this show. And I wouldn't want anyone to say that wardrobe is falling down on the job, but I do have my own signature style. It's who I am."

It's who I am . . . Wasn't that a perfume slogan from three years ago? Jeez, Deanna really fell apart without the scriptwriters to put words in her mouth.

I grabbed another carrot and headed off to change my clothes. I was still so buzzed from hitting my mark on the scene that I really didn't care that Deanna was being a bitcho supremo. Let her whine and complain and give orders and send her assistant off for more Diet Coke. She was going to be stuck here till Friday, while I was free for the rest of the week.

I wondered if those gowns I'd liked at Lord & Taylor would be going on sale for Memorial Day. I remembered one that fit like a glove, a ballroom gown in diva red satin. It would be perfect for the Daytime Emmy Awards ceremony.

Oh, yeah. Did I mention that it was off-the-shoulder?

22

Alana

"**I**'m always fighting oil in the T-zone," I told Karo as she massaged an astringent wash into my face. "It's a never-ending battle, but they say at least my skin will remain young looking."

"I hear you." Karo's hands worked expertly, dabbing with a cotton ball, then rubbing gently with her fingertips. "Baby, I have customers who would kill for skin like yours. You just keep doing what you've been doing, but be sure to moisturize."

"Twice a day," I said. With the agent's card in my pocket and my hand-modeling career off to a strong start, I decided to give my poor feet a break and take a seat at the Bare Shoulders counter. Karo had obliged me with a quick facial that would show off the Bare Shoulders line of skin care.

"How's that feel?" she asked.

"Nice, but I think I like the Exotic Cucumber mask best. It feels so clean, and it really soothed my sore sinuses."

"Umm . . . excuse me, ladies?"

I knew that angry voice. I opened my eyes to find Marcella on fire.

"What do you think you're doing?" she reached around me and started capping the Bare Shoulders bottles on the counter. "This is not the way you were trained, either of you, and—"

"I'm sorry," I said quickly, realizing how bad this must look. "But I already signed out. I meant to finish out my shift, but my feet were so tired, and I really am interested in the Bare Shoulders line, and Karo offered to demonstrate. And the main thing is that I don't work here anymore." I decided to spare her the really bad stuff—that the perfume was irritating my sinuses and that serious shoppers didn't want to bother with a spritz and that I no longer wanted to be employed by a celebrity who had been photographed licking tigers. Really, no reason to be such a downer, and it was so nice of Marcella to get me the job in the first place. "I'm quitting," I finished in a bright voice.

"Well." Marcella folded her arms. "You don't have to take it that far."

"No, I want to quit. I have to. I'm going to need every spare minute to pursue my new career." I held my hands off to the side, posing them delicately like a ballet dancer. "I'm going to be a hand model."

"Oh. I'll call Greg and let him know." As if changing gears, Marcella looked at my face, my hands, my face, then back at my hands. "Oooh. I've always said you have perfect hands. But honey, how are you going to go about this endeavor? Do you know anybody in advertising? You're going to need an agent—"

"Got one!" I waved Daryl Malkowitz's card.

"Daily manicures—"

"Already a sacred ritual," I admitted.

"An insurance policy on your hands. After all, those mitts will be your bread and buttah."

"I didn't think of that. Do you know anyone at Lloyd's of London?" Both Marcella and Karo shook their heads. "I'll bet Daddy's insurance guy could help me out." I touched Marcella's shoulder. "You're a genius. You really are. Bon Nuit doesn't know how lucky they are." I leaned into the mirror to rub in a smudge of cream Karo had missed. "And now that I'm self-employed, I'm free to head out to the Hamptons house ahead of the holiday traffic. I've been wanting to go out a few days early and make sure the new furnishings are in place for my parents. Memorial Day weekend is always their first time out for the season."

"I thought your father cut off your shopping sprees?" Marcella said.

"But I purchased a ton of stuff before he lost his mind. And I figure, if I set things out with just the right touch, he'll begin to understand. He'll change his mind like that." I snapped my dainty fingers. "By Memorial Day, Daddy will be begging me to decorate the rest of the house."

I leaned closer to Karo to confide, "My father is so clueless when it comes to design."

"Well, what do you want, honey? He's a man."

"Please! Don't get me started on our issues." I didn't usually make small talk about family matters, but Karo was so sympathetic and the relaxing facial had broken down some of my inhibitions. "If Daddy would just accept that he's from Mars and I'm from Venus, it would be a start. I don't know how my mother does it."

"Some men will never get it," Marcella said, rubbing a little cucumber cream into the back of her hand. "They come to things from a totally different place than we do. That's why we have to reach out for them and pull them in. It's like they're drowning in the water, thrashing around, and they need a hand to pull them to shore. They need us. But we can't stand on the riverbank and preach at them that they should learn to swim. They're fucking drowning! It's not about wanting to learn to swim; it's about knowing how to do it. And they don't. So it's up to us. We can save them, girls."

I put my hands on my hips, amazed. "Oh my Lord, that is the most enlightening explanation I've ever heard."

"Yes, honey." Karo was nodding. "Mmm-hmm. You tell it right, girl." She went off to deal with a customer who beckoned at a nearby counter.

"Marcella, you must be an old soul," I said.

She shrugged. "Whatever."

At that moment, I realized the downside of quitting my job at Bon Nuit. Marcella! I would miss being around her. Which gave me an idea.

"You know, the Hamptons house is huge," I said, turning to face her. "Why don't you come out sometime? Come out for Memorial Day? We need to stay in touch, honey. Lunches and shopping quests and whatnot."

"Definitely, cookie. But I gotta work Memorial Day."

We compared schedules and it turned out that Marcella had the next few days off, before she worked the holiday weekend. "Perfect! I talked to Hailey, and she's got off, too. We can all drive out together tomorrow and you guys can take the Jitney back whenever you want."

"That could work. Let me talk to my sister. I was supposed to watch my little nephew, but my sister, she'll get over it. Girl's gotta live."

"Please! You work hard all week. You deserve a vacation. And we can shop the outlets!"

"Look, I got to get back to linens. Some idiot put the

new Ralph Lauren sheets on display without steaming the creases out. Moron."

"Ralph Lauren sheets?" I perked up. "What are the new color schemes? Oh, never mind, I'll go take a look on my break. We need some new linens for the Hamptons. Come to think of it, I could use sheets in my apartment." Not that I wanted to apply my measly three hundred dollars to new bedsheets, but who could resist a peek?

23

Hailey

When I got to my dressing room, there was a note on my table from Susan Laslo, the girl who played the troubled teen, Lizzie.

Saw your scene . . . bravo! You rock.

—S

I smiled. Susan was a girl of few words, but I was beginning to realize that there was a solid, spirited person stuck in the role of Lizzie Slate. Since we were both minor players, we shared a dressing room the size of a Mini Cooper, which was just fine for both of us.

I dashed off a little note about enjoying the long weekend, since no one would be taping on Monday, then left it on her dressing table. Susan was scheduled to tape for the rest of the week, but I was done until next Tuesday, with a chance to go to the Hamptons with Alana.

A real vacation, with the promise of acting work when I returned; it was a rare luxury.

I turned toward my skinny closet, threw my arms into the air, and did a little hip-swaying dance. I had nailed an important scene, and now I was free, free, free!

Why didn't my mother ever call to check in at victorious times like this?

Leaning into my closet, I sorted through the emergency clothes there and decided to leave just about everything until next week. My pink polka-dot shoes were coming with me, along with three bottles of Evian water I'd snitched from craft services. You could never get enough bottled water in this city, especially when the weather began to warm up and the subways and stores held on to the stale winter heat.

Just then there was a knock on my door and I straightened, knocking my head against the top of the closet.

"Come in!" I called, rubbing the tender spot.

Antonio Lopez filled the doorway, his short, dark hair slicked back to appear in his pseudomobster scene. He wore a double-breasted, pin-striped suit in a pale shade of gray—sinister spring fashions. I know it's wrong to judge a person based on looks, but I couldn't help myself.

I loved him.

"Hilly," he said in his beautifully accented voice, though I couldn't remember if he was from Spain or Portugal or Argentina. Like that mattered anyway. "May I come in?"

"Sure!" I squeaked, stepping back and nearly falling into the closet. As he gracefully squeezed into the tiny space, I quickly closed the closet door to prevent further bodily injury. "How's it going?"

"Excellent." There was that killer smile, subtle and over-the-top sexy in one simple flash of the teeth. He was magnificent. "I just had the privilege of seeing your scene with Deanna. I wanted to tell you how fantastic it was." He pressed one hand to his chest. "I was genuinely moved."

"Me, too," I said without thinking. Oh, like that made sense! Jeez, was I an idiot! "I mean, *Et tu?*' Like Shakespeare?" Which made even less sense.

Come on, dinglebrain! Pick yourself up here!

"But thanks," I said. "I didn't even know you were watching. And coming from you, well, it means a lot. Thanks."

"You're welcome."

In that moment, I realized that a box of tampons had spilled open on my table, and I sort of leaped forward to block it from his view. Not that Antonio didn't know about those things, but I didn't want to go there with him.

He held up his arms, as if blocking me from bolting out the door, and we both laughed nervously.

"I'm sorry," I said earnestly. "It's just that I'm not used to having stars like you in my dressing room."

"Stars? There are no stars here." He reached out and tucked a strand of hair behind my ear.

"Well, there's Deanna . . ." I said.

"OK, one star. The rest of us are just actors." His face was just inches from mine now. "But I wanted to say, I admire what you're doing."

I was about to say "me, too!" again, but realized it would be doubly stupid a second time. He seemed to want to kiss me, but he paused, his eyes smoking and glazed. I couldn't stand it. I reached up, wrapped my arms around his shoulders, and kissed him.

He moaned, his lips dewy and moist against mine. Antonio was a fabulous kisser—I remembered that from our one scene together. He had the ability to transport me, to lift me to another place and time with the nudge of his sweet lips.

I was so into it, I barely noticed that my butt was crushing a row of tampons against the makeup table.

He ended the kiss and hugged me close. "We need to get together," he said. "May I see you this weekend? Outside the studio, of course."

"Oh, but I'm going out to the Hamptons," I blurted before I had the good sense to change my plans. "I'm leaving tomorrow, but I'd love to see you."

"I have a little condo there," he said, lifting my hand to kiss my knuckles. "East Hampton. Perhaps we could meet there? There's a club on Main Street that really rawks."

I nodded like a bobblehead. "Yeah, sure! Sounds great!"

We set it up for the following night, then Antonio stepped to the door. "I have a tedious scene to do. Taking another bad guy hostage, I'm afraid."

"It happens." I tinkled my fingers in a wave.

"Oh, and just a word of advice? You might want to keep our involvement under wraps around here. At least for now. Don't want any unnecessary studio scuttlebutt circulating."

I was impressed that Antonio knew what "scuttlebutt" meant, but I nodded as he blew me a kiss and ducked out the door.

Big sigh, then another thought. He had said "involvement," hadn't he?

So we were involved?

Antonio Lopez and Hailey Starrett, a new soap couple. *Soap Opera Digest* would run a feature on us. We could do one of those joint interviews on *Soap Central.* Together we would be a powerhouse!

My hands shook as I flipped open my cell and speed-dialed Alana.

"You'll never guess who I'm hooking up with tomorrow night. . . ."

24

Alana

"Who ever decided that the streets in Brooklyn should be named? It's too confusing. Was that Mr. Brooklyn, or what? Are you sure this is the right address?" I asked Hailey as I edged Daddy's car dangerously close to the bumper of a parked car and veered into a spot by a hydrant. The street Marcella lived on was narrow, dark, and, well . . . tacky, with a crummy little deli, a cleaners, and an Off-Track Betting center on the corner. Men clustered around the outside of the OTB—ill-dressed, slovenly, grayish men in clouds of cigarette smoke. Disgusting.

Hailey was already on her cell, ringing Marcella. "We're here! Or at least, I think we are. There's a cleaners on the corner and a deli and . . . yes, I see the men. OK. We're parked at the hydrant. OK." She flipped the phone shut. "She'll be down in a minute. She says roll up the windows and don't talk to the OTB losers."

I was already rolling up my window, annoyed that their smoke was drifting into the car. My father loved this old Mercedes, an ancient black sedan built like a tank. I'd tried a million times to get him to trade up to a newer model, but that was Daddy, clinging to his old stuff. I adjusted the side-view mirror and caught sight of a man spitting on the sidewalk. Yucky. I felt sorry for Marcella, having to live here. It had to be unpleasant walking past those men every day, though I knew Marcella could hold her own.

"This block is creepy." I leaned toward the mirror and straightened my hat, a teal blue open-weave sinamay trimmed in a white satin sash. My collection of hats was justifiable, since they're the best way to keep sun damage from the face, and this particular hat went well with my Adrienne Vittadini beachwear—teal-and-white-flowered capri pants, a long-cut white duster, and matching low-heeled Dolce & Gabbana sandals with peekaboo straps. The outfit was exceedingly bright for this dingy Brooklyn street, though it was fabulous beachwear. Not that I intended to be near any real beaches; I can't stand the grit of sand under my nails, and with my upcoming career, well, damage to the hands was a big no-no.

"She said it's the building right over the cleaners." Hailey tipped her sharp white Kangol hat back and peered up at the building. "What's keeping her? Maybe we should lock the doors." Coming from a woman in a crisp white mafioso hat, the comment struck me as funny.

"Not to sound weird or anything, but do you think Marcella is poor? I mean, this neighborhood and everything . . ."

Hailey tapped her chin with her cell phone. "I think Marcella is sort of normal. This is no worse than that Washington Heights dungeon I lived in before I moved in with you. Marcella is average. You're the one who's different. You've never had to worry about money."

"Until now," I said, thinking of how the money from my spritzing paycheck had somehow shrunk to less than three hundred dollars just from buying a few lattes and taking a few cabs to work.

My funds were frighteningly low . . . especially since I hadn't been able to cash in on the return of my "buying spree" items, which had been a total shock to me since I had all my receipts, none of the tags had been removed, and I had brought the merchandise back to the stores within twenty-four hours. Imagine my dismay when the first clerk I approached at Bon Nuit told me she couldn't hand over cash on the spot?

"What? No cash? But I have receipts!" I chirped.

I was told that it was store policy. The clerk would be happy to credit the account—which meant the money would go right back to Daddy.

"No! That won't work at all!" I had protested, demanding to see a manager who politely told me the same two words: "store policy."

As I made the rounds with my returns, "store policy" became the mantra of the day. Most retail establishments agreed to give me the money back, but it would have to be processed through their credit department, which would issue a refund in three to six weeks.

That was three weeks ago, and let me tell you, I was feeling the crunch. But money things always have a way of working out for me. I calculated that, just about the time the checks started rolling in, I would be seeing a big advance from my hand-modeling jobs. And of course, by that time, Daddy would have seen the magic I can do with the help of a few charge cards and would reinstate my credit line.

I turned toward the squarish, pedestrian brick apartment building that rose over the cleaners in time to see Marcella emerging from the narrow vestibule. In a smart black-and-white ensemble, she could have stepped right out of the pages of *Vogue.*

"Well, shame on me, I take it all back. Just look at her. Those houndstooth checked pants could be an ad for Talbots' classic collection."

"I could die for that vanilla alligator bag," Hailey murmured.

"Definitely a Furla. And look at that hat! If that isn't the cutest." It was a bucket hat in black-and-white buffalo check with a floppy, flirty brim. "I can't place that hat, but do you recognize the sleek, draped black tank?"

Hailey and I glanced at each other, then said in unison, "DKNY."

"And her luggage. What is that?" Hailey gasped, but Marcella was already waving and bouncing her rolling suitcase down the stone steps.

I unlocked the car doors and stepped out, more to see her perfectly matched luggage than anything else.

"Sorry I'm late," she called. "It's hard to get out the door with a baby in the house, even when it's not yours. I just love holding the little querido."

The demure tote was made of smooth leather in a buttery shade of honey. There was a matching cosmetic bag, just the right size to hold tall bottles of shampoo, conditioner, lotion. I couldn't resist touching the large suitcase on wheels—butt soft.

"Where did you get this?" I gawked as Marcella lifted them into the trunk. Riding alongside these enchanted bags, my old Giacomo tapestry pieces would probably curl up and whimper all the way east.

"It's the sort of luggage you'd expect Julia Roberts to carry," Hailey said as the three of us popped into the car. "Or J-Lo. Or Jennifer Aniston."

"Hailey, honey," Marcella chastised her, "do you

really think any of those people carry their own luggage?"

"Well, I can tell you one thing," I said as I tipped my sunglasses down and followed the signs to the BQE. "Those men outside the OTB certainly got their pickles tickled today, seeing the three of us out in our spring finest with our hats and all."

Marcella slapped her thigh and turned toward Hailey in the backseat. "I'm sure they didn't believe their eyes."

"I'm still stuck on that luggage," Hailey said. "Our producer keeps talking about going on location, and if we do, I'm going to need something nice. The old college backpacks don't cut it anymore."

"Time to step up," Marcella advised.

"OK," I said, cutting to the chase. "So we're dying to know where you got it."

"Bon Nuit, of course. It was ridiculously overpriced, so I kept an eye on it until Silly Sale Day." Silly Sale is when everything—and I mean everything—at Bon Nuit is fifty percent off. It's a wonderful thing. "That morning I zipped in there as soon as the doors opened, and with my employee discount, I got it for a song."

Hailey and I oohed in admiration. An exquisitely beautiful purchase is one thing, but an exquisitely beautiful purchase at deeply discounted prices? Sheer magic.

"I forgot about the employee discount," I said, mentally ringing up those Ralph Lauren sheets I'd liked minus twenty percent. "Are you allowed to include friends and family members?"

"Bon Nuit is very strict about that," Marcella said. "I'd help you, honey, but I can't afford to lose my job."

"No, of course," Hailey said politely, but I could hear the disappointment in her voice. It killed me, too, knowing that all those employees had a discount that I couldn't get. Sometimes life is incredibly unfair.

"There is nothing like a great bargain," I said, ramping up the speed as the expressway began to clear. "I still remember the most fabulous deals of my life. I can just about smell the perfume I was wearing that day, even remember my shade of lipstick. The memory is that vivid."

"OK." Hailey put her hands on the console and leaned between the two front seats. "Let's tell shopping stories. The most incredible buy of your life. Alana?"

"Hard to say." I told them about a two-hundred-dollar cashmere sweater I had bought for Daddy one Christmas at Macy's. It was already on sale but I had so many coupons and one-day savings tickets that it rang up to be seven dollars and seventy-eight cents with sales tax included. "At that price," the salesclerk had teased, "we're almost paying you money."

"Jimmy Choo boots down in the Village," Hailey said. "They were red-tagged, double discount, eighty percent off. I think they were from the previous season, but I didn't care. Those boots fit me so perfectly. I still have them."

"Remind me to toss them out of your closet when we get home," I said. "Boots from two seasons ago? Have you lost your mind, child?"

Marcella's best buy was a Hermès scarf on the clearance rack in that little accessories boutique in Bergdorf's. "Or actually, it was last night at Sears when I got this tank top and these slacks."

I gasped in disbelief. "You got that outfit at Sears?"

"Can you believe it? Sears. I went with my sister to get a crib for the baby, and I was wheeling him around and I almost ran into this sales rack. Next thing I know, I had him in the dressing room and nobody believed how fucking great this stuff looked on me."

"That's amazing," Hailey said.

"Tell me about it. It was a nightmare getting that crib home in a taxi, but we made it. Dragged that thing up the stairs ourselves. My brother-in-law had to work overtime."

I think Hailey and I were still recovering from Marcella's outstanding Sears acquisition when she revised her best bargain scenarios.

"If you want to talk designer, I think it would have to be the Kate Spade bag that I found at this boutique on Madison that was going out of business. Or wait! Do housewares count? I got a Cuisinart Deluxe food processor at fifty percent below retail. I was dating the salesperson at the time and I talked him down. The relationship ended fast, but I still have that food processor and it's fucking great!"

As we laughed and compared anecdotes, I had to be honest with myself. Hailey and I were excellent shoppers, but Marcella Rodriguez had the golden touch; this woman was truly gifted.

And I basked in the glow of greatness.

Two hours later the Mercedes rolled past the rosebushes that marked Rosebud Lane, and my parents' summerhouse came into view. Six years ago, while Mama and I were off in Europe, Daddy had picked the place himself—a U-shaped, cedar-shingled charmer with a white wooden porch that wrapped around the front of the main wing. Two cars were parked near the garage, which used to be an old carriage house, and I remembered Mama had mentioned that the housekeeping staff would be cleaning and stocking the place as scheduled. As we drew closer, I noticed that the porch was littered with large brown boxes.

"Looks like a UPS convention," Hailey teased.

Gravel crunched under the tires as I pulled up to the steps, swung my door open, and lifted my sunglasses onto my head. "Giant boxes! I love presents." Navigating the stone path delicately in my D&G sandals, I hopped up the steps and sprang onto the porch to examine the shipping labels.

"Fortunoff! The Source!" I threw my arms around a box and pretended to hug it. "I almost forgot! It's the outdoor patio furniture I ordered to replace that hideous aluminum junk Daddy bought last year. Oh, I can't wait to see it," I said, tugging at the lip of one huge box.

"Excuse me?" Marcella swung her black bag atop one box and scowled at the label. "Who delivers packages without getting a signature? Who leaves thousands of dollars' worth of merchandise out on someone's front porch? You are so lucky someone didn't drive by and cart this off in their truck."

"The cleaning crew probably signed for it," I said, shoving a key under the giant staple. "And it's the Hamptons. People can't just drive up to your house without raising suspicion."

Hailey's hands were on her hips. "Alana! Don't break a nail! Remember, your hands are your future."

I jerked my hands back as if they'd touched fire. "You are so right. We'll work on these later. Let's get settled in first."

25

Hailey

"Let's get unpacked and head over to Southampton," Alana said, leading the way to the main wing. "They're bound to have a few early Memorial Day specials, don't you think? The boutiques are still quiet this time of year, and I have to say, some of my all-time favorite swimsuits were purchased in the shops out here."

"Forget it," Marcella rolled her chic luggage over the oriental rug. "I'm in a store all week long and it's gorgeous out and we're here at the ocean. Let's go to the beach."

What? No shopping fix?

Alana and I exchanged a look of confusion.

"But I thought you were a veteran shopper," Alana said. "Besides, the beach is right out there beyond the dunes. We can do the beach anytime."

"Listen, cookie, the stores will be there later, too." Marcella removed her hat and flicked her pixie cut into place. "So where's my room, honey? Don't leave me hanging here."

I think Alana was a little discombobulated, but she led us into the main wing, where the bedrooms were redecorated a few years ago with trendy themes such as the tie-dye room, the art deco room, the moose lodge room, etc. The art deco room was one of my personal faves, with its neon lighting and plastic spaceship chairs, but when we got to the top of the stairs, Marcella won the toss. I was relegated to the tie-dye room, a scheme reminiscent of my electric Kool-Aid acid parents.

"Like a regression to my childhood," I muttered as I headed down to the end of the hall. "Did I ever mention that this room has ghosts for me?"

"Don't worry," Alana called after me. "No skeletons in that closet. We keep the family secrets buried in the basement."

I was about to answer when I heard a voice. A man's voice, coming from this end of the hall.

"Did you hear that?" I stopped and turned back to my friends. "I think there's someone here."

"Don't be a lily-livered ninny!" Alana waved me off. "Ain't nobody here but us chickens."

OK, then. I pressed on and paused outside the door at the end of the hall.

"You know it," came a man's voice.

Was there a TV in the room? I didn't remember. Maybe someone had left a television on.

"Judge Marshall-Hughs?" I called, feeling a little creeped out. I didn't think Alana's father would be here, and when he did come, he always stayed in the master bedroom, the south wing. I felt like a character in a horror movie, walking into a really bad situation. But Alana and Marcella were already unpacking in their rooms. I was being silly.

Pushing open the door, I saw light streaming through the grape tie-dyed curtains . . . onto the tight buttocks of a black man who stood facing away from me, his hands in the dark hair of a woman kneeling at his feet. A woman wearing jeans and sneakers and a crisp blue cleaning smock. A woman who probably couldn't hear me over the man's moaning.

"Oh, my God!" I gasped as I realized what was happening.

"Oh, Miss Alana!" the woman cried, mistakenly.

"What? Oh, no!" The man swung his head around toward me. It was Trevor, Alana's cousin. "No, don't stop!" He told the woman, cupping her face.

I stepped back, stunned.

"Hailey!" he shouted.

"Yes?"

"Close the damned door!"

"What in the world has gotten into you, Trevor Marshall-Hughs?" Alana was red-hot, in his grill, her finger jabbing at the air, her head wagging. "Getting your groove on with the cleaning lady in my Daddy's house! My Daddy's cleaning lady! My parents' house! And you just drive out here and bust in without calling anyone or asking permission and you drag that poor woman off to bed like a grunting Neanderthal?"

"We weren't using no bed." Trevor stared off at the ocean, cool and resigned, his arms crossed over his untucked polo shirt.

Marcella, Xavier, and I were twisted around in our lounge chairs to watch, although the scene was bound to be ugly and regrettable, like a twisted car wreck.

"I told you he wouldn't care," Xavier said. He turned back toward the ocean and reached down for his water bottle. "The man shows no remorse. Throw the book at him, Judge Alana."

"I am going to be throwing a lot more than a book at you, Mr. Trevor Marshall-Hughs," Alana continued.

"Don't talk to me," Trevor said, heading off down the beach. "I'm in no mood."

"Apparently you were in the mood a few minutes ago! And I can't believe what that bitch was doing in my Daddy's house. I have half a mind to fire her ass."

"Don't even think about that."

"Just watch me!"

Marcella and I had to twist around the other way to watch them go. Alana traipsed after him, hustling in her chiffon wraparound skirt to keep up with his long-legged stance. Occasionally the wind carried her voice back our way, but it seemed to be more of the same speech.

"I've never been so embarrassed in my life," I said, though I knew it wasn't really true. I'd been plenty embarrassed, plenty of times.

"He's the one who should be embarrassed," Marcella said.

Xavier laughed. "Come on, ladies! No harm done. The lady was willing, both parties are single, and if you subscribe to cable TV, I'm sure you've seen juicier scenes than Trevor with his pants down."

"I guess." I thought about it for a minute, then cracked a smiled. "Yeah, sure. I mean, it wasn't sexy." I laughed. "Actually, it was sort of comical."

Xavier gave a mock sigh. "That's what all my women say."

By the time Trevor and Alana returned, our little beach party had grown into a dozen or so people, some neighbors, others just walking along the Dune Road beach and deciding to get in on the conversation and free drinks. The sky was clear and sizzling blue, and the temperature was veering into the seventies. Definitely sneaky sunburn weather, so we all lathered up, though the breeze off the ocean made it too cool for swimsuits just yet. Marcella had befriended a swarthy fabric designer from Chelsea and a couple who represented artists for children's books. Xavier and Trevor flirted with the women, a group of flight attendants and some grad students who were preparing to spend the summer as camp counselors on the North Fork. Alana had the attention of a former Navy Seal who now ran a charter boat for local fishermen; I couldn't tell if she was interested in him or simply wanted to know the best time of the week to purchase fresh fish.

I joined in the conversation occasionally, but most of all, I closed my eyes and let the sun warm my skin as I tried to focus on the sound of the waves smashing on the shore. My heart wasn't into the party scene at the moment; my thoughts were too wrapped up in someone else.

Antonio.

OK, maybe it was infantile, a goofy little crush, like the posters of Brad Pitt that I'd hung up in my locker in high school.

Only this time, I didn't have to hang up posters. It was the real thing. Well, sort of.

I tried to pin down the facts, think of the real relationship qualities, as Alana had advised. What did I know about his personality? His background, aside from the standard bio in the tabloids? His likes and dislikes?

I knew I could answer some of those questions. Of course I could! But at the moment, the prospect of spending an evening with Antonio was such a bright light on the horizon that it overwhelmed every detail around it.

"Yo, people!" Xavier called, clapping his hands. "Ladies and gentleman, if I could have your attention for one moment."

I lifted the brim of my floppy beach hat and found Xavier standing in the sand, working the crowd.

"My name is Xavier Goodman . . ."

"Hi, Xavier!" a few of the flight attendants shouted back.

He pointed to them, nodding. "And I'm a fun-aholic. Now, I know, that probably sounds as squeaky clean as the Beach Boys in their hey-day, but it's gotten to the point where you can't say anything anymore. Can't say party, baby. Can't say ecstasy. Can't say snow. Can't say blow, for two very good reasons."

Marcella and I glanced over at Trevor, who was doubled over laughing. Alana didn't seem quite so amused. She stared down at her chaise and brushed sand from her skirt.

"You OK?" I asked her as Xavier went on.

She plunked her sunglasses down and let her head roll back on the chaise. "I just wish he'd stop. Why does it always have to be about him? I mean, here we are, hanging on the beach, and X has to turn it all into a show. He always takes control and makes it all about him."

"You know what?" I said softly. "I think you two are just too much alike. That's the problem."

"Please! That is not at all what it's about."

Xavier's jokes rolled on. "Then there's the whole range of names that are no good anymore. Let's see: Peter, Dick, Johnson, Willy, Woody, Murphy. Yeah, I met some Irish guy who called his thing a Murphy. What's that about? I told him, no brothers ever do that, but he told me, what do you think Sean Combs did? I mean, you think it's a Puff Daddy for nothing? Puff Daddy. I like the sound of that. Sure beats a Murphy."

I recognized some of the jokes from his performance at the club. Others seemed to be spontaneous, improvised for the people on the beach. When he came to two grad students who were obviously a couple, Xavier shook his head and warned the guy.

"Beware the American princess! She will let you eat cake, then tell them 'off with his head!' "

Alana bolted up in her chair and swiped her sunglasses off to glare at X.

But he went on, joking about how there's an American princess in every crowd. Like a spider, she seduces her mate, then eats him for breakfast.

Alana leaned forward on her arms to confide, "Can I kill him now? I don't think I can wait for breakfast."

I shrugged as she stood up and smiled wide for the crowd. "And I'm sure you all recognize Mr. Xavier Goodman's type. He's the Joke That Wouldn't Die."

The beach grew quiet as Xavier squinted over heads of the group, watching her.

"I'm sure you have a friend like this," Alana coaxed. "As a boy, he told you the same knock-knock joke over and over again until you ran screaming into the woods."

That got a laugh.

"As he grew up, his jokes improved. People actually gathered around him at a party—at least for the first hour or so. But the problem is he never stops. He's like a CD on auto-replay. You could go to the cleaners and come back and still find him playing the same tired material. Over and over again."

This time, even Xavier forced himself to smile, though he wasn't comfortable being upstaged.

"This is the friend who's loaded with self-confidence," Alana went on. "It oozes from his pores, an overabundance, probably the result of a hormonal imbalance, so common in men. If you could bottle and sell his self-confidence, you'd see a hell of a lot more female comics out there. . . ."

I watched in amazement, sure that Alana was hating

every minute of this. Although she liked to be the center of attention, she wanted to be singled out for her beauty and fashion savvy, not for her public display of twisted logic.

There was a lot of anger brewing between Alana and Xavier, even Alana and her cousin Trevor. I didn't understand it, but one thing I knew for sure: it was dangerous to cross Alana.

26

Alana

Somehow I managed to restrain myself from burying Xavier and Trevor in the sand and leaving only their heads exposed, with a honey glaze and a jar of fire ants nearby. And believe me, that required a great deal of restraint.

After we returned to the house and I had a chance to relax in the spa shower that Mama and I had modeled after a spa at the Tokyo Ritz, I realized it was wiser to spare their lives, especially considering that I needed their help getting my new furnishings in place. Part of the master suite, this spa was off-limits to everyone but my parents and me, and I thanked my lucky stars that Trevor hadn't chosen my serene Japanese garden when he decided to have the cleaning lady polish his knob. With the fresh scent of shampoo in the air, I reconfigured our sleeping arrangements, deciding to let the guys stay in guest rooms of the main wing (way to ruin the tie-dye room for Hailey). We would move to the north wing, where the bedrooms hadn't been redecorated since I was in college, but at least we'd have our privacy.

While my friends showered, I hollered up to the guys to get their butts downstairs and earn their keep. Trevor plodded down the steps, barefoot and yelping about not having a moment's peace when women were on the premises. Xavier came behind him, wearing only olive cargo shorts and smelling lemony clean.

I stepped back from the landing of the stairs, a little distracted by the view. All that chocolatey skin and rounded muscles, slightly pumped but not so swollen that the bloated things wanted to leap out of the skin.

The man was fine. Delicious. And so out of line to come downstairs that way with my friends and me in the house.

"Would you get yourself decent and get back down here before I wallop your ass?" I crowed.

"I *am* decent. It's eighty degrees out there. This is decent for eighty degrees."

"*I* can't work with you that way," I insisted.

He tossed back his head and laughed . . . all the way up the stairs.

Now what kind of response was that? Was I supposed to feel embarrassed or annoyed? I tell you, these two brothers deserve each other.

To my surprise, when it came time for the heavy lifting, Trevor had a smart attack and found a dolly out in the maintenance shed. Like regular repairmen, he and Xavier wheeled those boxes around to the screened-in pool side atrium and popped those nasty giant staples out with long, flat screwdrivers.

"Oh my Lord!" I gasped as X lifted out the first chair, an all-weather natural wicker armchair with sumptuous cushions patterned with palm trees, orchids, and tropical flowers. "It's beautiful! Coco Island Escape—just as I planned." The design theme had slipped my mind, but now that I saw the warm coffee tone of the wicker, it all came rushing back. "I'm going to get two potted palms from the local nursery, and I've got tiny little turquoise lights to string along the far fence. I'm modeling everything after a little oceanfront café in the Bahamas. I haven't been there yet, but *Condé Nast Traveler* rated it the number one getaway for 2004."

Trevor stepped away from the huge cartons and pulled one of the green aluminum chairs away from the table, causing a spine-tingling scratch on the concrete. "What's wrong with these chairs? These look new!"

"Please! Daddy got those hideous specimens because they were on sale and they were green. The set is called Lime Freeze. Doesn't that say enough?"

Trevor sat down in one. "They look okay to me . . ."

"He wanted something to match the grass!" I said, gesturing to the short-cropped green lawn beyond the pool patio. "You don't match grass, you accent it. The coco wicker will work so much better." I went to the largest carton. "This must be the table. Some assembly required, but there's a toolbox in the maintenance shed. Do you think you can manage it before dinner? I'd love to dine alfresco tonight."

"Can I manage it?" Trevor sat back and crossed his arms behind his head. "I'm liking the green chairs. And if you don't like the chairs, what's wrong with the table? It's just a glass top with white legs."

"Am I speaking in a foreign tongue, or what?"

"I think we can handle the table," Xavier conceded.

"You go handle the table, X," Trevor said, looping one leg over a green chair. "I'm happy as a green salamander right here in my green chair. Wouldn't mind a beer or one of those fancy cocktails with a little umbrella in it. How 'bout you make it a melon ball daiquiri. Or a green apple martini . . ."

"If you would like to eat dinner this evening, you need to help your friend assemble the table," I told my cousin as I smoothed a hand over the cheerful tropical print on the newly unveiled chair. I sat down and closed my eyes, recalling photos of the Bahamian paradise from the magazine spread. Ahhh!

"What about the green furniture?" Xavier asked.

"Send it out on the surf." Even as I said it, I worried at how ecologically depraved that sounded. "Actually, just put it in the shed? We'll get someone to cart it away after the holiday weekend."

After the coco wicker was unpacked and assembled, Xavier and I spent some time refining the pool side layout while the others prepared dinner. Trevor grilled steaks, Marcella boiled fresh Silver Queen corn and set the bread she'd brought from the Brooklyn Bakery in baskets, and Hailey assembled a salad—her specialty.

As we sat down to dinner, sunlight angled over the north lawn, painting the carpet of flowers with yellow light. The orange marigolds, the colorful impatiens, Mama's favorite trellis of white roses, and the wall of lilac bushes along the far fence—this garden was one of my father's favorite sights on earth, and from now on he would be able to enjoy it in comfort and style. Daddy would be so proud of me.

"You never did tell me what brought you guys out here," I said as we passed the steak platter. "Mama didn't mention that you were coming."

Ignoring the serving utensil, Trevor fumbled with a steaming ear of corn. "I didn't know it myself, until your Aunt Nessie sent me through the roof."

"Oh? When you're in trouble, she's my Aunt Nessie?"

"She's a nutcase, that's what. And with the mood I

was in today, I knew I had better get the hell out of there before I said something I would live to regret. A man's got to know his limitations, and I'm not lying when I tell you that today, she pushed me damn close to mine."

"You could have talked to her," Xavier said. "She's a reasonable woman. No reason to fly off the handle and blow out of town like that."

"Oh, talk to her? Talk to her, bro?" Trevor dismissed him. "Get the hell out of here. I didn't see you try to do any talking with her."

"I didn't have a gripe with her."

"She always liked you best, X," I teased, causing Trevor to flick a crumb at me. "How rude." I glared at him. "Didn't your mama teach you anything?"

"She taught you to work out your differences," Xavier said. "But you just ran. Besides, why you gettin' so upset about a stupid computer program? If the woman wants to keep notes, let her keep notes."

"She was the one getting upset," Trevor answered. "Hitting buttons on the computer, then pulling the plug out of the wall. Can you imagine?"

My Aunt Nessie can throw quite a tantrum when she's upset. "She must've really let you have it," I said.

"I couldn't stick around there a minute longer. Mama was that crazy." Trevor rolled his eyes. "She's all 'you do this and you do that and you do it now, boy.' The woman may be a great cook, but she doesn't know jack about business."

"Don't you be talking that way about your mama," Xavier chastised him. "That woman raised you. Practically raised me, too, and did a damn fine job without a man to support her."

"That doesn't mean she's not crazy, though," Trevor pointed out.

"My parents are totally crazy," Hailey said. "When

they left New York, I think they were legitimately looking for some peace and quiet, a relief from the superstress, but they went overboard with the no-phone, no-TV thing. I'm surprised they still have electricity, though I'm waiting for the day when Dad starts to worry that he's picking up signals from Mars through the toaster."

"Yeah, well, we're all a little whacked now and then." Xavier put his fork down on the edge of the plate and put his hands on his lap. "I will never forget the way Nessie took me in. Nearly adopted me when I had nowhere to go."

"Is that how it happened?" I teased. "And here I thought you came for an overnight with Trev and just never wanted the party to end." From the old Great Neck days, it was truly the way I remembered it, with Xavier suddenly camped on the bottom bunk in Trevor's room, Xavier appearing at Sunday suppers, Xavier running through the sprinkler barefoot and soaking his shorts along with the rest of the neighborhood kids on hot summer days. Then, Xavier in a necktie and tight jacket at our Christmas supper—a sacred family tradition—and my surprise and curiosity that there was a package for him under Aunt Nessie's tree. "You know, I always wondered what happened. The neighborhood story, with the car crash and all." Local legend being that X's parents died together in a horrible accident on the Long Island Expressway. "Was it true?"

"Nah." Xavier lowered his eyes. "It wasn't that simple. My mother, well, you know, she had her problems. Fell into the heavy stuff, and the cops caught her dealing one day. Before they could send her to prison, she was into the wind. My guess, she tried to get to California, since she always talked about Hollywood. Don't know if she ever made it, though."

Xavier's mother had always frightened me a little,

Zebra Contemporary

To start your membership, simply complete and return the Free Book Certificate. You'll receive your Introductory Shipment of FREE Zebra Contemporary Romances, you only pay $1.99 for shipping and handling. Then, each month you will receive the 4 newest Zebra Contemporary Romances. Each shipment will be yours to examine FREE for 10 days. If you decide to keep the books, you'll pay the preferred subscriber price (a savings of up to 30% off the cover price), plus shipping and handling. If you want us to stop sending books, just say the word... it's that simple.

If the FREE Book Certificate is missing, call 1-800-770-1963 to place your order.

FREE BOOK CERTIFICATE

Yes! Please send me FREE Zebra Contemporary romance novels. I only pay $1.99 for shipping and handling. I understand that each month thereafter I will be able to preview 4 brand-new Contemporary Romances FREE for 10 days. Then, if I should decide to keep them, I will pay the money-saving preferred subscriber's price (that's a savings of up to 30% off the retail price), plus shipping and handling. I understand I am under no obligation to purchase any books, as explained on this card.

NAME _____

ADDRESS _____ APT. _____

CITY _____ STATE _____ ZIP _____

TELEPHONE (_____) _____

E-MAIL _____

SIGNATURE _____

(If under 18, parent or guardian must sign)

Offer limited to one per household and not to current subscribers. Terms, offer and prices subject to change. Orders subject to acceptance by Zebra Contemporary Book Club. Offer Valid in the U.S. only.

Thank You!

CN026A

THE BENEFITS OF BOOK CLUB MEMBERSHIP

• You'll get your books hot off the press, usually before they appear in bookstores.

• You'll ALWAYS save up to 30% off the cover price.

• You'll get our FREE monthly newsletter filled with author interviews, book previews, special offers and MORE!

• There's no obligation – you can cancel at any time and you have no minimum number of books to buy.

• And – if you decide you don't like the books you receive, you can return them. (You always have ten days to decide.)

Zebra Contemporary Romance Book Club
Zebra Home Subscription Service, Inc.
P.O. Box 5214
Clifton NJ 07015-5214

ll..l.,.lll....ll.l.l.l..l.l..l.l...l.l...ll..l

PLACE
STAMP
HERE

with her red leather gloves and tight cornrows and cold stare. Once when she yelled at me for pushing my cousin Dan-Dan away from my tricycle, I ran into my mama's skirt, crying from the unfairness of it all.

"Yeah, you got a bad shake, bro." Trevor tore a piece of bread in half and slathered it with butter. "Things might have turned out different if your mama hadn't pushed your daddy out."

"Another one of those 'what ifs' that we can't control." Xavier took a long draw on his water glass as knives clinked against plates and Hailey passed the salad down the table. The dining went on, but we all seemed to know that the moment belonged to Xavier, that it was his time to trip back to the past. "My old man, he meant well. He tried to make things work, tried to do right. Drove a truck, hauling things cross-country. My mom hated that schedule. Began to hate him. Last time I saw him, he'd brought me a baseball glove. I remember it, 'cause I was five and the glove was so big on my hand, I could shove most of my fingers into one section." He swiped a hand over his jaw, his eyes distant, far away. "Man, I loved that glove. The day he gave it to me, my Dad cried. His eyes were so wet, he made my shirt soggy when he hugged me. I didn't get it, didn't understand why he was so sad, why it was different from any other time when he came by to visit. It wasn't till years down the road that I put it all together, that it was the last time I ever saw him. He must have known that at the time."

It was such an unusually introspective moment for X that everyone at the table was quiet for a minute; just the bittersweet strains of Lenny Kravitz and the spring breeze moved through the atrium. It was that time of day when the cool breeze stirred the warmth from the earth, mixing the smells of soil and concrete, grass and ocean salt in a pleasing swirl.

I put my corncob down and licked some butter from my lips, suddenly feeling a twinge of sympathy for Xavier. Somehow I'd never put it all together—that he was living with Trevor and Aunt Nessie because he had nowhere else to go. Damn. That explained some things. It also made me feel like a selfish jerk, treating him like a leech all those years.

Well, maybe not all those years.

I admit, there had been a few stages in adolescence when Xavier was my crush. Really, who can resist the boy who appears in every theater production at the high school, the guy who wins the talent show because he can crack up even the stone-faced principal. Xavier had a presence, a bright light around him, and for a time I longed to be in that light. I had wanted to be his girl.

But I was just Trevor's cousin, like family. From his end, it wasn't going to happen.

"Let's clear this stuff away, and I'll make some coffee," Marcella said as the moment passed. "I'm stuffed, but I brought the most delicious dessert from this bakery in Brooklyn. They make the best cannolis."

"Cannolis? Damn!" Trevor dropped his corncob and wiped his hands on a napkin. "What's a hot Latin lady like yourself doing with those sugary Italian weenies?"

"Oh, honey, you'd be surprised." Marcella grabbed a stack of plates and disappeared into the kitchen.

I picked up two bowls and followed her, leaving X still staring off toward the tulips and impatiens and lilac bushes, their glow growing softer in the dying light. Maybe I didn't hate him so much anymore, after thinking about all the stuff he'd gone through. After all, he wasn't a bad person.

Just bad for me.

27

Hailey

"**C**an we go?" I called impatiently through the screen door, then paced some more on the wooden porch. I usually don't worry about being on time, but I was supposed to meet Antonio at the East Hampton club in twenty minutes, and I had no idea how far it was or if the guys would ever finish getting ready.

I was nervous.

And what if I was late?

What if he left?

What if he thought I stood him up?

"What's with the ants in your pants, girl?" Alana stepped out on the porch, her dark skin gleaming against a ruby red bustier that she wore over a loose print skirt. She slipped into a short-cut jacket and checked her watch. "Oh, shit! You've got to meet Antonio! Why didn't you say something?"

"I didn't want to rush everyone." My right hand flew to my mouth, and I tugged it down before I could nibble on the tips of my nails. Bad, Hailey! Down, girl, down!

Alana opened the screen door and cupped her hands to her face. "Trevor! Xavier! Cut the primping and get your sorry asses down here or you're driving your-selves." The door bounced against her bottom, and she stepped away to let it shut. "Marcella is just finishing up with her sister." Once again, she shouted inside, "Marcella!"

Our red-headed friend appeared, waving her hands to shut up Alana, her headset clipped on like a switch-board operator. "Would you just listen to me, because I am telling you that you got to sit him up and let him di-gest or it's gonna burn like a motherfucker. Babies can't just eat lying down and go to sleep. Did you even try to burp him?"

She nodded and sighed as the answer seemed to come through. "I know. I know you're trying, honey. You can only do your best, but in the future, don't give him his bottle lying down. You wouldn't eat chicken fricasee in bed, would you?"

I turned to Alana as Marcella headed out to the car. "Marcella has a baby?"

"It's her nephew, but her sister's a nervous wreck . . . a young mother, and the baby has colic."

Climbing in the car, I eavesdropped on Marcella's advice and marveled at how the woman exuded calm and control. Maybe I should have asked her about my choice of wardrobe tonight. I was wearing tapered jeans with a Hugo Boss tailored shirt—gray with white pinstripes and three-quarter sleeves. The daring part about it was that I wore nothing underneath it and it was unbuttoned to the bottom of my rib cage. The gray was severe and serious, my hair was wild and loose, and the amount of skin and cleavage revealed was daring and so seductive that I had felt a sting of embarrassment when I first faced the mirror.

I'd thought about changing, even went back to my suitcase, but I wanted to do this. I wanted to try a sexier look. This was my chance with Antonio Lopez, and if I didn't give a clear message now, he wouldn't be waiting around for a PS.

By the time X turned on to Main Street in East Hampton, I was a nervous wreck, a knee-wiggling, lip-biting wreck. "We're late," I said. "He's already been there for ten minutes."

"Who's been there?" Trevor turned around from the passenger seat. "Who's been where?"

"Antonio," I said. "Are we almost there?"

"It's just up ahead," Xavier said. "But who knew all these people would be out here partying before the season has even started."

"Antonio who?" Trevor asked. "What's happening?"

"Antonio Lopez, you dillhole," Alana snapped. "She was supposed to meet him ten minutes ago, and she would've been on time if you two would've paid attention."

Trevor held up his hands. "I didn't know! Antonio Lopez . . . mmm-mmm. The hot Latin lover. Is he really that hot in person?" he asked me.

"Hotter," I said.

"What about on the show? You think he's gonna find the serial killer terrorizing Indigo Hills? Or is he next on the killer's list?"

"She doesn't know that!" Alana snapped. "Would you get us to the club already?"

"I have to give you credit, Trevor," I told him. "I can tell you've been watching our show. Catching up on the serial killer plot."

"Yeah, well, there's nothing else to do while I'm

waiting around for Mama to update her records on that goddamned clipboard."

The car lurched to a stop and Xavier hit the horn. "Goddamn! Did you see that? He stole my spot!"

"Just park," I said desperately.

"There's nowhere to go. The lot's packed to the gills."

"Then pull up by the door. Now!" Alana demanded.

X spun the car round to the door of the club.

Marcella was the first out of the backseat. "Don't worry, honey," she told me, "it's better to be late and make an entrance."

I was such a bundle of nerves, I began to wonder why I was here. "Why am I doing this? Antonio is out of my league."

Alana spun around and grabbed me by the arms. "Get a grip, girl! There's a gorgeous specimen of man waiting in there, and he wants you. Now get your butt in there and grab his ass before some other sister does it for you!"

She really didn't leave me much choice. With a deep breath, I flicked my hair back over one shoulder and pushed through the door.

The dance floor was dark, lit mostly by a revolving disco ball, and the dance music boomed with that throbbing beat that guaranteed a headache within the hour. What was I doing here? I'm so bad at clubs—especially disco-type places where it's all about body language and not at all about real language. If I had to dance my way into a relationship, I'd still be sleeping in my little twin bed back in Wisconsin.

I searched the crowd—a succession of very young faces, most devoid of the artistry of plastic surgery.

"Looks like frat night," Alana said. "I guess most of the colleges are out already."

Someone banged into me, and I fell against a table. "Where is he?" Panic. "He's not here."

"It's early, and it's a big place. Marcella went to look in the other room. We'll find him."

Not tonight, I thought. It was silly of me to think this could work, that Antonio might actually . . .

And there he was, cutting through the crowd, his eyes locked on me. Behind him, Marcella waved and pointed. Found him! She was beaming.

I nearly choked on my own breath. He was smiling at me with such an amazing look, like I was the most precious gem he'd ever seen.

"Hilly! You made it. I'm so happy you're here. Would you like to dance?" As he spoke he took me by the hand, pulled me close, and kissed me once on both cheeks.

"Not just yet," I managed to say.

"Good. I have a table in the other room, a little more quiet. Would your friends like to join us?"

I snapped out of the spell to look for them. Alana was already talking and strutting with some guy on the dance floor. Marcella stood near the door with Trevor and X, but when I caught her attention she mouthed "bye-bye" and waved.

"We can hook up with them later," I told Antonio, who slid one arm over my shoulders and ushered me up the steps and past the bar.

In the attached room, dark wood tables and tall booths were the haven for people who wanted to talk. I could barely take in the people or the atmosphere in the glow of Antonio. His touch lit my nerve endings, his killer smile was blinding. And as we crossed the room, I just knew that everyone was watching us . . . eyes on us, Antonio and his girl. The couple. Antonio Lopez and Hailey Starrett.

Hailey Starrett-Lopez. Hailey Lopez? No . . .
Hailey Starrett-Lopez.

And there in the corner was a dark booth, our spot.
He gestured for me to slide in, then he sat beside me,
dropping his hand on my knee with a natural, easy
warmth.

"Is sherry OK?" he asked. "It's a personal favorite.
The best ones are made in my country, but I find that so
few Americans appreciate its lush, sweet qualities."

I told him that sherry was fine. His hand remained
on my thigh as we talked, and I found myself wishing it
would slip lower, travel down to the inseam, grab a
handful of thigh. I was surprised at myself, having
such a case of ants in my pants, but I wanted to be with
Antonio in the worst way, and part of me just wanted to
have that initiation over so that we could move on to
the less jittery, more chummy stage of the relationship.

We chatted about the show: the camera crew, the
writers, the new caterer in craft services. Antonio told
me a little about his background in Argentina, about
the early days when he modeled for shaving-cream
ads. He talked about nosy photographers, adding that
the Hamptons were a hot spot for pesky media. But
more than anything, he loved his fans. Soap opera fans
were so loyal, so loving, so devoted.

I made up a story about being the child of reclusive
artists in the Midwest. I figured that the pertinent facts
were true; he didn't need to know that my parents' "art"
was blackberry jam.

When the conversation hit a quiet spot, he turned to
me and dropped his head to my shoulder. "Oh, Hilly,"
he said in a tone that squeezed my heart like a sponge.
"I have a confession to make." He lifted his head so
that his smoky eyes met mine.

My heart thudded hard, rising up to my throat.
"What's that?" I nearly wept.

"You are so beautiful," he said. "I want to have you." With that, he reached a hand right into my blouse and cupped one breast.

I nearly choked at the sensation of his warm palm, so quick and intimate, pulling me into a dark, delicious passion. His lips pressed against mine, nipping lightly as his hand tested the fullness of my breast. Sighing, I dropped a hand to his jeans and loved the bulge I felt there. Oh, yes, he did want me. I was tickled. I'd never made love to a celebrity before, and somehow, his fame made each sensation that much more titillating.

He undid the next button on my blouse and lodged his face inside to suck on my nipple. I was afraid someone would notice, but it was dim and we were in the corner and it felt so good, I had to close my eyes and stop worrying. When he'd sucked me to a frenzy there was more kissing, more groping, including an awkward unzip of his pants so I could reciprocate. With his pants open, I felt free to explore the playground, my hand gliding over the smooth, bulbous head, down the shaft.

"That is . . ." he sucked his breath in between his teeth, his dark eyes nearly closing, "so good when you touch me there." He lifted his hips to stab at my hand, and his hard penis seemed to pop out of his pants.

So Antonio had skipped the underwear phase tonight, too. He'd anticipated something like this. Knowing that gave me a boost of confidence. He wanted to make love to me. Antonio Lopez wanted me. That thought alone gave me the tingle of preorgasm.

I felt my muscles squeezing tight for him, wanting him inside me, here and now. Impossible, I know, especially with the news that photographers were lurking about. But the heat coursing through my blood didn't heed common sense, and Antonio didn't seem to care much that his pants were open under the tablecloth.

What can I say—passion is crazy.

"Listen," I whispered, grabbing him hard. "I want you. But not here."

He moved his fingers along my inner thigh, up along the zipper, then tugged at my belt buckle. "We have to go," he said. "Will you come to my place?"

"Yes," I whispered, confident that I would be saying that word to him time and time again. There would be a lot of yeses in our future.

There were knowing smiles from my friends as Antonio led me around the dance floor to the door. I smiled back, loving that everyone in the club had their eyes glued to us. We were the celebs of the night.

As we stepped out into the parking lot, a man popped out onto the sidewalk and Antonio tugged my hand. "Hilly! Paparazzi!"

I pretended to duck a little, but really I was moving a little closer to Antonio, thrilled to be photographed with him. Who cared if our picture appeared in *Soap Opera Rumors*? We were soap opera stars engaging in a real life love story, and I wasn't at all ashamed of that.

OK, I admit that we had sexual chemistry, but with Antonio it was about more than sex. I was beginning to feel as if his every touch were transforming my life.

This was the stuff soap opera dreams were made of.

28

Alana

It takes me about five minutes to rate the crowd at any given event, whether red-carpet or beach party. There's your snubbish faux-punk fashion crowd, the commercial fashion crowd who are still snubbish but much more buttoned-down, the downtown antichic kids who think they'll defy fashion by wearing truckers' hats, the blue-blood debs who have the misfortune of premature aging caused by dry skin and unfaithful men, the television crowd who long to become film people, usually mixed with the film people who protest that television is trash driven by corporate sponsorship . . .

Please! Add in a few Broadway stars and billionaire entrepreneurs and you've got more egos than even Freud could handle. And the killing part is that most of them don't know how to dress. Sad, isn't it?

Unfortunately, the crowd at the club that night was none of the above. Aside from Antonio, who was now long gone, Marcella and I quickly established that there was not a worthwhile man under the roof. Furthermore, most of the college girls who'd turned out that night looked as if they'd applied their foundation with paint rollers.

Clearly we were not going to make any new best friends, and with Xavier and Trevor ensconced at the bar, engaged in deep "guy" conversation, Marcella and I really had no choice but to dance.

"It's a shame," I said as Marcella and I moved to the edge of the dance floor. Here I'd worn my popping red bustier and would probably never wear it again, and no one worthwhile had even seen it. "Another wasted night."

"Didn't I tell you? Don't expect to meet anyone worthwhile out at a club, honey. You've got much better prospects in other places. How about that guy with the boat you met on the beach today?"

"Not my type," I said. "But sweet."

"Well, I liked Donovan. Do you know he's worked for Pierre Cardin and Barney's? We're going to have lunch in the City sometime. But someone like Donovan wouldn't be caught dead in a place like this. He was going to a private party tonight. A house party. That's the way to go."

"I need another drink," I said, heading over to my cousin and X.

"What you need is a good night's sleep. Save yourself for better things, honey. Tomorrow, I'm going to work the beach and get us an invite for a party that's worth our time."

"It's never worth it," Trevor sputtered, his eyes bleary. "Never worth the time."

"Somebody's been hammering at the booze," Marcella said, sidling up to the bar between Trevor and Xavier.

"Do you think I'm drunk?" Trevor asked. "Because

I'm just getting started. Bartender . . ." He motioned for another round.

I noticed that Xavier had a pint glass of seltzer with lemon. "Easy on that stuff, pal," I teased, taking the empty barstool beside him. "You don't want to lose control. Oh, wait, that's right. You're always in control. In control and controlling."

"I'm driving," he said.

"In control and in the driver's seat," I added. "Unlike my cousin, who never misses an opportunity to lose control, whether it's with women, alcohol, or drugs."

"Don't be a bitch. I'll get you all home. And Trev, just leave him the hell alone. The brother's got some shit to work out."

"Please! How many times have I heard that one? Poor Trev! He's shooting up and he sold his gramma's jewelry for drug money, but let's not talk about it because poor Trevor has things to work out. Issues."

"Would you cut it out?" X said quietly.

"Hey!" Trevor piped up, lifting his head. "You talkin' about me?"

"Yes, I am, cuz. But you can go back to sleep. Don't want to wreck your buzz."

"Fuck that." Trevor pushed back and teetered off the bar stool. "This party's dead. I'm getting the hell out of here."

"OK, good night, sweetie!" Marcella called after him. "Safe home and all that."

"Go ahead," I told Xavier. "Go on after him. It's your job to save him."

"He won't get far." X turned around to watch Trevor weave through the stragglers. "He's got no car keys, and most of the other bars have closed for the night. He's probably just going to the men's room."

"I'm surprised you're not rushing out to hold it for him," I said.

Behind X, Marcella mouthed an "ow!" at my words, then turned toward the bar to ask the bartender something.

"Why do you think I'm responsible for Trevor's problems? Am I the reason he's all fucked up? Yeah, you can blame me if you want, but is it really about me?"

"If we knew the source of his suffering, maybe it could be healed," I said. I knew this wasn't the time or place to discuss Trevor's personal situation, but Xavier had drained his quota of my patience. "The truth is, Trevor coddles his pain. He doesn't want to get better, not really, and if he's not going to champion his own recovery, then we can all beg and cajole and baby him till the day we die, but it's not going to make a bit of difference. So excuse me if I'm not the voice of sympathy, but I've been down this road with Trev a time or two."

"Oh, have you?" Xavier scowled. "Because honestly, Alana, you are totally clueless about Trevor's world. Step out of your bubble, girl. Maybe you should spend a little less time sitting in judgment and just think, *think* about the personal demons this man is trying to fight."

"Demons! How can I feel sorry for a man who's got it all but time and again tries to trash it?"

"Honey, I don't know about demons," Marcella interrupted. "But right now I think there's something bad going down for Trevor."

We swung around to see. Trevor leaned against the wall and peeled bills out of his wallet as he spoke to someone standing behind a divider.

"Oh, no." I didn't want to believe it. For all my harsh words, I wanted to believe that Trevor was past the worst of his addiction, that he was just hiding in the legal addictions—sex and alcohol—until he could pull his head up out of the dirt. "Is he buying drugs?"

"Fuck!" Xavier bolted from his barstool and marched to the back of the bar. Marcella and I flew behind him.

"What the fuck you think you're doing?" Xavier slapped a packet out of Trevor's hands and pushed him against the wall.

Trevor's eyes opened wide in shock. "Easy, bro." He seemed angry, then the fight left him as his head lolled against the wall, his eyes closing.

Xavier spun left and shoved at the other guy, a heavyset white brother with a Santa beard and receding hairline. Bad Santa stepped back, rubbing the shoulder of his leather vest. "Get the hell away from him!" X shouted. "What's your problem?"

"No problem." Sweat beaded on his forehead from the effort of trying to bend down over his belly and pick up the packet of coke. "It's cool, OK? Just keep your hands off me."

"Excuse me?" Marcella pushed between Trevor and X and planted both hands on the dealer's chest. "You think it's cool? You think this is OK? Because let me tell you, pea-head, this is not cool at all. What do you think you're doing selling this crap—and to my friend?"

He tried to edge away. "Lady, look . . ."

"Don't give me no crap." She pummeled his chest. "Do you know what you are? Let me tell you. A waste to society. A monster! Does your mother know you're out dealing drugs?"

Bad Santa shot Xavier and me a desperate look. "Will you take your friend and go?"

It was time to get Trevor home, but Marcella wouldn't be silenced. "Do you want to know what I think? I think you should get the hell out of here before I call the cops. Actually, why don't you stay, and I'll get them here right now." She pulled out her cell phone and punched in some numbers.

"That's not necessary," the dealer said, edging toward the rest rooms. "No harm done, right?" And he raced down the hall to the exit.

"What an asshole," Marcella said.

"He wasn't so bad," Trevor said groggily.

Marcella scowled at him. "Not him, sweetie. *You!"*

Despite my criticisms of Xavier, I was glad to have him around that night. Besides the fact that he was the only one still sober enough to drive, he managed to get Trevor up to bed with no problem and promised to sleep in the same room to keep an eye on him.

Pulling back the old freedom quilt on my bed, I realized I was exhausted. Through my anger, I still loved my cousin, still wanted to help him, though it felt as if my hands were tied.

During the car ride back, he'd leaned on my shoulder and cried real tears, blathering apologies over and over again. He was sorry for being a problem, sorry for messing up. He begged me not to hate him, begged forgiveness.

"Come on, Trev, you know I don't hate you," I told him repeatedly. "But I can't watch you fuck up again. You've got to make a change."

And as Xavier drove us down pitch black country roads, Trevor kept promising that he would change, kept promising he was going to straighten up and live right.

"Not for nothing, honey, but he won't remember any of this in the morning," Marcella told me. "Trevor, shut up and go to sleep. We'll talk tomorrow."

"Not gonna talk, I'm gonna do something! Do something with my life!" he shouted.

It hurt me to see Trev that way, crying and broken.

For the first time, I guess I realized how real his pain was. I couldn't relate. In some ways Xavier was right. I had lived my life in a safe bubble, a bubble that Trevor had popped tonight.

Tonight I had realized that Trevor could not go on this way. If he didn't change his life, this addiction was going to kill him. It seemed so obvious. So why couldn't he act on it?

I didn't want to lose him, but I didn't know how to help him.

I slipped under the quilt and pulled it around my shoulders, hoping to squeeze some familiar comfort out of it. This had used to be my room when Dad first bought the house, and most of the items had remained intact—the old collection of CDs, my four-poster bed with canopy, my quilt, and my stuffed tiger.

I hugged Tigee and went back to the old days, the squirt-gun booth at Adventureland where I'd won Tigee when I was seven or eight. Trevor was there, his ankles popping from the jeans he was always outgrowing. Aunt Nessie let us get soaked on the water ride, then we feasted on corn dogs outside on benches overlooking the Ferris wheel.

"I'm not goin' up there," Trevor always used to say. The Ferris wheel frightened him. Too high to go when you can't fly.

I guess he'd forgotten that rule.

Turning on my side, I pressed my face against the soft-worn pillow sham and tried to come up with a plan. What could I do for Trev?

He loved his neckties. I would buy him a fabulous tie at the outlets tomorrow. A small gesture, but at least it was something positive.

The outlets . . . that was another problem.

After the bill at the club, I was down to a hundred

and sixty dollars. (Yes, we should have skipped the last two rounds!) How could I find anything with one hundred and sixty measly dollars?

I noticed a stack of old magazines from my youth on the night stand. *Teen People. Mademoiselle.* Eek! I went to push them off, then saw that they were combined with a stack of junk mail. The cleaning crew had probably just dumped this stuff in here, since it was my old room.

It's amazing, the quality of junk mail these days, the paper stock, the airbrushed art. I picked up one envelope with a photo of a dad building a sandcastle on the beach with his kids. *Build your SUMMER dreams!* the caption said.

What a sweet thought. Vigilant about protecting my hands, I used an emery board to open the envelope and unfolded the letter, a light blue wash set against a border of effervescent royal blue bubbles.

A lot of fine print with boring numbers, but the headlines were appealing.

Make a splash with your new, limited time 0% APR!

Not sure of the difference between APR and April, but whatever.

Your credit is preapproved.

Well, I liked the sound of that.

Hot Days! Cool Cash!

Liked the sound of that even more.

OK, time to read the fine print. What was the catch? The astute shopper knows there's always some snag.

Now's the time to dive in and enjoy all that the warm weather has to offer—especially since your new National Bank of Integrity Viva account gives you easy access to the funds you want. Your new, low 0% Annual Percentage Rate (APR) . . .

Well, there, I just learned something, though I still don't know what it means . . .

. . . features instant checks, ATM withdrawals, and cash advances. Summer cash to use however you like.

Now there's an abbreviation I understood. ATM! ATM!

Use your credit line to travel to a vacation hot spot and cool off oceanside—or cool down in the Great White North.

It was all too good to be true! The only snag—when I flipped through the enclosed papers, there was no shiny plastic card enclosed. I checked the envelope and confirmed that yes, it was addressed to me. This nice bank meant for me to have this card. And the 800 number printed in large, boldface type was hard to miss. I yawned. Would they still be up at Bank of Integrity?

I tried calling, and a very nice person named Val assured me that my bank provided customer service twenty-four/seven. Val helped me through the application process, a piece of cake, really. The only thing that made me hesitate was household income.

Hmm. The card was for me, and I didn't really have an income, but you'd have to count the money Daddy pays for the co-op. Something like three thousand a month.

I was about to answer when Val coached, "They mean, the total income of all the people living in your household."

I sat up in bed. That included Mama and Daddy— that's what Val said. "Well, I'm not exactly sure, but let me give you a low estimate." My parents' salaries, plus interest from investments and annuities . . . "I'm guessing thirty thousand?"

"A year?"

"A month."

"Oh! OK, then." Cheerful Val needed a minute to run it all through, then she came back with a warm welcome to Bank of Integrity. Not only were they sending me a card with a white dove on it, but Val would give me my account number so that I could start "cashing in on summer fun" right away!

Considering the bond I'd formed with Val, it was hard to say good-bye, but I knew she'd be there twenty-four/seven just in case I ever needed her. I turned the light out and lay down with a smile. Maybe I couldn't fix the problems of the world overnight, but I'd made progress. I'd awoken that morning with a measly two hundred in my pocket, but I was going to sleep with a healthy twenty-thousand-dollar credit line.

I slept like an angel.

29

Hailey

"I have never found a pair of sunglasses I really love." I was turning a rack at the Sunglass Shack outlet, having tried a few and dismissed them all. "What is it about sunglasses? They make such a strong statement." I tried a squarish pair. "Bossy. Aggressive." An oval pair. "Nerdy."

Marcella nodded. "Schoolmarm."

"Try these." Alana handed me some crescent-shaped tortoiseshell frames, which made us all laugh. I fanned my fingers past my face, Travolta-like. "OK, give 'em back," Alana said. "Why is it that they look fine on me?"

And they did.

"On you they say 'intellectual, astute, artistic.' On me, they're like 'did you get a message from your planet yet?' "

Marcella placed a pair of rhinestone frames back on the carousel, then nodded. "OK, ladies. Let's move on. Banana Republic?"

"But we didn't buy anything." Alana handed Marcella a pair with neon frames. "We just got here."

Marcella tucked the neons back on the rack. "Don't you have sunglasses?"

"Sure. But I like these tortoiseshell frames."

"Do you need them?" Marcella pressed. " 'Need' means, can you live without them?"

"Well, that's an odd question," Alana said, modeling the shades for us.

"Honey, you're the one worried about budget and all. That's all I'm saying."

"I know, but aren't they fabulous?"

I nodded. "You should get them."

"Should I?" Alana beamed.

Marcella put the brakes on. "How much are they?"

"Who knows? They're great." Alana removed them to check the tag.

Marcella snorted. "And they call that a discount? Honey, you do what you want, but I'm telling you, we carry the same line at Bon Nuit, and they'll be half that price on Silly Sale Day. Think about it, 'cause I'm trying to save you some money."

"Oh." Alana seemed crestfallen, but she lifted the glasses and plunked them back onto the rack. We headed toward the door, but she turned back and gazed longingly at the sunglasses. "I think they need me."

Marcella crooked her arm through Alana's and guided her toward the exit. "Let them go, honey," she said soothingly. "Someone will find them a nice home at a farm somewhere. A very expensive farm."

Banana Republic was a festival of fashion.

No Manhattan girl can resist a black linen blazer, especially in the crisp yet casual styling of the Big

Banana. There's something so "I don't give a fuck" about the lines and fabric of their clothing; it's so New York.

I was trying on my blazer when Alana passed me on the way to the checkout counter, her arms loaded down with a heavy wad of items. "You hit the mother lode!"

"Just a few things I had to have." Marcella popped out from behind a display of silk tanks and Alana added, "Things I need. Yup. I totally *need* this stuff."

"How do the khaki boot pants fit?" Marcella asked.

"I think they'll be good. I'll try them on at home."

"What?" Marcella was flabbergasted. "Why?"

"It takes too much time to wait in line here, and I'm not in the mood. I'll just return anything that doesn't fit."

Marcella was shaking her head. "Oh, no. No, no. You are not wasting your money on things you won't ever wear." She pointed to the dressing room with a stern look. "March!"

To my surprise, Alana listened. I grabbed my black blazer and red hip huggers and denim stuff and hurried behind them. It didn't seem like a good idea to cross Marcella, and I was curious to see what she thought of my black linen blazer.

Half an hour later, the three of us stood in line with very select purchases and a new feeling of pride. Marcella had taken us through the paces, critiquing each outfit, checking out the seams, the drape, the fabric, the care instructions.

My linen jacket had not passed Marcella muster. "Who wants to see a soap opera star in a droopy linen jacket all bagged out like a potato sack?"

Ouch.

But we had found a linen blend that Marcella assured me would not wrinkle, and I couldn't wait to wear it to work. Maybe I'd run into Antonio in the coffee shop across the street from the studio . . . maybe I'd wear it to his apartment . . .

I was leaping ahead, as usual, but I wanted him in my life so desperately, especially after the night we'd shared. The hot groping we'd done in the club had fired up to mad movie passion at his place, and we'd twisted and rolled through the sheets, two playful lovers.

And to think I'd been so nervous at the start of the evening, so worried that I'd do something stupid and he'd realize I was a klutz and a fraud. But Antonio had a gift for making you feel like you were the only person on the planet, the only one who mattered. When we sat down at that table in the club and started talking like two old friends, I felt that bond, that connection with him. I knew he was into me, but I wasn't sure how much, how deep his commitment was. I mean, some women were good at playing the casual game, that "if it feels good do it" thing, but not me. When I fall for someone, I start planning out forever. Neurotic, I know, and it had driven more than a few guys away, but I can't really invest in someone without thinking long-term.

The question was, how could I make plans with Antonio without pressuring him too much?

So far, he was still doing the initiating, and had asked me to dinner tonight. Marcella promised to help me find something special to wear at Liz Claiborne or DKNY. But I worried a little about how things would play out when we returned to the City. Would he have me over at his apartment, or come to mine? Would we spend whole nights together? Move in together? There I was, pushing again.

Marcella went to the register first with her single item—a pair of black faux linen pants in a size six, stretchy so they fit well over her "J-Lo butt" as she called it.

Alana stepped up to the next open register and started her transaction.

I moved up when Marcella was finished and handed the clerk my card. "Sorry," he said. "They're not taking this for some reason."

I gulped. My credit limit, maybe? Hadn't I paid the minimum on my cards? I did! But maybe that was before I'd bought my new swimsuits for this weekend. And the massage at Armitage.

How embarrassing. "Oh," I said with minimalist brilliance. "Sorry."

"Here, put it on mine," Alana said, reaching for a slip of paper across the counter.

"But I thought . . ."

"I have a new charge card," she said proudly. "My very own."

"Congratulations! What a big step." It was a move in the right direction for Alana, taking financial responsibility. After all, she'd gotten a job, and she was even pursuing a career that interested her now. Hand model. Who would believe it? "I can't believe you got your own credit card," I said. "Kudos, honey."

"Oh, it's not just a card," Alana said, tucking the slip of paper carefully back into her wallet. "It's my ticket to summer fun."

Part Four

**EXPLOSIVE SAVINGS AT OUR
FOURTH OF JULY SALE!**

30

Alana

As I followed Hailey onto the set of *All Our Tomorrows*, I tried to think of nice things to say, things that would imply that I was impressed without my totally lying. The truth? This cavernous old building was a dump.

"Exciting, isn't it?" Hailey's eyebrows shot up. "I still remember the first day I was on the set. I felt like the new kid, but no one seemed to notice. I changed in the bathroom because I didn't know I could use a dressing room. I was so dumb. Deanna ordered me to get her a Diet Coke, and I did." She hugged herself. "This place has such memories for me."

"I can see that," I said; a lame comment, but I'm not a very good liar.

I forced a smile as we got shoved back by two workers carrying a hollowed-out refrigerator. Not to complain, but there was nowhere to sit unless you counted the furniture on the actual sets, which was strictly forbidden territory unless a scene was being taped. Besides, the decor of those rooms was so unappealing, you wouldn't want to hang there, anyway. The living-room set was pat and tweedy, sort of June Cleaver-meets-the-Stepford Wives. The doctor's office was so Gothic, I'd swear they were storing Frankenstein's brain in that filing cabinet. And the pub-style lobby of the inn . . . whose idea was the green theme? You'd think a leprechaun had tossed his shamrocks. Didn't these people know that primary green was deadly?

"Alana!" Rory stood paging through a script with two guys on the crew. "Darling, how are you?" He rushed over and kissed me on each cheek.

"Oh, darling yourself," I teased. "You're so Hollywood in New York, and I love it."

He preened. "The attitude goes with the Botox lips. What in hell are you doing here?" He gasped. "Not a hand shot for us? Will your hands be appearing in today's show?"

"Not yet. But I have an audition today."

"It's her fifth audition," Hailey added. "She's really jumped into this hand model thing. You should see her at home. No one takes care of her hands the way Alana does."

"What can I say? They're my future. My agent, Muriel, thinks something will come through soon."

"Let's see, let's see! Strike a pose!" Rory insisted.

I folded my hands across my chest (mind you, I was showing just a teensy bit of cleavage) and Rory burst into applause.

"Isn't she great?" Rory motioned to get the attention of the crew people he'd been talking with. "Aren't those hands perfection? She could be the hands of our serial murderer!"

"Very nice," one man said. "Except that our murderer is a white male."

"Oh, that!" Rory waved him off. "You must catch

me up, doll. It's been a while, and I haven't heard one word on you from our friend Hailey, mostly because she's been detained elsewhere."

Rory and I smiled at Hailey, whose face blushed strawberry pink. "Don't stare. So I've been busy. And happy. Antonio is wonderful."

"So when are you going to share the wealth?" Rory asked. "Bring him out to meet the friends? Dinner? Lunch? Cocktails? Skinny-dipping? You two are one of the soap world's best-kept secrets."

"Why do you think I'm here?" I plunked down in a high director's chair, one of the few places to sit aside from the living room furniture on the set. "It's the only way I'm going to meet the man."

"Don't sit there!" Rory and Hailey exclaimed.

I stood up and looked behind me. "Cooties?"

"Double cooties." Rory took my arm and guided me away. "It's Deanna's chair. If she caught you there, you'd be banned from the set."

We wove behind the scenery to a table of pastries, muffins, yogurts, and fruits, along with juices and a large coffee urn. Rory offered me coffee, but I declined, having read that caffeine dries out the skin, and I was working to keep the hands in mint condition. I did succumb to a bowl of strawberries, and settled into a molded plastic chair.

"What's in the offing for the Fourth?" Rory asked. "A rooftop barbecue? Anyone know of a party overlooking the fireworks on the river? Or are you gals heading out to the Hamptons again?"

"The Hamptons won't be happening anytime soon," I said. "I don't think Daddy has quite recovered from our last trip."

"What's this?" Rory perked up. "Don't tell me you girls trashed the house? Bad girls! Bad!"

"The house was no worse for the wear," I said.

"Alana made it better." Hailey tore off a piece of bagel. "She found this gorgeous wicker furniture for the pool terrace. Comfortable, with a Caribbean look. Beautiful furniture! We ate dinner out by the pool."

"Stop! You're killing me!" Rory held up a hand. "I miss the days of basking in the sun, but you're talking to a guy whose dermatologist won't let him go near cancerous rays. It's the Irish curse."

I had heard the Irish curse used to describe a small penis, but I didn't think Rory would want to go there at the moment.

"What was Dad's problem, then?" Rory asked.

"Still money issues," I said. "He doesn't want me to spend it."

"I hate when that happens." He turned to Hailey. "Were you there for the showdown? Did the judge pitch a fit? Were the police called?"

"I was already back in Manhattan," she said. "Alana had dropped us at the Jitney the day before. Marcella had to work, and I had made plans in the City with Antonio."

"Let me tell you, my fun crashed to a halt when they left. I went back to the outlets and bought up a storm, but it didn't help. I covered the quaint shops on Southhampton's Main Street, found some fabulous swimwear. Oh, and that's where I got those dangly earrings, hand-made by some tribal Indians on Long Island. And shoes . . . Dolce & Gabbana on sale! Who could resist?"

"Doll, you're rambling worse than a Tuesday story line," Rory said. "Where in this shopping spree does the judge come in?"

"Enter Judge and Mrs. Marshall-Hughs, Saturday morning," Hailey offered. "Alana was still in bed."

"Another one of my father's pet peeves—the work ethic. He thinks that getting up at the crack of dawn is a prerequisite to hard work. Anyone who sleeps after eight is a slacker."

"I guess I'd be guilty in Daddy's court of law," Rory said.

"Well, I couldn't sleep for long. I was cozy under my quilt when I heard a scream from the pool terrace. It was my father, and he sounded awful. I was sure he was having a heart attack. I rushed downstairs and it was all about the patio furniture. Where were his green chairs? He wanted his green chairs back. And how much did the coco wicker furniture cost him? When I mentioned the three-thousand-dollar sale price, I think he almost did have a heart attack."

"But she got it on sale," Hailey pointed out. "Alana's father is an educated man, but sometimes the facts elude him."

"I tried to show him how the new furniture was superior. More comfortable and atmospheric, but he didn't want to hear it. He dragged it to the side of the house and marched out to the shed to retrieve his old furniture, the hideous green chairs. Mom seemed to like the wicker, but after Dad's outburst she was afraid to sit in it."

"A colorful scene!" Rory said. "I can just imagine the judge rearranging furniture on the pool deck."

Hailey knew the other details—the more painful ones. How Daddy said the new furniture resembled a "goddamned movie set." He didn't understand how his daughter possessed the poor judgment to sink his dollars into such frivolity. How Daddy had called me a lazy parasite with a vicious sense of entitlement. That had hurt. How could he not see that my days were bursting, full of activity? I wasn't lazy, and to compare his own daughter to a life-sucking organism . . .

Mama wasn't much better. She sat me down in her kitchen and told me to face the fact that I had a serious problem, one that needed counseling. Professional intervention, she called it, unable to look me in the eye. I should have stopped the conversation then. Never argue with a parent who cannot look you in the eye.

"I need to see a shrink because I have a talent for design and home decor?" I asked her.

"Your shopping addiction has become a problem."

"Shopping isn't a problem; it's what I do best. And half the time it's therapy for me. Why would you want to spend hundreds of dollars on a therapist who'll try to dredge up bad feelings when I can spend the same money on clothes and shoes and handbags that will make me feel happy?" I asked. "Where is the sense in that, Mama?"

In response, Mama, the college professor, told me that it was not a subject for further debate.

Helloooo? Whatever happened to a democratic society?

I had tried to make a dramatic exit.

How I had wanted to peel out of the driveway, spraying gravel behind me!

But my purchases had bogged me down. I had to make four trips to the car, traipsing through the house with bags and boxes. The shoe boxes were the worst, bulky and difficult to hide. I considered leaving them behind, and believe me, I would have if I'd been able to part with my good friends Dolce & Gabbana.

At one point, Daddy came running around the side of the house to gawk into my open trunk. "How?" he gasped in horror. "How did you pay for all this merchandise?"

"I'm taking care of it," I told him. "My new career pays well."

"What new career?"

I slammed the trunk closed, letting my hand rest

near the Mercedes symbol. "I'm a hand model now," I said, stretching the truth. "People have always said I have exquisite hands."

"That's not a job! A job is hard work."

Again with the puritan work ethic. Sometimes I wonder how I ever survived my parents' inability to have fun.

"So . . . another trip to the Hamptons is not in the cards for the Fourth. Maybe Labor Day? Daddy should have returned to his senses by then. He's got to be realizing how clashy and uncomfortable those green chairs are."

"Green chairs." Rory shook his head. "Of all the issues that drive a wedge between people, this is the first time I've ever heard of patio furniture providing such controversy. The way you talk about it makes Janet Jackson's boob and Mayor Bloomberg's policies pale by comparison."

"Those chairs are symbolic of the lack of 'aesthetics' in my father's world." I had given some thought to this problem, and the word "aesthetics" had such a nice ring to it. Not that I'd been able to run it by Daddy, since we weren't exactly on speaking terms.

"Well, gals, if we're all going to be in town, let's do something fun for the Fourth." Rory tapped his chin. "The beauty of the New York summer is that Manhattanites flee. The city will be our playground."

"Yes, let's do something!" Hailey clapped her hands together. "Maybe Antonio will join us. I'm really dying for you to meet him, Alana."

"And I'd love a peek at the real Antonio," Rory said mysteriously.

"Speaking of which . . . where is he?" I checked my watch. "I have to be crosstown for this audition. I'm going to have to go."

"And we have to get to makeup, Ms. Ariel."

Hailey shrugged. "Sorry. I guess we'll walk you out."

We were passing by the dressing-room doors when the man in question appeared striding confidently down the hall. Usually, the classically handsome men are a bit too polished for me, but Antonio broke the mold. Tall, dark, handsome, and exuding fire . . . I could see why Hailey fell for him.

"Antonio!" She rushed ahead to throw her arms around him, but he turned his head abruptly. Hailey's kiss landed awkwardly on his chin.

"Hilly . . . I'm late for wardrobe."

"I wanted you to meet my best friend," she said, introducing us. He shook my hand and looked me in the eye, but the man was obviously not at ease.

"I must go." He turned away, then called back, "Nice meeting you."

"Cute, but reticent," I said as he disappeared. "What's his problem?"

"I hear he's a very private person," Rory said. "But you would know better than I. Is he incredibly secretive? As mysterious as those dark, exotic eyes suggest?"

Hailey laughed. "He's not mysterious. Just sex-starved."

"Wheeeew!" Rory and I squealed.

"He's totally different in private," Hailey went on. "Much more relaxed. Whenever we're in public, he clams up. I don't get it."

"Can't be sure," Rory lowered his voice and motioned us close, "but I suspect it's about Diva Deanna."

"What?" Hailey croaked. "They're not an item. Deanna is married."

"Like that'll stop her," Rory scowled.

"Did they have a thing?" I asked.

"Off the record?" Rory nodded. "About two years ago, and the diva is very possessive of her exes."

"How could they have had a thing?" Hailey seemed baffled. "She's married. I didn't read about it."

"Hailey . . ." Rory shook his head. "Sometimes you just can't take the Wisconsin out of the girl."

I tinkled my fingers good-bye, limbering them up for later. "Wish me luck. I have a good feeling about this audition."

"See you later," Hailey said forlornly, obviously thrown by the revelation about Antonio and Deanna.

"Break a leg, doll!" Rory crowed. "No, make that a fingernail!"

I glared at him.

"Oh, just go and wow them with your stuff!"

My plan, exactly.

31

Hailey

"Maybe I should have that line," Deanna said. "It just sounds Meredithy, don't you think?"

"You already have so much dialogue in this scene, Big D," Percy said. It was his day to direct, and I sensed that Deanna was wearing away his aura of cool with her relentless changes and demands. "Don't want to bog you down."

"It's not a problem," Deanna insisted. "Have I ever had trouble remembering my lines? Look at me. You don't see me walking around with a script, do you?"

That's because one of your peons carries it for you, I thought.

"What's the line?" Percy asked.

" 'I knew the real Skip,' " Sean read. " 'I knew his heart and soul.' "

It was supposed to be my line, but Deanna wanted it, along with the emotional drive of the scene. She was trying to rob me blind, but I knew better than to fight her on it. Around here, you did not argue with Deanna and live to see the next sweeps week.

Percy made a mark on Sean's script and frowned. "Fine, give the line to Meredith. OK, people are we ready to roll tape? Tell me we're ready. I need you to be ready."

"Ready!" Deanna crowed proudly.

"People, take your marks," Sean shouted.

On my way to my cue outside the door to the inn, I passed Rory, who was to be positioned at the piano.

"Hey, doll, do you even have any lines left in this scene?" he asked, a twinkle in his eye.

"I'm not sure," I said. "I may have to learn sign language."

"Are we rrrready?" Percy asked.

"Ready, Percy," I called.

"Yea-huh!" Rory signaled.

Sean counted it off, "In five, four, three, two . . ."

Deanna opened the scene with a long monologue in which she spilled her feelings about the supposedly dead Skip to Stone, the sympathetic piano player. I tried to listen for my cue, but much of the dialogue had changed and, honestly, I was rattled by my earlier discovery about Deanna and Antonio. Yuck! How could he have had a *thing* with her? Personally, I didn't want her anywhere near his *thing*, but I didn't want to make a big deal out of something long past.

Anyway, I was trying to focus, but Deanna's lines were pretty repetitive now. Stuff like "I knew Skip so well," and "I loved him, I really loved him," and "It was a once-in-a-lifetime love," and "You know how it is when you meet someone you feel you've known forever?" It was hard to tell where she was in the script, especially since her voice was so mellifluous. Through the scenery, it sounded like "Blah-blah-blah-blah-blah. Blah-blah-blah, blah-blee-blee-blah-blah."

As I stood there, anger at Deanna roiled inside me. I was so frustrated, I wanted to cry. What was this scene about now, anyway? That Meredith was the best? That she had loved Skip more than anyone? And that my character was just some interloper who wanted to torture poor Meredith?

Sean pointed at me—my cue.

I opened the door and walked in, spied Deanna sitting by the piano, looking the victim.

As I crossed to her, my eyes stung. I couldn't help it. I just burst into tears, letting out a sob as I paused before the diva.

Rory's eyes popped with surprise. Deanna seemed a little disarmed, too.

"I know what you're saying about me," I sobbed, trying to calm myself with a deep breath. "I know how you felt about Skip."

"I knew the real Skip," Deanna said passionately. "I knew his heart and soul."

"Then hold on to that," I said, veering away from the script. "Cherish that memory. But please, I'm begging you, leave a few scraps for the rest of us."

On her look of shock, I doubled over sobbing, and Percy yelled, "Stop tape!"

I sank to the floor, too emotionally overwrought to worry that I'd botched the scene and that we would have to tape it all over. Deanna was wearing me down; I had succumbed in front of everyone, and I wasn't quite sure how to pull myself back together.

"Fantastic! Fabulous!" He gave a thumbs-up to Deanna. "Hey, Big D! Your script changes worked beautifully. Wunderbar scene. Let's move on, people."

Deanna stepped on my dress as she walked by, but didn't say a thing. Pissed, I guess. Oh, well.

"Where's my Diet Coke!" she yelled, and two of her

peons emerged from the crew to follow her to her dressing room.

Rory extended a hand to me. "I don't know what you did, kid, but you done good."

Sean stood beside him, extending a box of tissues. "Thought you might need one of these."

"Thanks." I pressed two tissues to my eyes, then laughed. "What a roller-coaster ride."

"You'll get used to it," Sean said kindly.

As Rory headed off to his next scene, Sean said, "Can I ask you something?"

I nodded.

"Would you like to grab a cup of coffee sometime?"

I smiled. "That sounds great." Sean had been nothing but supportive and fair during my time on the show.

He bit his lower lip, nodding. "Good. How about next week?"

I was about to agree, then I wondered how that would look. What would Antonio think? Would I appear disloyal, like I was cheating on my boyfriend?

"Um . . . let me check my date book," I said cheerfully.

"Yeah, sure." Sean's smile was tentative, as if he could read my doubts.

I'm so sorry! I thought as I headed back to my dressing room. Why was it that the sweet, smart, kind guys only came out of the woodwork after you hooked up with someone else? Sean could be a friend, but I was totally in love with the sexiest man of the decade, and I wasn't about to do anything to jeopardize that passion.

32

Alana

Wouldn't you know it, the crosstown traffic moved along at a good clip, and I found myself at the Soho address with forty-five minutes to spare. Not wanting to appear too eager, I ducked into a Starbucks and decided to splurge on a latte. I hadn't had caffeine for two days now, and I missed the buzz.

From my window seat, I had an anonymous view of people on the street. The handbag vendor, a Hispanic man with wary manner. The buttoned-down editorial grinders in pleated skirt and denim jacket. The clueless hetero male in T-shirt and Gap jeans. The freelance artist with wide leather portfolio. And the endless leagues of students or displaced personalities with piercings and tattoos and tutus and sculpted, shocking pink hair.

I'm sure they all thought they dressed just fine, but watching them walk past, I had to wonder, Who dressed these people? What a shame that Mayor Bloomberg didn't institute a mandatory course for third graders—

because you can't start too young—called "Finding a Fashion That Fits You." I would help him design the curriculum, with special attention on the diverse fashion needs of various body types, skin tones, lifestyles, and seasons. With, of course, a compulsory exam at the end of the year that each student would be required to pass in order to go on to fourth grade. (Really—the course is a prerequisite for life, so anyone who cannot pass the final exam must repeat it until they get it right!) Because, looking at the people of New York, I am so sorry to say that even down here in funky Soho, they're getting it wrong.

At ten-twenty I crossed the street to the building of converted lofts and climbed the stairs (since the caged elevator was frightening) to the second floor, where two women sat on a carpeted hump.

One of the women looked up from her magazine to tell me, "You're supposed to sign in."

I leaned over the empty desk and wrote my name on the clipboard, astutely noting that Claudette and Pucci were ahead of me. Taking a seat, I eyed the competition. The girl by the window seemed withdrawn and dazed, as if lost in some Buddhist chant. Was it some trick of the hand-modeling trade? From here, I couldn't see her tools, but I would have ventured a guess that her fingers were long and slender, like her legs.

The girl with the magazine was a type A, thrill seeker, risk taker. How did I know? Any hand model willing to chance a paper cut moments before an audition . . . well, let's just say, those hands belong in another profession. Might I suggest sugar cane farming or diamond mining?

A harried girl with little twisty barrettes all over her head came out of the studio. "Oh, hey, did you sign in? We're running a little late. Be with you in a minute."

How hard could it be to review a pair of hands? How

long could it take? Palm side now. Just the pinkie! Flex
the thumb . . .

"Oh, and there's coffee in there," Barrette Girl said.

I poured myself a cup of coffee and sat on the hump
to read the covers of the magazines. I checked out the
ceiling tiles—mundane. I wondered what the studio
was like inside and knew I could turn this waiting area
into a comfortable haven. Or a sleek, hip meeting
place. What would it cost? For starters, there would be
the demolition crew . . .

Claudette was called, and the dazed girl fell out of
her trance and loped into the studio. Then there were
two.

I sipped the surprisingly strong coffee and yawned.
How was I going to keep my audition energy up with
this delay. Were they examining Claudette's index finger yet?

Pucci yawned too. I imagined Barrette Girl emerging from the studio to find Pucci and me asleep in each
other's laps.

It was after eleven when I was finally called into the
studio. After the wait, my expectations were high, but
it was a boring space, functional and bare, stripped
down to the brick and support beams and lined with
lighting equipment, backdrops, and a scaffold for lights.

"Hi, Alana! I'm Nadine." A young woman in a black
knit tank and scarlet print skirt greeted me from a distance, and I noticed that she didn't offer her hand. Rule
number two, never touch the hand model. "Right this
way."

Following her, I noticed that she had two-inch cuts on
the backs of her ankles. Big ouchies. What could those
scabs be from? Boots that didn't fit? A shave with an
old razor? A fall down the stairs? Or worse . . . maybe
she was a cutter, one of those girls who mutilated
themselves as a way of owning their own bodies.

I blinked. Why was my mind racing ahead like a toy truck?

"Right here." Nadine stood beside a table draped with blue velvet and placed her hand on the cloth to demonstrate. "We're going to do five shots. One open palm. One back of the hand. One fist. One wearing the bracelet. And one holding the necklace. OK?"

"Got it." I smiled and stepped into Nadine's place by the table. "Piece of cake."

I placed my hand on the velvet and tried to exude energy through my palm.

The photographer looked through the lens. "Could you lift the hand, please? Above the cloth. Don't rest on the table."

I pulled my hand up and held it there. Shaking.

"It's OK," the photographer said. He glanced up from his camera and smiled. "No need to be nervous."

But I wasn't nervous; I had a case of the caffeine shakes. I jiggled my hand a little, tried to gain control, tried the shot again. The camera snapped twice.

"Next shot."

I flipped my hand over and tried to hold it steady. My blasted ring finger quivered like a baby chick in the snow.

"Can you hold your hand steady?" Nadine coached.

"I'm trying. But you know what? I think I drank a little too much coffee today."

"S'OK." Nadine nodded. "We'll get you next time."

"Why don't I come back tomorrow? Or maybe later today? I'll detox with water."

But Nadine was already trying to walk me to the door. The photographer walked away from his camera to talk on his cell. Clearly, my time was over. "We're about ready to wrap up here, but thanks for coming."

At the door, I caught Nadine's eye. "Look, I've been counting on this job. Can't you help me out here?"

"Sorry," she said sadly. "It's really not up to me. But you have very nice hands. Ease up on the coffee and try again next time."

Try again next time.

It sounded like the booby prize at a rinky-dink arcade game—unacceptable for someone accustomed to winning the giant stuffed bear. Totally unacceptable.

33

Hailey

Antonio caught me as I was heading into my dressing room.

"Hey, you! What's going on with you, honey? Alana was so excited about meeting you, but I could tell you weren't interested."

"May we step inside?" He pointed to my dressing room. We stepped inside and he closed the door behind him.

"You can sit in Susan's chair," I offered, since there were only two places to sit in the cramped space. "She's off today, and she won't mind." As I sank down in my own chair a heaviness overwhelmed me.

"Hilly? Are you all right?"

"I've been better. Look, Antonio, I heard some things today that didn't sit well with me. About you and Deanna."

"Aah." He glanced down, nodding.

"And then, when you acted so weird with Alana. And in the month that we've been together you've never come out to meet my friends. And come to think of it, we don't go out as a couple much." And when we did, it was to obscure little places—Antonio's favorite Argentinian restaurant on East Thirty-sixth Street or a dark hole-in-the-wall spaghetti place in Hell's Kitchen. "Antonio . . ." It hurt me to voice the question, but I had to ask. "Are you ashamed of me?"

"No, Hilly. No! Don't think that. It's just that I work hard all week, and when the work is done, I'm not much in the mood for going out on parade." He kneeled down before me and rested his head on my knees. "Don't you know I love to be with you?"

"But why do you hold back? Why don't you want to be seen with me? And, I'll be honest with you, it was very upsetting to hear about you and Deanna."

He lifted his head, chin on my thighs. "I know. Sorry. It was a long time ago."

"But she was married. And she has kids."

"I know. It happens. But it's over with her. At least, I have no feelings for her. Deanna, what can I say? She likes to keep a grudge. Which is one of the reasons I want to keep you a secret. She might be terribly mean to you just to get back at me. I have seen her do these nasty things, and I can't let that happen to you, Hilly."

His hand cupped my knee, then slid up along the inside of my bare thigh, his fingers fond and hungry at the same time.

I fell back against the chair and sighed, wishing I understood Antonio. So open and communicative when we were together, he became an indecipherable enigma when I stepped away—like the stranger who had greeted Alana in the hall this morning. Did I know him at all, or was I simply seduced by fingertips working their way up my thigh, eager to give me pleasure?

"I love to pleasure you, Hilly. And it's my job to protect you."

"But she can't hurt us," I said, rubbing my hands along his arms. "Don't you see? If we're together, if we're strong, she doesn't have a chance against us."

His dark brows lifted, his eyes sad. "I don't want you to be in danger. Even if it's only danger of harming your career." He reached forward and ran his fingers over the scalloped edge of my panties, down along the g-string to the most erotic zones.

"Antonio . . ." I closed my eyes and fell into the fantasy of danger and escape and passion, allowing him to coax me to sweet satisfaction.

34

Alana

Disappointment is not good for my soul. Some people seem to wallow in it as if it's a warm fuzzy blanket on a winter night. But me, I have no patience for bad feelings, and as soon as something like that hits me, I run fast till the stink of it wears off.

Of course, if you're running through the cosmetics section at Saks, the stink wears off that much faster.

That was where I started my therapy after the bad audition—first floor Saks, accessories and cosmetics. A girl can't have too much face cream.

Then, I did a big naughty. I strolled right down Fifth Avenue in the bright July light, turned right at Fusion's holographic door, and rode the elevator up to three, where I stepped into the very chic, close-your-eyes expensive, appointment-only Fusion boutique that featured clothes from the newest, craziest designers.

"Alana!" Vespa has a shrill, nasal voice that she cracks like a whip. "I didn't know you were coming in today. Welcome! Sit! Let me get you a coffee. Sumatra or Black Sultan's Roast?"

"No coffee, no, thanks. I need a . . ." I dropped my shopping bags down beside the green-velvet couch and sought to put words to the longing in my soul. "I need . . . something special."

"Aah, but you don't know how to describe this elusive object of your shopping quest." Vespa's violet eyes glittered under her pouffy auburn bangs. "You need that je ne sais quoi."

"Yes!" I clapped my hands together as that tiny bit of college French came back to me. "That I-can't-say-what." I sat down and crossed my legs with a feeling of accomplishment. "Can you show me something like that in a size six?"

Sitting back on the couch, I began to feel human again as Vespa shimmered out with a high-waisted Chanel skirt, tiered ruffles covered in silver and gold spangles. Not me. The second Chanel radiated my palette—antique satin in blanched stripes of copper, gray, and gold. The skirt was looped with beaded cords and black and copper spangles, but the drop waist was a problem. Never put a drop waist on a big-butt girl. Next!

That was when it appeared—a black cashmere skirt and jacket that took my breath away. The skirt was a delicate full swirl screened with glittery gold feathers that fanned out over the hips—an exquisite design, a perfect cut for my body.

All the familiar symptoms arose within me, the accelerated pulse, slight warming of the face, slight tickle at the nape of my neck. I had to have it.

"Ah, this is the one, is it not?" Vespa laid the garment in my lap and my hands savored the rich folds of cashmere. "It's a Giles Deacon. Do you know him? A new designer from the UK who had his first show just this year. He fancies his designs 'misplaced chic.' "

"I like it!" I said.

In the fitting room, I discretely stole a look at the price list. The skirt was only $970! The jacket, a tad more at $1500, and I wasn't as crazy about it—a double-breasted design with gold buttons and gold epaulets that hung down to my knees. Unusual, yes, but really not me. Still, did I dare break up the set?

Vespa and I were debating the merits of black Chanel heels or nude Manolo Blahniks when my cell chimed "Celebrate." I checked the caller ID—Dad. Oh, blast it. Did he have a camera hidden in my Louis Vuitton bag? Or maybe he was calling to invite me to the beach. Wouldn't that be a relief? In the thick of July's heat and humidity, nothing was better than the cool nights in the Hamptons.

I flipped it open. "Hi, Daddy."

"What on earth do you think you're doing?" he growled.

I smiled over at Vespa, trying to think of an honest answer. "Therapy. Some serious therapy."

"You talk on your cell phone during therapy?"

"I miss you, too."

"Don't get cute with me!" Daddy had gone ballistic. I tried to think of what I'd done to set him off. "We've intercepted a letter for you here and I'm calling to learn the meaning of this correspondence."

The man was a federal judge, and he still did not know the language of the people. "What was that, sir?"

"You know," he went on in one of his familiar ranting tones, "I thought we taught you respect and responsibility, but from what I see here, you . . . your . . . oh, damn it all! You talk to her!"

"Alana, we just got to the Hamptons house and there's a bill here from the National Bank of Integrity.

Looks like a Viva card. Have you any idea what this is in reference to?"

"Oh, let me think . . ." But I had changed the address on the account! I'd been receiving mail from them at my apartment. They'd sent me my shiny new card. Why were they ruining my life? "Of course, I remember. Do you want to pop that in the mail for me?"

"What's this about, Alana?"

"Mama, I will take care of it." Silence. "It's my own account, OK? I'm trying to demonstrate my new sense of responsibility." A scuffling sound over the phone line. "Mama? Don't you open my mail, Mama . . ."

"Seven thousand dollars?" she screeched.

Seven grand? And that was without my new Giles Deacon suit, which would add another twenty-five hundred. And what else had I purchased recently? I was usually on top of inventory, but the phone call from my irate parents had thrown me.

"Alana, when did you get this credit card?"

"Now didn't I just tell you I would take care of it? But no, you have to go and open my mail without permission when . . . That's not fair, Mama. I said I'll take care of it."

"You're damn right you will. You will take care of this bill, and you will see a counselor." Her voice held an unusual edge—Mama Godzilla.

"A counselor, Mama? I've tried those people. Wanting to blame all my problems on you and Daddy, that's what they do."

"I'm talking about a financial planner. You're a big girl now, Alana, and it's time you learned how the financial world operates."

I rolled my eyes. I wouldn't mind ringing that bell to open the stock exchange one day, but otherwise, the financial world bored me. Oh, and the jackets those traders wear on the floor? Please!

"I'm going to call right now and make an appointment for you. Carol recommended someone, says he's excellent."

"Carol recommended her? Carol Graystone? Then she must be expensive. Does the counselor have an office in Bergdorf's? Or maybe a suite at the Stanhope."

"The name is Lee Leventhal, a downtown address."

"Mama, this is crazy! Don't you want me to stop spending money? You do, and I hear these financial wizards are pricey. Very expensive."

Silence. Had I won?

"You can put the fee on your new Viva card."

And then, for the first time in my life, my mother hung up on me.

35

Hailey

That night I was sort of glad to head off to dinner with my friends without Antonio, who had to work late. Rory had scored a table at Mosquito, where we were all sure that Jackie Chan was dining in the booth behind us with a woman who might or might not be Tina Fey, and it was fun to be with just the gang, celeb-spotting and speculating.

"It's her, honey," Marcella said, reaching for the olives. "It is most definitely her. How many beautiful women do you know who wear those fugly glasses?"

"Who cares about her?" Alana turned casually to her side to adjust a bracelet and spy. "Oh, he's so cute," she hissed, "in that Chan kind of way. I hear he has joints like putty."

"And that would be good for what reason?" Rory inquired. "Feel free to illustrate your example with a sketch or diagram."

"See, now you're teasing me, and after the hellacious day I had." Alana eyed Rory coyly behind her sour apple martini. "First I get snubbed by Hailey's boyfriend. Then I blow an audition. Then my parents call to tell me they're doing some freaky kind of financial intervention. I'm being sent to the Betty Ford Clinic for shopaholics, and now I have to face verbal abuse from a soap-opera star?"

"We in the biz like to call it daytime drama." Rory placed a coaster under his highball glass of Dewar's. "Say it with me, children. Day-time dra-ma . . ."

I still felt bad about Antonio's uncoolness when I'd introduced him to Alana, and despite his satisfying attempt at an apology, I still had lots of questions for him.

Especially after an odd occurrence on the set that afternoon.

"It was really quite bizarre," I told my friends. "I stood at the door, watching Antonio leave. He had a scene to do, which was one of the reasons he needed to, you know, save his energy."

"What a man!" Rory lifted the cherry from his Dewar's and popped it into his mouth with zeal. "Saving it for later, like a prizefighter before the big match."

"Anyway, there I am, thinking about my next costume change, when I see something move in the shadows. I called out, 'Who's there?' And a figure emerges. Deanna. She was hiding out there, waiting and watching."

My three friends looked at each other open-mouthed and gasped, "Stalker!"

Sipping my cosmo, I nodded. "I think maybe. The way she scuttled out, like the wicked witch of the west, and with none of her munchkins around . . . It was all very weird."

Choking on his Dewar's, Rory pressed a napkin to his face. "Love the casting! We'll have to get Jodi to whip up a black hat for Deanna next week."

"It's funny, yes, but also a matter of some concern." Marcella squinted at me. "Did she threaten you, honey?"

"She told me to leave him alone. That's what she said, and she was referring to Antonio. But he already told me that it was over with Deanna a long time ago."

"This is one juicy story." Alana tore her eyes away from Jackie Chan. "What else did she say? What did you do? Did anyone break a nail?"

"I stood my ground," I said proudly. "I looked Deanna in the eye and told her, 'You're a married woman, remember that?' "

Rory and Alana groaned.

"What's wrong with that?"

Marcella patted my hand. "Nothing wrong with what you said, honey."

"If you're Mother Teresa," Rory said. "Think about it, Hailey. Does Deanna care what you think about her moral standards? Do men like Antonio lie to women to balance romance and personal freedom?" He shot a glance at the booth. "And do you think Jackie Chan might show us some of those joints of putty?"

"So then what happened?" Alana asked. "How did it end?"

I thought of the twisted contortion of Deanna's face. "Her eyes shot fire at me as she backed away. And she hissed at me like a cat. Said I was foolish. 'You foolish, foolish girl!' "

"Nasty bitch," Marcella said.

"And that was it. After that she disappeared."

"Melted into the floor, right?" Rory teased. "Would that be when you threw a bucket of water on her?"

"Joke all you want, but I'm a little concerned about my friend Hailey." Alana patted my back. "If this Deanna woman is going to throw her muscle behind some sort of harassment campaign, Hailey could get hurt. Certainly, it could be damaging for your career, right?"

I shrugged. "She's got a lot of clout."

"And she had you shit-canned before," Rory pointed out, "over what? Did you spill her Diet Coke or something?"

"Oh, that woman is a nightmare," Marcella popped a maraschino cherry in her mouth and shook her head. "I've been taping the show and watching it while I feed my nephew, and let me tell you, I don't like that Meredith Van Allen. Saying all those nice things about Skip when you know she killed him. That woman is definitely up to no good, and if you ask me, so is the bitch who plays her."

"I wish the rest of the viewers saw it that way," I said. "Deanna is always the soap actress featured on the cover of women's magazines, on the morning talk shows, on Oprah. Somehow people don't see that inside that perfect size-two Barbie-doll bod lurks a spoiled monster."

"Well, I see it," Alana said, "and I am here to tell you I won't let her railroad you. My father isn't a federal judge for nothing. If she so much as wags a finger at you or breaks wind in your general direction, we'll be all over her. Nobody is going to mess with my friend. If you need me, you know I'm here for you, Hailey."

"We'll break her ass." Marcella cracked a breadstick. "We're all here for you, honey."

I looked at Rory, who squirmed in his chair. "Some of us do have careers to look after," he said, hiding behind his glass of scotch, "but if the need arises, I know you'll give me a jingle. And don't forget, you've got el buffo, macho Antonio on your side. I'm sure he can play matador to Deanna's bull."

"Uh, he's from Argentina, not Spain."

Rory waved me off. "I always sucked at geography."

As our salads were served, Alana recounted her day in detail. She had been surprised by the phone call from her parents, doubly surprised to hear of her seven-thousand-dollar balance.

"I'm only surprised they didn't whop your ass," Marcella said. "How are you going to pay that balance off?"

"From my hand-modeling money," Alana said defensively.

"Um, excuse me? Have you seen one cent from any jobs yet?"

Alana stabbed at a sliver of apple, suddenly fascinated by her salad. "I'm not panicking. Money always works out for me."

"Because your old man bails you out," Marcella chanted in a whiny tone. "Not for nothing, honey, but you can get in serious debt with those credit cards. Way over your head. The only way to use credit cards is to know you have the money in the bank when you make the purchase. You pay your balance each month, end of story. No interest to pay, no annual fee. That's the way to go."

"I'm planning to do it that way," Alana said. "Just as soon as my earnings catch up with my expenditures."

"And what if they don't?" Marcella asked. "What if you never get a modeling gig?"

"Marcella!" I blinked at her. "That's brutal."

"Please!" Alana held up a hand, today manicured with tiny rhinestones. "If all that bad stuff happened, I'd eventually have to make some changes. I'd give up my gym membership. And low-fat muffins. The carbs are too high, anyway. And manicures."

I rested my fork on my plate. "Alana is really trying hard." I turned toward her. "We know you are, honey. And no matter what, no matter how much I'm making, I will not let you go without a manicure."

"Oh!" Tears in her eyes, Alana threw open her arms and we hugged. "You're so sweet."

"I think this is what Hallmark would call a bonding moment," Rory said dryly.

"I'm glad you love each other," Marcella said. "But you two are the worst money managers I've ever met. You spend way too much on clothes, some of which you don't even have the time or the desire to wear. What the fuck is that about?"

I peeked over at Alana, and suddenly we began to laugh.

As Alana dabbed at her tears with a napkin, Rory tried to explain. "Sometimes, my dear Marrrrrchella, it's not about the merchandise. Sometimes, the shopping is everything."

36

Alana

The next day I felt every inch the loyal daughter and dutiful financial citizen as I headed out to meet with the financial guru. To prove my earnest desire to reform, I even resisted the passing cabs and walked to the bus stop. Now, this seemed like a shrewd, money-saving measure, but with bus fare having been notched up to a solid two dollars, I had to wonder if cab fare would really cost me that much more.

I would have to ask Suze. I mean Lee.

Although Mom's finance chick was named Lee Leventhal, I was already envisioning Suze Orman, that blond, bright, brash cable TV money person who tells people that they'd better start saving money. I'd spent my time in the shower making up little jokes to tell Lee about my recent spending spree. How I wanted to make sure my card worked. How I'd heard you needed a personal charge card to build a credit history. How shopping was therapeutic for me, and if I happened into a sale, it was often less expensive than a session with an analyst. Besides, I could walk away from my retail therapy with a much nicer pair of shoes.

And then there were the clever lines in those perky letters inviting me to open a charge account and "spend, spend, spend!" Of course, I knew they were just an advertising come-on. But really, how creative . . .

Today, life gets better . . . when you use your credit card and save on purchases.

Or . . .

Write today, save today! Use the attached checks to access your credit line.

And this one, with a picture of a tiger:

Unleash your wild side. Get a gold card from the Safari Collection.

Oh, Lee and I would have a good laugh over how the credit card companies tried to seduce customers into irresponsible spending sprees. We would recognize the high regard for material goods in American society, the competitive spirit of fashion, the desire of women from ages eighteen to forty to feel good about their bodies and, consequently, the clothes they wore. (Hey, I didn't get into Harvard based on my SAT scores!) I would acknowledge to Lee my awareness of all these factors.

And then, with an emotional glaze in my eyes, I would confess that on occasion I engaged in impulse buying. I purchased unnecessary items for the thrill of the sale.

Lee would nod knowingly. She would reassure me that this is normal behavior. Girls will be girls. She might express an interest in meeting with my father, exploring his awareness of the cultural significance of shopping in American society.

I would wish her luck on that.

Then we would hug, maybe go for a cappuccino, or stroll through some of the art galleries in her Soho neighborhood. We could choose our favorite pieces, maybe dare each other to buy a piece of art. (This last thought as the bus headed downtown, past a strip of tiny galleries.)

We still hadn't approached the address of Lee's office building, but we were moving out of Soho. I must have misjudged that one. Hmmm. The offices here were squarish and old, and I realized we were rolling into the courthouse neighborhood. City Hall. Federal Building. Big snooze.

I stepped out of the bus and located Lee's building—boring as cement and glass could be. Inside, there wasn't even a doorman, just a buzzer system. Poor Lee must have hit some hard times. Maybe she herself had a shopping addiction?

All the way up in the stuffy elevator, I tried to ignore the smell of floor wax and to focus on the good things that happened when Suze Orman fixed someone's life. Financial fixes were good! Focus on the prize, forget the pitted linoleum floor.

On the fifth floor, there was one receptionist for a dozen or so people. I told her I was here to see Lee, and she took my name and asked me to sit down. I crossed to the leather sofa—no, scratch that, vinyl—and thought twice about letting my gorgeous new Giles skirt meet the worn synthetic surface—a surface that was bound to be infested with all sorts of microorganisms.

I decided to stay on my Manolos.

It wasn't long till she sent me into Lee's office— third door down on the right. I crossed the threshold and extended my hand. To my shock, an old, crotchety man with an *enormous* nose sat in Lee's desk.

"Oh, hello," I said, dropping my hand to my gold-glittered skirt. "I was looking for Lee Leventhal."

"You're in the right place," he said, smiling under

that nose. "Have a seat, Ms. Marshall-Hughs, and I'll be right with you. Just wanted to start a file on your case, take some notes."

I flopped back into the chair, stunned.

This was Lee?

How could Mama have done this to me—to her own daughter? Hadn't she researched this place? It didn't take a Rhodes scholar to see that Mr. Leventhal was not of the caliber to work with a Marshall-Hughs. Especially not one as savvy as me.

Lee was friendly enough, but I zoned out from word one. Fortunately, instead of taking information, he decided to start with his overview of personal finance. Blah blah, blah blah, blah blah.

I knew I should be listening, but I could not take my eyes off that nose. It was unnaturally large, with red veins and little pockmarks.

How did a nose get pockmarks? I wondered as Mr. Leventhal launched into a lecture about the importance of a monthly budget, debits, keeping records . . . stuff I knew, although I did not know how a nose could become so engorged and disproportionately large.

Had he been injured by shrapnel during a war?

The man seemed ancient, and for a moment, I wondered if he was old enough to have fought in World War II. Perhaps stationed on an island, somewhere in the South Pacific.

Shrapnel, or maybe it had been some type of exotic insect inhabiting the tropical foliage on the island. The rare, pockmarking, nose-attacking island chigger.

Or perhaps it was a replacement nose, plunked on by a doctor back in the days before plastic surgery had been perfected . . . like the eighties. Maybe Mr. L had been a factory worker involved in an accident. Or a Mafia don who took a bullet in the nose.

"Excuse me," Lee Leventhal said when the phone

rang. As he spoke on the phone, I gestured that I'd step outside.

And step outside I did.

"Miss?" the receptionist called after me.

I didn't look back. Not to be rude, but I wasn't about to waste any more time pretending to accept advice from people I did not admire.

I would call Mom and lay down the requirements.

Send me Suze—or take me as I am.

37

Hailey

"**O**h, not here," I whispered, glancing at the door to my tiny dressing room. "What if Susan comes in?"

"Susan is a big girl." Antonio's dark eyes were intent as he pushed me back onto the dressing room table and wedged himself between my legs. My robe fell open as he slid a hand along one thigh and dipped into the trimming. "Besides, it's too late. You're all wet and I'm hard as a rock." He kissed me hard, sucking the resolve from me. "Come on, Hilly. We won't be long."

With a moan, I slid my arms around him and kissed him back. "OK, but I'm almost out of condoms."

"Not a problem." He produced a packet from his pocket, which he tore open and expertly applied. "I come prepared."

The foreplay was minimal, the penetration abrupt and deep, but it was a routine we'd fallen into, and I felt my breathing quicken to match the rhythm of Antonio's pumping. I closed my eyes and gave myself over to the image of this beautiful man making love to me.

Within five minutes we had both climaxed and were laughing together about the bottles of lotion that Antonio had knocked to the floor in a fit a passion. "It's a good thing they're plastic," I teased him.

He pulled up his black boxers, zipped his jeans, and reached out to hold me close. "Hilly, I'm so sorry I have to go. I have a lunch date with some people who want to talk about a film."

"With you starring in it?" I felt a little rush of excitement. "That's pretty darned terrific."

"We'll see." He shrugged. "Many times, these things fizzle out."

I couldn't help but wonder if there might be a part for a young, blond ingenue in Antonio's movie. It would be great to work with him off the set of *All Our Tomorrows*—a real bonding experience for us—but it seemed a little premature for me to weasel into his deal. Besides, Antonio was still a little secretive about his career, and I found it amazing that we could be sexually free and intimate while he closed the gates when it came to other aspects of his life. Chalk it up to the enigma of men.

After he left, I curled up in my little chair and flipped through the latest issue of *Soap Opera Diaries*. Every time I opened one of these tabloids, I expected to see the photo of Antonio and me sneaking out of the club in the Hamptons. Actually, I was dying to see the photo of us together, longing to be linked to him in the press (no matter what Deanna thought about it) and realizing how a photo in any paper would provide a major boost to my career.

But once again, no coverage for me. It was so unfair. Obviously, none of the trades had bought my photo from the photographer when he passed it around town weeks ago.

I sighed. What law did a girl have to break to get some exposure in this biz?

There was a knock at the door, and I assumed it was Susan being discreet. "Come on in."

The stiff facade of Gabrielle Kazanjian appeared in my doorway. "Hailey? It's been a long time."

I uncurled my legs and closed up my robe. Oh, God, was I still smelling of sex? I quickly leaned down to retrieve two of the bottles Antonio had knocked over.

"May I come in?" Gabrielle asked.

"Oh, sure! Absolutely! You just caught me taking a little break."

"Sorry to disturb you," she said, her usual deadpan fish-face indicating nothing. Was she being sarcastic? Had she heard moans and groans coming from my dressing room just minutes ago? Or was she totally sincere?

Why was I so paranoid?

She stepped in and closed the door behind her. "I thought we should have a personal talk."

I forced a tight smile. Again, paranoid.

"There've been some changes at the network that I thought you should know about."

"Changes?" I sounded like a trussed chipmunk.

"In the next few weeks, we'll be getting a new director of daytime programming on the East Coast. Keep it under your hat, of course, but I've already met with him and he's very concerned about the demographics of our audience."

"Right." I nodded, wondering how this would affect me.

"Essentially, he wants to bring in a larger sector of the youth audience, and we all know that young people like to watch other young people. Like you."

Me? Yes, I was young. Yes, yes, yes!

"Now, we both know your Q rating isn't the highest," she said.

Oh, not the dastardly Q rating! I didn't want to go there.

"But our new director of daytime wants to get behind you. He'll instruct the writers to come up with a walloping new story line centered around you." She smiled—a wonder her skin didn't crack. "Do you think you can pull it off?"

I nodded furiously. "Sure! I mean, pinch me, I'm dreaming!"

"Yes, well, remember that this is not public knowledge just yet," she said, turning toward the door.

"Not a worry!" I assured her. Normally I'd have followed her to the door, but I was feeling a little ripe from my encounter with Antonio. "I'm on it!"

She nodded sagely. "I see that."

38

Alana

Thank God they let me into the studio. I couldn't find Rory, and Hailey was in the middle of taping a scene, but I didn't mind standing at the edge of the set to watch. After my brush with the largest nose ever born on a human head, I felt soiled and sad. Disillusioned. I wasn't really sure why, except there was something about my parents' lack of trust in me—a mushy, sensitive feeling that hit me every time the parents made a move, and it was a swampland I didn't want to cross at the moment.

So I waited at the edge of the set, watching the director call out shots and make some last-minute changes with the actors. There was something about CPR—Hailey's character had to resuscitate some-one—so some guy on the set was giving her tips about where to place her hands, how to breathe, stuff like that.

One of the crew adjusted the lights, and some of it spilled over to me, catching the glimmering gold-feather embossing on my skirt. I lifted my hands into the white pool, admiring the smooth surface of skin, the pearly nails shaped like little almond slivers. Why didn't some commercial genius see the beauty of these hands? From what I'd seen at my auditions, those casting people were morons.

When Hailey's scene started, it was hard for me to see with all the camera guys and cord holders getting in the way, but I could tell she was in the groove, and the director and crew people seemed to like her a lot. No wonder. After you've worked with a prima donna like Deanna, any normal person seems eminently reasonable.

"Help! Someone help!" a lady in the scene called out. "He's not breathing!"

In a flash, Hailey stopped wheeling her little meal cart down the hospital corridor and rushed to the ailing man's side. "Go, get a doctor," she told the woman. "They're in a conference in the north wing." As the woman ran off the set, Hailey helped the man to the floor, straddled him, and started alternately pumping his chest and then breathing into his mouth. (Well, I guess she was pretending on the CPR, but I was convinced.) While Hailey worked on the dying man, somehow she managed to fit in a little speech, persuading him not to give up, to cling to life with all his strength. I wanted to jump in beside her and shout, "You tell him, girl!" It's not every day you see a hospital aide save a man's life, but Hailey made it look real.

Apparently, the rest of the crew felt the same way, because when the scene ended, the director started them applauding and the guy with the clipboard told her what a great job she had done. I rushed over to compliment her, and she threw her arms around me and gave me a big hug.

"I'm surprised to see you here, sweetie," she said.

"Didn't you have your meeting with that Suze Orman person today?"

"Don't ask! When everything fell apart I didn't want to be alone. I thought maybe we could go shopping?"

Her blue eyes glimmered. "I have a VIP shopping pass, good all day at Bloomingdale's."

"That's the best thing I've heard all day. Can we go now?"

"I'm done here. Just let me get out of this costume and—"

"Hailey . . . wait!" A short, dark-haired woman with a measuring tape around her neck split off from the director and chased after us. "Don't forget, you need to get that fitting done now. The big wedding scene is coming up and I can't have your boobs popping out of the gown."

I leaned close to Hailey. "Why not? Bound to improve ratings."

"Go over to my closets and find a dress," the woman ordered. "I've got a meeting, but I'll meet you there in an hour and mark the alterations."

"OK, Jodi," Hailey said politely.

I frowned at her.

"Jodi's the costume designer," Hailey explained. "And this is a great excuse for you to see all the things she's got in her closets. A real treasure. Almost as much fun as shopping."

Honestly, I was in no mood to indulge the obnoxious woman who'd just ordered my friend around . . . until I stepped into the "closets," an endless, two-tiered train of clothes racks. At first sight, it was a bit overwhelming, like stepping into a warehouse of Salvation Army clothes. But on closer inspection, the quality and the styling of these garments were unmistakable.

I staggered to a rack of summery whites: pleated skirts,

scalloped tanks, halter dresses, slip dresses, wispy lace tops. Beside the whites were gowns, short and long, print and solid, conservative black and glittering beaded, spangled explosions of color. I flicked the hangers along, pausing to soak up the dramatic styling and rich fabrics.

As if the fabrics and styling weren't enough, the labels were to die for: Chanel, Vera Wang, Oscar de la Renta, Caroline Herrera, Michael Kors, Zac Posen, Narciso Rodriguez.

"You're awfully quiet," Hailey teased.

"Almost speechless." I stepped away from the rack and stared up and down the line of clothes. "I'm trying to absorb it. I am looking at the mother lode—a shrine to fashion."

"And this is just the formal wear."

I held a sheer black D & G gown under my chin, thin straps and a low back, trimmed with gold cord and rhinestones. "Is there a dressing room? Or should I just strip down right here?"

"There are some curtained sections in the back," Hailey said. "But we're not supposed to fool around with this stuff. Jodi freaks when we don't take the costumes seriously."

"Oh, come on, Hailey. A little dress-up won't hurt anyone, and Jodi won't be back for an hour. She told us that."

"Oooh . . ." She vacillated, but I knew she would give in. She couldn't resist, either. "I've always been dying to try on this gray linen duster by Anne Taylor. OK."

I collected a mound of fabulous gowns and nearly ran to the curtained area in the back.

I tried on the black Dolce & Gabbana. Elegant.

A beaded turquoise Oscar de la Renta sheath. Stunning.

A charcoal gray satin Chanel with an ornamented bustle bow. Thrilling.

Hailey was laughing, trying sexy neckline-plungers that her character Ariel would never be allowed to wear. "And look at this one," she said, kicking out from under a high-cut gown. "It's slit right up to the patootie. Don't you love it?"

"My supply is dwindling," I said, hitching up my satin skirts. "Gotta get more."

I ran for more clothes and came back with an armload of treasures from a small room off to the side. "Look what I've found! Did you know there's a little room off to the side with—guess what?—Prada gowns! Our favorites—and this one in these russet tones. I'm getting choked up just looking at it."

"Wait. From a separate room? You can't try those on."

"Why not?" I was already prying my beautiful earth-tone Prada ballroom gown from its hanger.

"They belong to Deanna. All her wardrobe is kept in a separate room. The vault, they call it. No one is allowed to touch it except Deanna and Jodi. And besides, none of those dresses will fit; they're all size two."

"Oh, what's the harm? Deanna doesn't ever have to know. Besides, she's got the best clothes in the whole massive collection. And—oops!—look at this." I finished zipping up the Prada gown and smoothed my palms over the tapered bodice. "Deanna's perfect size two fits me like a glove. What does that tell you about Ms. Deanna Childs's trademark *tiny-two* shape?"

"You're kidding." Hailey gaped. "She's a fraud? She's not even really a size two?"

"Not even close." I twirled in the mirror. "I adore this gown."

"How do you think Deanna pulls it off?"

"Well, Jodi must be in on it. And maybe she uses the

big hair to distract. With that mass of fat curls, her body looks small by comparison."

"I've always wanted to wear this gown," Hailey said, pulling out a shell pink beaded sheath.

"Now's your chance. And I have to try this one. It's a Christian LaCroix, and I saw some celeb wearing it in *Vogue.* Hers was white though." I slipped on a black lace LaCroix, a short dress that revealed an eye-popping amount of leg, as well as seductive portions of bare skin under lace.

The effect of black lace against my cocoa skin, along with all that leg . . .

"That dress is a man-killer," Hailey said.

"Grrrr," I teased. "This is a dress you definitely do not take home to Daddy."

"That would be if you could take it home. Remember . . . we're playing dress-up. None of this can be for keeps."

"Who cares?" I laughed. "Really? I don't feel the need to own any of these magnificent creations. I'm just loving the chance to play in them."

And what did that say about me and my shopaholism? I liked spending money, I had to admit that. But as I slid into sexy silk gowns and unrolled the layers of frou-frou red feathers of an Ungaro, the textures and styling—the tactile aspects of the garments—brought me immense satisfaction.

Maybe it wasn't all about the victory of a purchase. Was there some other payoff? An aesthetic aspect that attracted me to shopping?

Besides looking fabulous, of course.

I strutted past the mirror in Deana's black lace LaCroix, lifting my head up and tossing my baby dreads over a shoulder. "Now here's a dress for the Emmys. Can't you picture me wearing this on the red carpet when we go to accept your award?"

"Only if I can wear this." She slunk up beside me in her shell pink sheath.

"Well, thank the Lord that gown has beads. Otherwise, I'd think you were totally nude."

"It fits like a body sock." Hailey wiggled her hips and the beads winked. "I *like* it."

"I'll just bet you do." The voice was cold, edgy, with the sarcastic bite of an angry parent.

Hailey spun around but I didn't need to turn to catch the hard lines of Deanna's face in the mirror. My heart sank at the sight of her monstrous scowl, her bulging-eyed anger. Party pooper.

"What do you think you're doing, touching my clothes, wearing my personal things?"

"We were trying on some costumes," I said. "Don't get your panties in a twist over it."

Deanna ignored me, glomming onto Hailey. "You're over the line. I'll have your job for this."

Hailey's face went as pale as her pink gown when she crossed her arms and bent down to pick up her clothes. I felt a twinge of regret as she ran from the room.

The party was definitely over.

39

Hailey

My hair flew behind me as I tore through the wardrobe closet, running in my bare feet. My only thought was to get to my dressing room before anyone else saw me in this gown.

"Hailey!" Jodi shouted as I banged into a rack of coats, nearly hooking myself onto a hanger.

"I . . . gotta go!" I couldn't stop now. "I'll be back."

"What are you doing? What are you wearing? That's not your gown for the wedding."

I knew she was probably putting it all together by the time I flew out of the closet, but I just couldn't stop. Adrenaline was pumping madly through my body, pushing me on. Sweat beaded on my forehead, and my heart thudded a message that I couldn't stand to hear: Deanna's got you now.

You crossed her line.

She'll screw you over.

By the time I reached my dressing room, I was gasping for breath, not so much winded, but feeling frantic. What had I done? Was I that stupid?

"Hilly?" Antonio popped out of his dressing room, his dark brows drawn up in confusion. "What is the matter? I just heard Jodi paging security to the wardrobe closet. Are you all right?"

"I'm scared," I admitted, swiping a hand over my sweaty forehead. "Deanna's after me. She's mad. She caught me wearing her wardrobe."

"What?" His gorgeous eyes went wide in horror. "How did that happen?"

"It's a long story." And I had a feeling it was getting more and more twisted by the minute. I opened the door to my dressing room. "Look, can you cover for me while I change?"

"I . . ."

Obviously, I'd asked too much. As he floundered for words I wondered at the level of his acting ability; was it so difficult to drum up a little improv in a pinch?

"I can't. I must go. Didn't I tell you? There's somewhere I have to be."

"Right," I said, hurt that he wouldn't defend me. "You go. Take care of your business. Don't worry about me."

He turned away without a kiss, without a good-bye. A total stranger.

Un-fucking-believable.

At least I had the bittersweet pleasure of slamming the door behind him.

That afternoon the streets of Manhattan roiled with rank humidity, the sticky, cloying air that tears at your skin and pinches your sinuses. As Alana and I walked out of the studio, it overwhelmed me. "Hell. It's the new theme of my life. I'm over my spending limit. Out of a job. Probably out of love. And now I'm wading through an urban swamp of sweat."

"Oh, honey, it's not that bad."

"Not that I'm complaining," I said. "At least I had a life, for, like, ten minutes. It'll be something to talk about over sewing circles back in Wisconsin."

"You're suffering from sunstroke. Come on. We need an oasis in the desert."

She led me to Henri Bendel's. The door whispered open with a puff of dry, cool air. I stepped inside the rarified retail atmosphere and felt a glimmer of hope refracting through the large gold bottle of perfume. Maybe my life wasn't over. I had an agent, right? So far, Cruella hadn't done much beyond carving off her twenty percent, but why couldn't that change? Today might be the day that she earned her salary. I was worth fighting for, wasn't I?

Without a word, Alana and I descended the stairs to the brown-and-white-striped ladies' lounge, a feminine refuge in a decidedly male metropolitan city. First I washed my hands and toweled my face with a cool cloth. Then, I chose a comfy chair and called Cruella.

"I don't care about Deanna Childs," Cruella said. "The last I heard, this new network guy wanted to see more of you in the shows. The youth thing. That does not include Deanna."

"But apparently she's got some weird clauses in her contract," I said. "At least, that's what Gabrielle told me."

"Gabrielle Kazanjian? You met with the executive producer?"

"Twice today. The last time, she told me I should just leave the studio before Deanna had a major hissy fit. Gabrielle was going to work on damage control, but she couldn't guarantee anything. She kept implying that Deanna could fire people. Is that true?"

"Unlikely but possible. Let me make some calls. I'll get back to you."

"At least she didn't yell at me," I told Alana.

"Of course not! You didn't do anything wrong."

"You know, you're right. I'll bet Cruella will get Gabrielle on the phone and straighten everything out. I mean, why not? I'm overreacting. And Antonio . . . he's going to realize what an ass he was." I laughed and collapsed against the chair as a tear slipped out. "What a day! I've been through the wringer, but maybe I'm making a big deal out of nothing. Once Deanna's tantrum winds down, the worst will be a stern reprimand from Jodi."

Alana took the chair beside me, folding her legs. She wagged the toe of her Dolce & Gabbana sandal playfully. "What do you think? Should we, maybe, shop a little?"

I rubbed my palms over the thighs of my jeans and took a deep breath. "You just read my mind."

A few purchases later, I stood tall again, my spirits lifted and my face refreshed with a tangy little moisturizer that could be applied right over daily makeup. Alana and I had both grabbed two bottles, then had them gift wrapped in the customary brown-striped boxes with bows—because we could.

The heat wasn't quite so oppressive as we headed out the door to meet Marcella, who was just getting out of work and wanted to lend her moral support in my time of crisis. She had picked a little French restaurant in the Fifties, and I walked with a spring in my step that wasn't caused by the heels of my Manolos. Shopping had restored my faith in the future; things would be fine.

As we came up to the restaurant, Alana slowed her step. "What is that, a line?"

I paused, equally put out. "I hope she made a reservation."

"Hey! You guys!" Marcella hollered down the block like a street urchin calling in his dog. "How's it going! I hate to ask, but have you heard anything?" she continued as we caught up to her. When I shook my head, she bulldozed on, "This place is always crowded, but worth the wait."

I was too tense to comment, and I think Alana was dumbfounded by the new dining experience as we squeezed through the lobby, staying with the line. La Bonne Soup was crowded with people clustered around tables the size of chessboards. Once we got a table, we had no space for our shopping bags and were forced to shove them uncomfortably under our legs. But the red wine and crisp salad plunked down in front of us were surprisingly good, and the soup that passed by our table smelled delicious.

"Soup when it's eighty degrees outside," Alana said, "who would think people would wait in line for it?"

"I love this place." Marcella pulled off a crust of bread. "You get a whole meal, plus drinks, for less than twenty bucks."

"And you choose a restaurant based on price," Alana said, as if the thought had never occurred to her. "Next time I'll know not to bring any packages. We're really stuffed in here."

"I was meaning to ask you, why do you have packages, anyway?" Marcella shot a look under the table. "And from Henri Bendel. Whatever it is must have cost you a pretty penny."

As Alana defended our need to shop, my cell phone went off and I fished it out. "Cruella . . ." I flipped it open. "Thanks for calling back. I was wondering."

"I don't know how you did it so fast, but sounds like you'd better plan your tomorrows without *Tomorrows*.

Ducky, I know you came from Iowa, but don't you know that you never attack the centerpiece of the show?"

"I'm from Wisconsin, and I didn't attack anyone."

A man with sweat-tipped bangs at the next table eyed me suspiciously. I turned away, realizing I was breaking one of my etiquette rules and talking on a cell phone at a table in a restaurant. It's so rude, but looking at the line blocking the door, I knew I'd never make it out.

"Make sure they have it straight," I went on in a low voice. "I would never hurt anyone."

"True, you went after her clothes, but to some women when you pinch the Prada you might as well be cutting out the gallbladder."

"They weren't her clothes. They were costumes. Did Deanna say they were hers?"

"Listen, Kansas, it's over for you at that show. The EP told me you're lucky they don't press larceny charges. Those clothes were worth a few shekels."

"Larceny! But I didn't take anything. Did you point that out?"

"They'll write you off next week. No more tapings for you, Montana. Now, normally they would have to buy off the rest of your contract, but I thought you might want to trade the money for their word in writing that they won't press charges."

"For what?" I rasped, trying to keep my voice low, my temper in check. "Costume abuse? Illegal fittings?"

"I'm glad you're taking this with a sense of humor," Cruella said.

Humor? I held the phone over my soup bowl and scowled at it. The diners at La Bonne Soup were about to see a woman spontaneously combust, and my agent thought I was coining quirky one-liners?

"Give me that." Marcella grabbed the cell away.

"You the agent? Well, let me tell you, honey, you had better get off your fat ass and do your job. Your client needs work, and what are you going to do about that?"

I watched in amazement as Marcella listened. "Don't give me that boollshit. And pardonez moi my French, but if you can't find Hailey a spot on another show, I will. . . . Oh, that's not a threat, honey, it's a promise." She flipped the phone shut and handed it back to me.

"Well!" Alana forced a smile. "Another problem solved. You never liked Cruella, did you? Bet you'll be glad to have her off your ass."

"I'm fired." I blinked, trying to grasp the reality. "I'm really off the show."

"And you're probably minus one agent, too," Marcella admitted, "but you can do better than that old goat."

"You know, Marcella," Alana eyed her shrewdly, "you should be an agent. You're tough and smart and diligent . . ."

"No, no way. Not interested. Retail is my thing. I know what I like and where I belong. But I would like to help you, Hailey. Actually, let's be honest here: you both need a lot of help."

Alana rolled her eyes. "You sound like my parents."

"Mr. Big Nose was all wrong for you, honey," Marcella said, "but your parents have their hearts in the right place. You're spending money you don't have—both of you. Look at you two! Both out of work and you spend the afternoon at Bendel's? Hellllloooo?"

"It was therapy for us," I explained.

"Retail therapy." Alana turned her wineglass on the table thoughtfully. "To be honest, it's the only thing that works."

"Not for nothing, but you both need therapy, and shopping is not it."

I was intrigued. "What's your take? What do you think we need?"

"Abstention. A total fast, for starters. Then you could ease back in on a sensible plan—like Weight Watchers or the South Beach Diet Plan."

Alana lifted her wine. "I'm horrified. And riveted."

"My friend Susan loves the South Beach Diet," I said casually, turning to glare at the sweaty man who was eavesdropping. I lowered my voice and asked Marcella, "Do you think we're fat?"

"Honey, you have perfect bodies. It's your loosey-goosey spending habits that are cluttering your lives with problems—and a hell of a lot of merchandise you don't even need. I hate waste. That's why I'm prescribing the Marcella Budget Plan. Let's call it the MBP."

"That's good," Alana said. "Everybody likes a trendy name."

"How do we start?" I asked.

She gestured us forward. "Put your credit cards on the table."

I opened my silver bag. "I'm down to one. I thought that would be a good thing, but I keep going over the limit, and then they fine me. And then I'm OK until I forget my balance and I go over the limit again."

Alana proudly clicked her card on the tabletop. "See the hologram dove? I got to personalize mine when I ordered it."

"Very nice," Marcella agreed. Then she slid the cards in opposite directions, handing Alana's card to me, mine to Alana. "You're going to hold on to each other's cards. I know you're good friends and you can trust each other to take care of them. But at the same time, you won't use them."

"But what about our expenses?" Alana asked.

"What expenses? You're on a budget now. You two can't afford all this cacky you buy. From now on, you are not to open your designer handbags."

I winced. "We'll starve!"

"You can use cash for bare necessities. Like milk. Or bagels."

"Starbucks," Alana added.

But Marcella was shaking her head. "Time to start brewing your own at home, honey. Those designer javas cost, and you don't have that much cash in the bank, right? You gotta prioritize. Make a budget and stick to it."

I slapped my forehead. "I am so bad at numbers."

"Not a worry. I'll help you," Marcella offered. "We'll help each other. Believe me, this is the first step to fixing all the crap in your lives."

"I believe, I believe!" Alana laughed.

I wasn't quite so enthusiastic. "I don't even know how to make coffee," I lamented. "Though I guess I'll have a lot of time on my hands to learn in the next few weeks." A lot of time.

Alana's cell phone rang, and she spoke with enthusiasm. "Guess what I'm doing? Going on the MBP with Hailey. No, it's not a cruise ship. Mm-hmm. You don't know what it is? Marcella told us all about it. Well, maybe I'll tell you about it someday. What's that?" She glanced up at us. "Trevor wants to know if we'll meet him and X at the Uptown Comedy Clinic."

"For starters, I don't think you can afford a night out," Marcella said.

"Can't we use our optional cash for it?" Alana asked. "I could really use a little lift."

"Give me that!" Marcella snatched Alana's cell phone and started barking at Trevor. "I have two financially overextended girls here, and I've got to tell you, the only way they will meet you tonight is if the evening is free. You promise? 'Cause if I cab it all the way up there and find out you're lying, I'm going to be steaming mad. OK, then. Yes, honey. We'll see you then." She flipped the phone closed and handed it to Alana. "All set. The night's on him."

"Wow. You really handled that." I slid my unnaturally flat wallet back into my silver Fendi satchel, feeling vulnerable. I was glad that Marcella was taking care of things, though she couldn't be with me twenty-four hours a day. How was I going to manage?

How would I survive without credit?

What emotional lows would I fall to without shopping therapy?

I couldn't stand to think about it. There would be time to worry tomorrow. And tomorrow and tomorrow.

Tonight . . . everything would be paid for. Time to celebrate like it was the last party on earth. For Alana and me, it was!

40

Alana

The uptown club was one of those high-energy places where you feel obliged to laugh and applaud because the lights are so bright and everyone else is having a roaring good time and you can't stand to be the only sourpuss in the crowd.

Yes, the club was hopping, popping high energy, and Trevor was wavering, waxing, low-energy drunk. The big news was that Xavier was flying out to Los Angeles in two days, a trip to start developing his comedy show now that the cable network had picked up his pilot.

"The networks usually do this in the early spring," Xavier told us in the bar outside the club as we lingered in the smaller room. "But in cable, anything goes."

"Right," I said, realizing that Xavier's departure was Trevor's excuse for falling into the bottle.

"I'm proud of you, bro." Trevor clapped a hand over Xavier's cheek, nearly falling off his stool. "Really proud. Stand-up, bro."

"That is so exciting!" Marcella raved. "I can't be-

lieve we're all gonna know a famous comedian with
his own show on TV."

"Yeah." I shifted from one foot to the other. "Aunt
Nessie always said you were a real comedian."

The hostess corralled us out of the bar and showed
us to a table inside. The comics hadn't started, and with
the lights up, I spotted a few acquaintances in the crowd.
Lydia Jackson, the daughter of one of my mother's
friends, would no doubt report back on everything from
the stiletto heels on my feet to the sheen on my face.
Izzy Daniel, an ex of mine, grinned across the room,
that big, warm smile that lets you know you're looking
fine. Izzy wasn't a bad guy, just a little too into his blues
creations to suit my lifestyle. Not that I didn't enjoy sitting on his mattress and listening as he wrote songs,
but there were other activities on my calendar, the more
basic being eating, sleeping, and showering. I waved
across the room, hoping he would stay on the other
side, then realized he was with a woman—Izzy had a
girlfriend. And from the way they seemed to be joined
at the hip, things were serious. Well, good luck to her!

I forced a smile for the two women I'd met on the
bar circuit, Nayasia and Sharon. Sisters, I think. They
always dressed to kill, with matching accessories,
shoes, earrings, etc. I'd give them an A for effort, but
the overall effect was way too pat and monochromatic.
Everything red with patent accessories. Or a profusion
of plum. For some reason, their look reminded me of
the hookers who work Ninth Avenue late at night.

Did I mention that people just don't know how to
dress themselves?

The sisters rushed right over to our table and made a
fuss over me, though I smelled the real lure. When you
travel with three attractive black brothers, you get a lot
of female attention. The sisters had no way of knowing
that one of the guys was gay, another wasted on booze,
the third wasted on ego.

"And who are these gorgeous escorts of yours?" Sharon asked. Tonight she was decked in peach, an unfortunate shade that made her look like the spokesperson for the Society of Easter Bunnies. Also, though I hate to sound catty, I would swear there was polyester in her skirt. Meow.

I introduced everyone, rising to the standards Mama had drilled into me as a child.

Nayasia wasn't so polite; she quickly scooted into the chair between Trevor and Kyle, leaving Marcella stuck with her Seven and Seven and a sardonic "can you believe this chick?" expression. Trevor managed to pull himself together enough to impress Nayasia. Or maybe she was smelling his mother's millions in the form of southern fried chicken. Hard to say.

After the show started, Xavier disappeared to the bar, and I sat between Marcella and Trev. Marcella found every joke hysterically funny, and Hailey laughed along, but I was distracted. Something about Xavier's success was bothering me, especially when I compared it to my lack of success as a hand model. It was all so unfair. Why couldn't I get a great offer like that?

Excusing myself, I pushed away from the table. I needed some fresh air. Maybe, if I cleared my head, I could come back and have some fun again.

But Xavier snagged me on the way out. "Where you going, girl?"

"What do you care?" I said as I passed through the bar.

Outside the air wasn't so fresh. Steamy. Superheated. With more than a hint of fragrances you don't want to think about. I sighed as X came out the door and nudged my elbow.

"What's up with you, Alana? If I didn't know better, I'd think you were having some sort of existential crisis. No, wait. It's a financial crisis, right? Well, that explains it."

"Right," I said sarcastically. "It's all that simple."

"Hey, simple as it is, people understand being broke. It's good material."

I spun toward him. "Don't even think about working it into your comedy act. I'm still furious over that princess routine. How could you, X? I mean, really."

The streetlight reflected blue on the side of his face, the overall effect smoky and ethereal. Underneath all that wickedness, X was a handsome brother. "Oh, chill, Alana. I can't believe you still haven't gotten over yourself. You've been one of my greatest sources of inspiration this summer. People love the princess routine."

"Do they? Well, score one for you, X. Your gain, my mortification."

"Now why do you have to take it so personally?"

"Maybe because it is personal?"

"Yeah, well, they say there's truth and pain in good comedy."

"Oh, now you're saying that princess bullshit is true?"

He shook his head. "Girl, I can do no right by you. I never wanted to hurt you. You're always so tough. Like one of those Hummers on the road."

"You're calling me a Hummer!" A little squeak popped into my voice, and I swallowed hard to squelch it.

"Lord," he said, "shut me up before the woman kills me."

There is nothing worse than a wiseass brother. "You're comparing me to a big-ass car?"

"It's not a car. It's a utility vehicle. Used to be for the military. Schwarzenegger was one of the first civilians to have one in this country."

Actually, there is one thing worse: a wiseass brother who thinks he knows everything. "Let me ask you something, X. Why did you follow me out here?"

"Now, see? You're assuming that it's all about you?"

I folded my arms. "The truth?"

He turned his head away. "I don't know what it is about you, Alana, but I just can't say no to the challenge. I mean, what does it take to get close to you? How much time? Let's see, I've known you since we were kids, so that's no good. Or is it candy and cards? Or what?"

"That's an odd question. You make me sound heartless."

"No, that's not what I meant. But the thing is for me, this TV thing in LA is a big deal. And, hey, it may totally flop, but before I go, I just wanted . . . I don't know, a sense of where we stand."

I nearly choked on that. "We?"

"You and I." He turned toward me, so close my elbows touched his shirtsleeves. That was when he put his hands on my bare arms, and I was surprised at how soft his palms were, how gentle his touch. So unlike the vicious barbs that flew from his mouth.

I closed my eyes for a moment, trying to resist the good feelings his touch evoked, wondering if my own life would ever make sense to me again. I hated this man, and yet I wanted him to move closer, to pull me into his arms, to kiss me.

The door squealed open behind me, and Hailey sucked in a desperate breath. "It's Trevor!" she cried. "Something's happened."

That night, for the first time in my life, I rode in an ambulance.

After Trevor had passed out in the men's room and couldn't be awakened, Kyle had dialed 911 right away. The ambulance came, and in the blur of flashing lights and a rolling bed from which Trevor's feet dangled over the end, the paramedics established that he was still breathing, at least.

"He's been drinking?" the female attendant asked.

It seemed like a rhetorical question. "And I found this in his pocket." Xavier handed her a prescription vial. Small, but it appeared to be empty.

"Will he be OK?" I asked.

The woman made a note on her clipboard. "They'll probably pump his stomach. Can't really tell you much more, except he'll be at Columbus Hospital. Anyone riding along?"

"I am." I tried to climb into the back, but Xavier was already in there with the other attendant.

"You can ride up front, with me," the woman said.

I climbed into the front seat and burst into tears. Without a word, she handed me a box of tissues, then put the truck in gear and plunged into the steamy night, sirens blaring.

At the hospital, the medical team took over, leaving Xavier and me stuck together in a nasty public waiting room. If the slippery plastic chairs weren't bad enough, there was always the clientele—arguing couples, punked-out friends of kids who'd overdosed, and the few normal people who kept their eyes averted. When X put his arm around me and pulled me close, I didn't object. In fact, it felt good to rest my head against his shoulder. I could almost close my eyes and doze off and pretend I wasn't here. Almost.

After a few hours of waiting, a young doctor summoned us to the desk. "Trevor overdosed on prescription painkillers," he said, taking his time to look us in the eyes. "That, combined with alcohol. I understand he has a history with this?"

I nodded.

"We're going to keep him for observation. He'll probably be groggy till morning, but you can go up to his room with him if you like. Tomorrow he'll receive a psych evaluation and we'll take it from there."

"But he's going to be OK?" I asked.

The doctor paused. "No promises. Has Trevor ever tried counseling? Detox?"

"A few times," Xavier answered.

The doctor nodded. "I would like to see him try it again, but that's always difficult. It's got to be his choice. He's got to be ready."

"He'll get there," Xavier said with a confidence I didn't feel. "He will."

When we got to Trevor's room, a nurse was there cleaning him up with a washcloth, though he was still passed-out. She finished up, found us an extra chair, then told us to try and let Trevor sleep awhile. Not a problem, since he was snoring like a bear and X and I were feeling giddy with exhaustion.

I pulled my feet up on the chair and snuggled into a blanket. I think I dozed for a while, but then Xavier was talking to me, asking me what I remembered from our high school. Did I think Trevor was using drugs then? Had it happened after Trev's father died? Was Xavier wrong to cover for Trev, wrong to take care of him?

"I think that might make me the evil codependent," Xavier said. "I worry that my going out to LA set him off, but I can't not go. I mean, for me, it's a lifelong dream."

My eyes still closed, I admitted that I wasn't an expert, that we needed some professional help. "Do you think Trevor will do rehab again?"

Xavier yawned. "I hope so. He told me he's sick of getting advice from everyone. All these people who say they love him, telling him what to do. I told him he's lucky to have people who love him."

"Sometimes I could just kill him," I said. "I used to

get so jealous. He's the savior of the family, but he keeps blowing it."

"Tell me about it." Xavier talked about growing up on the fringes of wealth, living with a family that had it all but personally never feeling any sense of entitlement. "It was like, I had to get out there and do it, prove to Aunt Nessie that I was worth her investment."

"That's why you worked all those hours at McDonald's?" I frowned. "And here I thought you liked those funny hats."

"It was the Big Mac that kept bringing me back," he teased.

We talked for hours, a sort of stream-of-conscious, sleep-deprived conversation. By morning, I was aware of the strange bond I had with X. Underneath his obnoxious attitude lurked a lightning-speed brilliance, a quick mind, and a slightly twisted sensibility I couldn't resist.

OK, in my semiconscious state, I had to admit I found him attractive.

"Let me ask you a hypothetical question," he said. "If you knew a guy who was headed out to LA with a big job and a fat expense account, would you hook up with him? I mean, would you find that kind of thing appealing?"

"If I had more energy, I'd smack your face. Are you asking me if I'm a whore?"

"No! No, never mind. It was just hypothetical."

A hypothetical question that reminded me how much I loathed him when he acted like a jackass.

Besides, even if I were in love, the new Alana had to beware of hooking herself on a man. It would be too tempting to find a new provider, a replacement for my father.

When I hooked up with someone again, I wanted it to be all about love.

Well, love, and a little great sex. Great sex can only help a relationship, right?

41

Hailey

Energy in, stress out.
Good air in, bad air out.

Light air in, heavy air out.

Folded like a sprouting pretzel, I sat on the floor of our living room and tried to relax. It was the first day of my new free life.

It was also Saturday, the day the messenger usually arrived with a fat envelope full of my scripts for the next week of taping. Despite my attempts at picturing a beautiful hilltop overlooking Sedona, Arizona, the image in my mind was of our apartment door—the one with the doorbell that usually rang on Saturday mornings, the one that I kept glancing back toward, hoping that the curse of the past twenty-four hours was just a bad dream.

But no, I had to stop looking. The doorbell was not going to ring. I'd been fired. The horrible, awful truth, but still the truth.

I pushed my hands out, resisting an imaginary wall. I had to resist. Must resist . . .

Oh, hell! I dropped my arms, snatched up the cell phone and called Antonio. Once again, I got his voice mail. Should I leave a message? The fourth one today?

No, I thought, clicking off. I was getting his message, loud and clear. He had dumped me. Our relationship was over.

My life was over.

I speed-dialed Rory's number and caught him on the way to the gym. "Gotta stay buff, doll."

"Can you meet me for lunch?" I asked desperately. "I'll treat," I said, before I realized that I had no way to pay for it.

"Pumped dudes like moi do not eat lunch. Especially after my weigh-in last night. If I don't watch it, the writers will change Stone's name to Boulder."

"Then give me information," I said. "Have you read your scripts yet? Does Ariel's destiny unravel during next week's tapings?"

"Well, I only skimmed."

"And . . . ?" I said encouragingly.

"It doesn't look good, doll. It's monkeypox."

"What?"

"Apparently you got a needle stick while working on a patient who flew in from Africa. Or maybe it was Ceylon. Anyway, you're infected with this monkeypox, which makes them put you in total isolation. I'm afraid your death is imminent."

"No!" I bellowed. "Maybe I'm just a little dead. A mistaken identity. Wrong body in the coffin."

"Oh, it's you, all right. They might even bring Skip back for a big sob scene at your funeral."

"They can't do that! Deanna will eat it up!"

"Exactly."

"Maybe I can go into a coma for a long time. Till Deanna goes on vacation."

"She won't stand for that," he said, his voice heavy with sympathy. "Sorry, Hailey."

"I can't let this happen. I can beat this thing; I know I can. I will take on the pox and win. Ariel can beat this monkeypox thing."

"Tootsie, you're preaching to the choir."

"I know," I said in a small voice. "Enjoy your work-out."

He grunted. "Like that's ever gonna happen. Later, sweets."

I let my head drop toward the floor, pushing the air from my lungs. My character was not going to rise up from this sad demise. Ariel was dead.

And I was dead meat.

42

Alana

After a few hours of restless sleep, I staggered out to the living room to find Hailey face-down on the couch, her chin propped on a pillow. She was watching an old movie with Kate Hepburn as ingenue. Beside her was a mug of something that resembled watered-down charcoal.

"I tried to make coffee," she said. "I think you need those paper thingies to make it turn out."

I scratched my head blearily. "Filters? Yeah, probably. Who makes coffee at home anymore?"

I opened the kitchen cupboard. No food, but a fabulous array of glassware and dishes, my favorites being multicolor earthenware I'd ordered from Kitchen Kaboodle. Fabulous dinnerware. Just no dinner to serve on it.

"How's Trev?" Hailey asked.

"He'll survive. If he stops abusing himself. He's agreed to go to rehab."

"That's a silver lining."

"We'll see. He's been there before." I closed the cup-board and drummed my fingers over the granite counter. "We've got to get out of here," I said. "I need to shop."

"But what about our doing the Marcella Plan?" Hailey sat up and folded her arms. "I'm not giving you your card back. Well, unless you really want it."

"We'll work off our savings. I can stop at the ATM and take out some cash. And then—I know!—we'll check out one of those budget places. Mandee or H&M or Blueberry's."

Hailey fell back onto the couch. "What has my life become?"

"It'll be fun. Come on, get your body dressed, girl. We're going shopping!"

Honestly, it took me a few minutes to make the men-tal adjustment. Blueberry's was cute as a Barbie's Malibu Beach House, but just as tacky, and it sort of disturbed my aesthetic sensibilities to see so many adorable things merchandised together.

Truly, I'd entered the mother ship of the Nayasias and Sharons of the world.

"I don't think I'll find anything here," Hailey said nervously. "Can we go? I think Macy's is having a sale today."

"Let's just take a look," I said, trying to think of something that would be safe. Socks? Hair scrunchees? "What about these mood rings? Aren't they fascinat-ing? I mean, it's something to talk about when you're stuck with a dud conversationalist."

Hailey shook her head. "They remind me of my par-ents. Mood rings and granola and incense. Talk about a lost generation."

I had never seen my friend in such a funk. Here we

were shopping and she couldn't find something to lift her out of that mood?

"I am going to grab an armful of—I don't know—some of those little shorty pajamas over there, and I'm going to try them on. You're welcome to join me when you come back to the human race."

I flicked the tag up on the pajamas and was shocked to find that they were more than twenty dollars. Twenty bucks here at Blueberry's? Didn't they advertise, *Don't get the blues, shop at Blue's, where the prices will lift your spirits?* What a crock.

On the way to the dressing room, I told Hailey, "Oh, and I'm going to need my card. I'll be back in a flash with a stash."

Hailey never did show up in the dressing room. When I reappeared in the store, I nearly dropped my selection of shorty pajamas.

"Marcella?" I tried not to sound guilty. "What are you doing here?"

Her face was puffed up with anger. "The question is, Alana, what are you doing here?"

"I called her," Hailey admitted, her face pinched. "Sorry, but I didn't know what to do, but it just seemed wrong to give back your credit card."

I scowled at her. "You . . ."

"Don't blame Hailey," Marcella cut in. "The only one you have to blame is yourself, coming in here and planning to burn money on more things you don't need."

"Excuse me? Can I wear pajamas, please?"

"Pajamas! Sleep in a T-shirt. Did you hear anything I said last night? The Marcella Budget Plan? Alana, you are broke, sister."

"I know." I put the pajamas on a rack of socks. The cheap brushed cotton fabric had shed, leaving little flecks of white on the front of my black tank top. "But that doesn't change anything. Shopping is what I do, it's like breathing or eating. You can't expect me to stop living."

And without even brushing the fuzz off my shirt, I tucked my Louis Vuitton under my arm and strode out of there, my head held high.

That Marcella had a lot of nerve, getting in my grill and telling me what to do. And Hailey, with her namby-pamby "I didn't know what to do" and "I'm so sorry!" I'd had about enough of them.

And doing this to me after I was up all night with Trevor. I marched down the street, thinking what a horrible city New York was when your friends turned against you.

Friends . . . huh! Telling me what they think I should hear. What did they care about me?

Again, the image of Trevor in the hospital bed came to mind, and I realized he had felt the same way. The people who cared about him were telling him something he didn't want to hear. Dammit if they weren't right, too.

I turned, and there were my friends, a few paces behind me. Yes, they really were my friends. Oh, I felt ready to kill them both, but I knew they meant well.

"I need a commitment from you," Marcella said, getting right to the point. "Either you want to work with me on this, or you don't. I can't make you do it, honey. Alana is the only one who can fix Alana."

"Yeah, OK, I'll do it," I said, "but you can't expect me to sit around all day and not go shopping. At least I can look, right?"

"That's the biggest part of the problem!" Marcella pointed a finger at me. "You have too much time on your hands. But we're going to take care of that right now. You need a job."

"Really?" I started brushing lint off my T-shirt.

"Great. Hey, how about if I get a job being a personal shopper for the stars? It's my specialty, and I could go out all day and spend someone else's money. Wouldn't that be great?"

Marcella shook her head. "Too close to your addiction. Come on, it's just two blocks this way." Already she was on the move, Hailey dutifully walking alongside her.

Oh, what the hell? I followed, picking my shirt clean and thinking that my Prada mules were feeling a little snug. Was it the humidity, or was it time for a new pair?

When Marcella started up the stone stairs of LA Minute, I wanted to shout my approval. At last, the girl had come to her senses and we were going to have lunch at the "hottest spot on the planet."

"What a great idea!" I called to them. "I'm parched, and they have the most delicious Hollywood salad here."

But Marcella shook her head as she held open the big glass door. "You can't afford to eat here anymore. I'm taking you in to apply for a job, honey."

I laughed. "What? Here? I can't cook."

"True, but you know what people like, you have a strong sense of style, and you know how the rich like to be treated. Doesn't hurt that you've got a damn pretty face. You'll make a great hostess."

"A hostess? What kind of a job is that?" I blurted out to a woman in a gypsy costume hooked up with a headset right out of mission control.

"It's a super fun job," she said cheerfully, acknowledging the three of us. "Table for three?"

"Oh, I'm not staying." Hailey shook her head in a panic, turning to Marcella. "I can't work here. It's too public. People will recognize me."

And I thought my cage was rattled.

Hailey was frantic. "They'll think I've given up," she blubbered. "I'll never get another role—"

"Don't panic, honey." Marcella put her hands on Hailey's shoulders. "I've got a different strategy for you. A little career advice. If you haven't heard, you were mentioned on *ET* and *Dateline: Hollywood* last night. You're the new bad girl of soaps."

"But I didn't do anything wrong!" Hailey protested.

"See, that's the thing. You keep proclaiming your innocence and people don't want to hear it. The public wants to hear how naughty you've been. People love fallen angels. I say you stop fighting this thing and go after the bad girl market. Exploit the villainess image. Go to another network and sell yourself as a stinker."

"It's so . . . *not me*," Hailey objected.

"Was Ariel you? Are you half fish, half girl?"

Hailey sighed. "I guess I could make it a game. Like acting."

"That's right, honey. What have you got to lose?"

"Hey? Sorry to interrupt," the hostess prodded perkily. "How about that table?"

"We're here to see Minute Man," Marcella answered, "about a job. Would you please tell him Marcella is here?" As the hostess radioed to a distant planet, Marcella was back on Hailey. "Now the first thing you do is call your agent. You tell her you have a three-point plan. You're gonna start with the trades, and she's going to set you up to be interviewed. . . ."

As Marcella spelled out the details for Hailey, I surveyed the lobby of LA Minute. Customers were whisked through here quickly; a good thing, because the lobby decor reminded me of the waiting room of a dentist's office—unsettling, with a promise of pain to follow.

"OK, I'm going to go call Cruella." Hailey held up crossed fingers. "Wish me luck."

"You go, girlfriend," I told her, giving her a quick hug. A minute after she ducked out the door, a heavyset man with slicked-back sandy hair sauntered out of the elevator.

"Marcella! What's happening, babe?" He lumbered over and kissed her on each cheek.

"Things are good," she said. "I just stopped by to save your sorry butt. My friend Alana is in the market for a job, and since you need a hostess, I thought I'd put you two together." She introduced us, and he shook my hand.

"The name's Danny Slane, but everyone calls me Minute Man." Danny's green eyes seemed to have a smile lurking behind them. "What do you think, Alana? We're a very service-oriented business. Do you think you would be happy here?"

"I can be happy anywhere, as long as I'm surrounded by style. And I like what you've done here. I've always enjoyed myself here—delicious food and a fun theme."

Danny grinned. "Great."

"However," I went on, "I have to be honest with you, Minute Man. Silk flowers in the reception area?" I shuddered. "And that doormat has to go. It just screams 'final sale at Kmart.' And the mints on the counter? Who are we kidding? Can you spell 'hepatitis law suit'? And that gypsy costume you make your staff wear?"

"Now, the costume is important. It's part of the theme," he explained. "We want them to look like extras in a big-budget film."

"From the 1940s? Please. That thing will make me look like a runaway slave. 'I ain't never seen no babies being birthed!' Is that the look you want for your staff?"

"Of course not, but we need to follow through on the theme."

"Then change the costume. I'm sure we can come up with something more flattering for the staff, a little classier for your establishment."

"Yes, please!" the hostess called over as she led a group of diners toward the stairs.

"I don't know." Leaning against a marble pillar, Minute Man scratched his chin. "You'll have to show me some designs for uniforms. But I have to say, I like your honesty. And you seem to have a sense of what people want."

"Trust me, I'm an experienced consumer."

Marcella nodded. "That's for sure."

"OK, then," Danny said, shaking my hand. "Let's give it a shot."

43

Hailey

"Zoe will be in soon," the receptionist told me as she paused in the doorway. She had just escorted me into the office of Zoe Lemonda, editorial director of *Soap Opera Diaries*, and my new pipeline to the world. At least, that's what I'd been hoping for when I set up this meeting. "Would you like something to drink?"

I grinned. "Do you have any scotch?" I got that response from Marcella, and it worked like a charm.

The receptionist paled, looking nervously out in the hallway. "Water, coffee, or tea?"

"Guess I'll stick with water, thanks."

I pushed the visitor's chair closer to Zoe's desk and sat down. None of that friendly personal space, Marcella had instructed. "Get right up in her grill, honey." I straightened the elegant beaded black Dolce jacket I'd borrowed from Alana. A totally new look for me, the dress and matching jacket revealed miles of leg and a tease of cleavage. I hadn't worn jeans for a week now.

Marcella had suggested that the new, bad Hailey needed a new look, and so far I was having fun stepping out in style—mostly in items from the depths of Alana's closet.

A young, pencil-thin woman with a blond pixie haircut came in and grinned. "Did you really ask for scotch! You boozehound!"

I laughed. "I figured it was worth a try."

"I'm Zoe," she said, extending her hand. "And I've heard that you've changed your look recently, but I must say, this is working for you. No more of that corn-fed midwestern girl, right?"

I crossed my legs. "I'm afraid we're not in Kansas anymore."

Zoe smiled. "Let's close the door. We've got a lot to talk about, I think. As you know, my specialty is behind-the-scenes info on the soaps."

I nodded. "And I've got a few dozen Deanna anecdotes for you. I've sorted them in my mind by level of severity from nasty to depraved evil, but you can do with them what you like."

Zoe's blue eyes went wide in amazement. "Do you mind if I tape you? You're the first person who's ever been willing to go on record with Deanna dirt. The woman is so powerful in this industry, well, not to scare you off, believe me, but no one has ever been willing to cross her."

"I used to feel that way, but she's crossed me one too many times. She's gotten me fired, she's intimidated my boyfriend—"

"Antonio?" Zoe turned on the tape player. "I'd love some juice on him, too. You can imagine, he's a big seller for us, too. But first thing's first: Deanna and her insipid evils."

"The thing to remember about Deanna is that she's truly the queen of mean. No one on the set is safe from her tantrums and orders. She's gotten makeup artists fired, and once she actually stuck a costume assistant with a straight pin."

Zoe was writing furiously, a look of amazement on her face. "Is it true that she demands rewrites?"

"Won't leave her limo if she doesn't get them."

"Ugh! I used to work production on a soap. No more. And the size-two costumes? I just have to ask . . ."

"Actually, size six." I nodded. "You heard it right. She's been lying all these years. God knows why. I'm a size six and proud of it."

"This is so great," Zoe said, holding her hands up like I'd scored a goal. "But I'll stop interrupting and let you dig into the whole stories. Like the time she threatened you. How'd that happen?"

"Well, she was waiting for me outside my dressing room, hiding in the shadows, when . . ."

I told the story with relish, careful not to inflate any of the details. In some cases, the truth was odder than fiction, and when I'd decided to step forward, I promised myself I wouldn't stoop to Deanna's level. I was sticking to the real story, period.

The old Hailey would have hated this, but the new me was ready to rumble. If Deanna was going to sling the mud, I was willing to get my fingernails dirty and slop it right back.

Fire away.

Part Five

**MAKE A SPLASH WITH AN
AUGUST SALE**

You Won't Want to Miss!

44

Hailey

There is nothing worse than having irate fans up your wazoo when you're buying feminine-hygiene products.

I had just placed my tampons and deodorant on the counter at the corner CVS when a woman behind me in line gave a loud sigh. I shot her a look.

"Oh, you're that mermaid girl," she said, loud enough for everyone in the line to turn around to stare. She had black hair that was growing in shocking white, making her resemble a skunk. I could only hope she was in line to buy some Clairol Dewy Chestnut. "You're that one who got caught stealing Deanna Childs' clothes," she said smugly.

I pulled my straw hat down over my forehead and muttered. "I wasn't stealing anything." Didn't anybody get that?

When I turned back to the cashier, skunk lady added, "Better watch her! She's a closet thief!"

The clerk's eyebrows rose, and I shook my head.

Sometimes, the bad girl image just doesn't work for you, but then nobody thinks of defending the rights of Mata Hari or Madonna to buy tampons in peace. I routed through the bottom of my bag for the thirty-seven cents in change. I would have to talk to Marcella about budgeting in some more cash for necessities.

"That's her!" The white-streaked woman pointed to the copies of *Soap Scandals* in the checkout-counter rack. She even stepped up and tapped my face, a photo of me leaving Mosquito with Jackie Chan, my face a little pale from overexposure, though Jackie looked adorable. We'd had a chance to meet him that night, and we just happened to leave the restaurant at the same time. See how the press twisted things? "She's Hailey Starrett, the thief from *All Our Tomorrows.*"

At least she got my name right. I turned slowly and folded my arms in front of me. "I didn't steal those clothes, and they didn't belong to Deanna in the first place. They were *costumes*, and I was in the *wardrobe* department doing fittings. I was just doing my job as an actress when Deanna Childs threw one of her famous tantrums."

I realized that the eyes of customers in the line were all over me, assessing my testimony. One woman with rectangular eyeglasses and a briefcase scowled. A girl with too much mascara was nodding in approval. One man from the back called out, "You tell her, Ariel!"

My testimony complete, I turned back to the counter and fished out the coins. I was waiting for the receipt to print (for Marcella) when the woman behind me added, "How about Antonio Lopez? Is it true that he broke your heart?"

Now that was too personal, and way too complex to answer in five words or less, though I was beyond the early scratch-his-eyes-out stage. By my count, the first seven days after any breakup should be termed as a cooling-off period, a time when each party needs to work through the hurt, rejection, blame, regret, disbelief—not to mention the tests for STDs, which may have been the cause of the breakup in the first place.

In my case, after that first week of misery over Antonio, I realized that I didn't miss him that much, and that the worst part of our breakup was the humiliation of allowing Deanna one more shot at me.

"You know," Skunk Lady said, yanking me back to reality, "you're not as pretty in person."

I turned to her and just rolled my eyes.

It was ironic, but ever since I was fired from the show, I'd been recognized more than ever. Marcella had been right about being unable to shake the bad rep. Not that I minded being the bad girl of soaps, but I wasn't even being paid for the honor or the invasion of my privacy. I wouldn't have minded the attention if I had a job!

"Is it true Deanna threatened you?" the woman asked.

"Read *Soap Opera Diaries*," I said, plugging Zoe's publication. "They're the only ones who got it right." Snatching up my plastic bag, I swept out the door, nearly snagging Alana's lilac silk print summer dress as I swept past the rack of *Soap Scandals*. It was an issue I'd already read, which quoted Deanna saying, "Hailey Starrett will not be back. If that girl wants to return to this show, she'll have to step over my dead body."

A tempting invitation, I thought. Very tempting.

45

Alana

"This is Alana sending five to the caves, party of five to the caves. Do you copy?" I spoke quietly into the headset mike, as I guided five female exec secs into the elevators.

"This is Bear. Copy that, Alana."

Bear was a nickname for Brandon, my associate manning LA Minute's third floor, which was otherwise known as the caves. Everyone employed at LA Minute had to wear a headset, and the lingo was just a shorthand that had evolved over the course of conducting hundreds of people through a multilevel facility. Today I was assigned to my favorite "hot spot," the main entrance, which was truly the land parallel to air traffic control. Here I got to meet and greet everyone coming in, charm them in the first thirty seconds, then hustle them along to "one of my favorite tables" with that high-voltage energy that was trademark LA Minute. In less than a month here, I had mastered the pace of one of the trendiest new restaurants in Manhattan. Perhaps it was just the flavor of the month, but LA Minute was the hot, hot, hot place to see and be seen, and I was fine, fine, fine at keeping on top of the friendly chaos.

I sent a few more parties off to their tables—the most stylish guests landing tables in the fountain room on the first floor, where all the stars and models and power players were seated. The main structure in the center of the fountain was shaped like an Oscar, the gold statuette given out to winners of Academy Awards. The second floor, called the balcony, was a little more quiet and reserved. The chairs were actually movie seats in rows of two or three. To break up the auditorium sterility, the tables were separated by screens made of rice paper, painted canvas, or stained glass. Somehow the overall look came together: kitschy, eclectic, and cozy. Chaos reigned in the caves on the third floor, designed to resemble a movie set for *Planet of the Apes* meets *Jurassic Park*. Our dark, wild dance floor and funky bar was favored by college kids and overage debutantes. The restaurant's owner, Danny Slane, affectionately known as Minute Man, offered incentives like half-price happy-hour appetizers to lure customers up to the caves, and people had responded in droves. I guess the lure of a discount works in the restaurant industry, too.

"Hello, Ms. Tong! Step in out of that humidity! Our garden is nice and cool today." Over my mike, I said, "Two coins for the fountain," and sent the local newscaster and her companion to the celebrity area.

I assumed that the next tall black brother in the lobby was a pro basketball player, until I got a look at his face.

"Trevor!" I gave him a hug, pounding on his back. "You're looking good, you bad boy!"

"Hell of a lot better than I looked the last time you saw me. And you're kicking some butt yourself, cuz.

Got yourself a job at the see-and-be-seen place in town."

I slipped out of Trev's embrace and noticed that Xavier was behind him. Somehow I'd known I would see him again, though it had bothered me to have the situation out of my control. For a guy who almost invited me to move out to LA with him, he had certainly dried up quick and fast. In fact, when I'd tried to get information about Trevor in rehab, I'd had to call his mama and try to sort fact from Aunt Nessie–fiction.

So what could I say to cover the awkwardness? "Oh, you." I didn't intend to sound so mean. "What, are you visiting from the West Coast?"

"Actually, I'm sort of bicoastal. You didn't think you'd be rid of me so easy, did you? Besides, someone had to spring your cousin from rehab."

"Nah, it's not that way," Trevor insisted. "It's my call now. I'm the one who's gonna make this work."

"Now, didn't they tell you in group that you can't do this alone?" Xavier objected.

Trevor held up his hands. "You're twisting my words, bro . . ."

"Whoa, wait!" I held up my hands. "Before you deck each other here in the lobby, let me get someone to cover and I'll go on my break so we can catch up."

I called in Ginger to cover and showed the guys to a table on the second floor, one of the very private screened-off tables near the kitchen door—not a great spot for clients, but secluded enough so that employees could take their meals without looking like slackers. Minute Man didn't like the idea of his people appearing in uniform in the local Burger Heavens and yogurt shops, and when I agreed that it looked unprofessional, I was able to talk him into accommodating staff right here in the restaurant. The boss was a reasonable man. Lucky for me, as I don't suffer fools gladly.

I placed an order in the kitchen, filled three glasses with Coke, and returned to the table. "I ordered us some pork chops, today's special."

"Pork chops?" Xavier tapped a finger against his dimpled chin. "Now what if we didn't want pork chops?"

"You'll eat them, and you'll like them," I said sternly.

"Same old Alana." Trevor stirred the straw around, making the ice in his drink jingle. "Tell me how you managed to walk into this place and become the boss so fast. What? You sleeping with the owner?"

"Minute Man?"

The guys nearly sprayed Coke out through their noses.

"I don't think so. Not that he's not a great guy, but I don't think Danny's wife and daughter would take kindly to me rolling down to their breakfast table. No, my rise to fame and fortune at LA Minute has been based on hard work and merit—hard for you to believe, I know, but there you go. I know there's no real future in the job, but I do have a knack for it. I guess it's just the party girl in me; I feel right at home in this venue."

"And you look right at home in that uniform," Xavier said. "It's a damn good fit."

"Probably because I designed it," I said, taking a sip of my Coke.

"You mean, like, in your dreams?"

"In my apartment." Stephanie served our pork chops with gravy and greens and apple sauce, and I said, "Eat it up while it's hot! It's a pet peeve of mine—can't stand it when they serve lukewarm food. It's always nice and hot here."

"Listen to yourself, Alana," Trevor said. "Did they brainwash you, or insert an LA Minute microchip?"

"Always competing with me, Trev. Does it bother you that I like my job, and I'm good at it, too?" I told them how the LA Minute uniform had suited none of the girls, with fabric that didn't breathe, no darts in the bodice of the white blouse, and a fat sash at the waist that kept dipping into customers' entrees. When I'd pointed out the problem to Minute Man, he told me to bring him some solutions. So I set to work with a needle and thread, trying various fabrics and styles. I adapted a white cotton blouse from a discount store, gave it three-quarter sleeves capped with pearlized buttons, a sewn-in bib in the front to cover any "nipplage," a jaunty collar, and plenty of darts to accentuate the female shape. When one of the waitresses modeled my design for Danny, he pronounced it "killer cute" and wanted the entire female staff to switch over, just as soon as I could alter twenty-some white blouses.

"That's when I realized the little Sew-Right that I bought from a late-night TV ad wasn't going to cut it. So I had to sneak into the parents' apartment when they were out east and pick up the sewing machine Daddy gave me for my birthday when I was taking ninth-grade home ec."

"They still had that old thing?" Trevor asked.

"You know it. Daddy is a saver."

"I remember when you got that," Xavier said. "Pitched a fit, didn't you? Made your poor father miserable."

"It was a dud gift. Thirteen years old, what did I want with a sewing machine?"

"But the way you cried about it," Trevor said. "Cried and cried till your eyes were little red onions. I was scared you were really sick or something, but my mama said you were just a spoiled brat."

"I was not!"

"Alana, you cried till your Daddy peeled some bills out of his wallet. A few hundred, as I remember."

"That doesn't mean I was spoiled. I just appreciated nice things."

The two guys exchanged a knowing look.

"Stop the collusion. Can I help it if I have refined tastes? People just don't understand me."

After we finished eating, Xavier excused himself to go out for a smoke.

"Smoking again?" I scowled at him.

He pointed a finger at me. "Don't even start on me, woman."

As Xavier disappeared down the stairs, Trevor nodded toward him. "Now there's a good man. He gave up drinking so he doesn't influence me in the wrong way. Only problem is, he's back on cigarettes. Unhealthy, I know, but he's doing it for me."

"Xavier's a nutcase in his own right," I said. "And how about you? What are your plans? I'm glad you're OK. Is there anything I can do to help you stay that way?"

"I don't know. Don't know what I'm going to do, just know I can't go on the way I've been. The family business is no good for me, and honestly, I'm probably no good for the family biz. Mama never wanted a million dollar business; expansion means nothing to her. She wants to cook and fill folks' bellies and bring them comfort. And you've probably heard the family scuttle-butt about me, how I lost her some money with bad investments."

I didn't want to admit that I'd heard and I'd chimed in with my own condemnation of Trev, partly out of cousin rivalry, but mostly out of jealousy. Trevor had an enviable gift for charming people.

"It's been a heavy burden, thinking that I had to fill my Daddy's shoes, that I had to prove myself and make Mama's catering business an even bigger success. And

all along, everything I did, she tore it down, worked
against me 'cause it wasn't what she wanted. I was banging my head against a wall, hating her, hating myself."
He wiped a hand over his face. "Man, I was really
down on myself. One miserable brother."

"Trev . . ." I put a hand on his back and rubbed between his shoulder blades, wanting to say more, wishing I could tell him I'd believed in him all along, but I
couldn't bear to lie when he was being so honest with
me. "I was worried about you," I admitted. "Sometimes
ready to kill you myself."

He let out a laugh, though his eyes were shiny with
tears. "Yeah, I bet. But at least you gave a shit. You
cared enough to want to kill me."

We both snorted. "Honey, I'll still kill you if you
start abusing yourself again."

"Fair enough," he said. "I'll count on it. You know,
I've always wondered how you do it. How you keep
pushing on, don't let shit bother you, you just keep
going and finding things that make you happy, smiling
and all. I mean, look at you in that outfit that you
sewed, and you sewed 'em for all the girls because it
seemed right and you knew what to do and you got a
kick out of it, too. That's a gift, Alana. To get yourself
out there and pick what you want from life, like it's
yours for the taking. And the joy . . . you really feel it,
don't you?"

"Don't you?" I asked.

"Nah . . . sometimes, I think this earth might have
been better off without me. I've wished myself away,
thinking it would have been better not to be born at all,
not to feel the pain we all have to go through."

"Oh, Trev, no." There was a catch in my voice as the
level of his pain hit me, and I squeezed his hand on the
bar and closed my eyes and tried to send him positive,
warm vibes through my palm.

After a minute, he complained, "Hey, you're squeezing all the juice outta me."

"Damn you, Trevor Marshall-Hughs. Don't you ever, *ever* think the planet would be a better place without you. And don't be telling me it's not worth the ride. The good times make it worth the ride."

He sucked in a breath. "I don't know, maybe I'm too numb to feel anything good anymore."

I smacked his hand. "Then give yourself some time. That numbness is going to wear off and that pain is going to lift, a little every day. And one day you're going to wake up and smell the fresh air and lift your head to the sun and say, damned if my cousin Alana didn't tell me I'd feel this good again one day!"

"You're full of shit," he said.

"Come on, brother, give me an alleluia and an amen."

"Get out!"

I curled my fingers at him. "Come on. Come on, come on, come on!"

He sighed. "Yeah, OK. Alleluia."

When he rolled his eyes, I smacked his arm playfully, all the while hoping it was true. My cousin couldn't go on with this heaviness in his heart; he needed relief, some source of joy.

"You are one sorry black man," I said. "But just you wait. A few months down the road, you're going to be singing it like you mean it."

"I hope so," he said. "I really do."

46

Hailey

"Not to imitate Donald Trump or anything, but, Cruella, you're fired." There, I'd said it, now I just had to say it to my agent's face.

I took a sip of my grapefruit martini and checked the time on my cell phone. I was early; those old habits died hard. When would I remember that bad girls keep other people waiting?

Cruella was right on time, smiling that brittle, cheeky smile of a skeleton whose lips are starting to stretch away from its teeth. "Hailey? You're looking well. I almost didn't recognize you. You've changed so. Is it your complexion has cleared, or you've lost that midwestern innocence?"

This time I refused to cower at her insults. "I thought I'd give you one last chance to buy me a drink before I hit it big and move on to another agent."

She tried to fake cool, but I could see the skin tighten above her eyes. "Yes, I guess you have lost that midwestern innocence. Waiter? A vodka mart, with three olives."

"So . . . not to point out your lack of accomplishment, but what have you found for me?" I asked her, feeling almost as if I were possessed by Marcella. "I wasn't joking about that deadline. With the way my face is in the press, I know I'm a hot commodity in daytime TV. Sometimes it just takes an agent who's willing to exert a little muscle, make a few calls, beat the bushes, as they say?"

Cruella got her drink and tipped half of it back as if it were water. "I think I've got something, but I wasn't sure you'd want it. They need a villainess to kill off one of their lame story lines, but you need to think long and hard about taking that sort of turn in your career."

"Who's looking?"

"One of the networks. *Days of Heartbreak.*" She popped an olive in her mouth as if it were the last piece of Lembas bread in Hobbiton. "They need a player fast for a two-week commitment."

"When do I start?"

"But dear, think about it. You could be acting yourself into permanent villainy. Typecast forever."

Did I have a choice now that Deanna had typecast me as a kleptomaniac?

I picked up a toothpick and stabbed an olive from Cruella's martini. I took my time swallowing, then smiled. "Bring it on."

I tucked my silver Fendi bag under my arm, pushed the check in front of Cruella, then walked out of the restaurant.

Funny, but being bad felt kind of good.

* * *

"I'm telling you, the bad girl act worked like a charm. Cruella almost choked on her olives when I left her with the tab," I told my friends later at LA Minute, where Alana had gotten us a piece of prime real estate—a large round table near the foot of the fountain, so close that the occasional breeze kicked up cooling fizz from the base of Oscar's gold feet. "So I start tomorrow on *Days of Heartbreak*!"

"You're going to be on *Heartbreak*!" Rory clutched his chest. "I'm smitten with jealousy. Take me with you!"

"It's great news, Hailey." Alana's dark eyes glimmered with mischief. "But I'm a little sorry you didn't get a chance to fire her ass. Cruella sounds like she needs a little attitude adjustment therapy."

"Good for you, honey," Marcella said. "You went for it and you got it."

"Thanks to you, all of you. I've gotten so much mileage out of Alana's wardrobe, Marcella's advice and Rory . . ." He preened. "Well, you always make me laugh."

"Is that it?" Rory flicked a drop of condensation from his water glass my way. "That's like getting an honorary award at the Emmys. One of those 'we don't know how to thank you, because we don't know what the hell you did' awards."

"You know what I mean." At the moment, I was feeling high on my success, giddy and happy and light. It was a gorgeous August evening, my friends were enjoying my victory, and the restaurant around us was buzzing with word that a celebrity was in the house. They were talking about me and this time I was thrilled. I was going to be in the limelight again, on a show. Just a two-week stint, but certain to lead to other things.

A photographer came over to take our picture, and

Marcella made sure they spelled my name correctly and noted that I'd be appearing in *Heartbreak*. It was exciting to think my picture might join the other celebrity photos lining the hallway outside the first floor restrooms.

"Look at it this way," Marcella pointed out. "At least it's not *in* the john."

"OK, now for the bad news," Alana said. "The kitchen tells me they're out of scallops, and the cold lamb salad has mint in it."

"Oh, the trauma," Rory pined. "Who can count when they're accompanied by mint jelly?"

"Deal with it," Marcella told him.

"I'm so glad you were able to reserve this table for us tonight," I told Alana. "It's nice to have reason to celebrate. And after this, I'll need to keep a low profile for two weeks. I've got a job to go to in the morning!" I felt so giddy with joy; nothing could ruin this evening for me.

Then I saw Alana tense. "What is it?"

One of the hostesses came over to our table, pushing her headset aside. "Houston, we have a problem," she told Alana, then whispered something to her.

"Oh, no, she doesn't." Alana tossed down her napkin, stood up from the table, and took the transmitter off the other girl's head.

"Are you OK?" I asked.

Marcella sniffed suspiciously. "What's going on?"

"Looks like they're patching through someone important," Rory said. "David Geffen? Ryan Seacrest? Mary-Kate and Ashley?"

"It's Deanna. She's here, and she wants seating on the first floor."

I let out a brittle laugh. "Oh, great. She wants to join us."

She pressed the button on the headset. "This is Alana.

Make sure Deanna Childs is annexed to the caves. Do you copy? Deanna to the caves. . . . What do you mean, you can't?" Alana glared up at Oscar. "OK, fine. I'll seat her myself."

"Alana . . ." the hostess called after her. "Ms. Childs always gets a seat in the fountain room."

"Don't worry, Sage. I'll take full responsibility," Alana said as she hustled toward the door.

But she was too late.

Deanna Childs already stood poised at the entrance to the first floor dining area, sucking the life out of the room with one of her trademark mincing expressions.

Just the sight of her gave me a little cramp in my stomach.

Then my eyes glommed onto her escort and I nearly choked on my cosmo. "Watch out," I said to my friends. "Any minute, steam is going to shoot out of my ears."

Marcella groaned. "Holy shit."

Antonio Lopez stepped closer to Deanna and linked his arm through hers. I could tell he was unaware of the controversy brewing on our side of the dining room, until he noticed Alana heading toward him.

Like falling dominos, he and Deanna got the big picture. Antonio's gorgeous tan face went yellow, while Deanna seemed to suck more power from the promise of a confrontation.

"Oh, dear," Rory sighed. "Looks like Mom and Dad caught us out with the Caddy again."

"Are you OK, honey?" Marcella asked.

"I just want to kill him, the snake," I said. "But first, I'd have to torture him. Years of torture. Somewhere secluded, with no cable or Starbucks."

"You know, this is all beginning to sound uncannily similar to a story arc we did in the late eighties," Rory said. "I really must get out of daytime."

Alana was talking to them a mile a minute, but Deanna shook her head, pushing past my friend.

"Hailey?" Deanna said in a snotty voice. She hustled within spitting distance, then paused, as if I were supposed to bow or curtsy. "I take it you're the reason these girls are reluctant to seat us here?"

"Do you think?" I rolled my eyes. "Because honestly, I don't give a rat's ass whether they seat you here or down in the Columbus Circle subway station. I'm beyond you, Deanna. Yup. I'm moving on to *Days of Heartbreak*, and it's going to be interesting, playing in a show that runs opposite yours."

"You don't have a chance," she said, dismissing me with a wave.

"Maybe. Or maybe I'm going to kick your sagging butt right out of the time slot."

It was satisfying to see her hand slide down, as if checking the sag of her ass. The power of suggestion.

"Guess I should thank you for giving me the kick in the pants I needed on *Tomorrows*," I said. "But you know what? I don't really like you enough to be that civil."

Deanna lifted her chin to answer, but without writers, I think she was at a loss for a dramatic rebuttal. Instead, she just huffed.

"So . . . move along. Go on," I said gently. "Scat, you two. Bye, bye, now. We're having a little celebration here, and I hate for you two to suck up any of the love flowing so freely here."

Deanna pivoted and stomped away, but instead of leaving the dining room, she wove around to the other side of the fountain.

Alana tossed up her hands. "What a piece of work!"

"Would you just go?" I asked Antonio.

He shrugged. "I can't control her."

"That's no surprise," Marcella observed.

Meanwhile Alana followed Deanna around the fountain. We all craned our necks, trying to watch the action.

"What about that table?" Deanna shouted, pointed over diners' heads. "Or that one. You know, usually they reserve a table for me. In fact, I wouldn't mind the one where your friend is sitting."

"I have a lovely table for you," Alana said. "On the third floor."

Deanna trudged on around the fountain, almost full circle now, like one of those figurines that circle a clock face on the hour before they get slammed back inside a little door.

"Young lady, I hate to have to do this to you, but I guarantee you, if you cannot find us seating by the fountain, you will not be working here tomorrow."

I started to stand up, but Marcella pulled me down. "Alana can fend for herself," she whispered. "Don't insult her."

With a big, gracious smile, Alana glanced around the room, then clapped her hands together. "Oh, look at that! There is a spot by the fountain."

When Deanna crossed her arms smugly, Alana stepped forward and gave the actress a firm shove.

"Waaaah!" Deanna shrieked as she fell back into the fountain, the spangled hem of her gown and her gold lame sandals flopping over the side like a fishtail.

"Holy fountain of youth, Batman!" Rory exclaimed without moving. "The diva is taking a dive."

Marcella and I grabbed each other's shoulders in shock.

"I don't believe it!" Marcella gasped. "I'm happy I was here to see it, but I don't believe it."

Antonio rushed forward to help her out, but a photographer was already there, snapping away at the many faces of Deanna as a drenched rat.

"You . . ." Deanna wiped her drenched curls back and rubbed her eyes. Mascara dribbled down her cheeks in an ashen fade, and one fake eyelash was hanging loose. "You!" She pointed at Alana. "You will pay for this!"

Alana crossed her arms and tossed off a shrug. "Yes, probably so," she said. "But it will be well worth the price."

47

Alana

Joe Allen's. I knew that. I was at the bar, with Trevor and Xavier.

How had I gotten there? That part wasn't so clear.

Not that it mattered. Here I was. Hailey was home asleep. Had to sleep for her job in the morning. Marcella and Rory, too.

Me? Don't need sleep. May never sleep again. May never work again.

And I liked that job at LA Minute. I really did.

Mr. Minute Man. What a pip. Nice guy. He hadn't fired me—yet—but he hadn't been there tonight. Took his wife and daughter to a baseball game. Nice guy. Wasn't there to see Deanna take a bath.

I started laughing. It was pretty funny. But not good for the restaurant. I knew that. Oh, what had I done? There's a moron inside me.

"I think I really fucked up," I said. "Oops!" Hand on my mouth. "Did I say that too loud?"

Trevor turned to me. "Did you say you are fucked

up? Or that you fucked up? 'Cause there's a difference, though I think both of them are true."

"Don't talk to me about drinking, you . . . Mr. Buddy." I pinged the pint glass in front of him on the bar. "Downing that stuff all night long."

"It's ginger ale. I'm done with all those addictive things. Well, everything except women."

"And women are the worst kind of addiction," Xavier added.

"I hear you," Trevor said.

I looked up at Xavier. Teeth so white . . . dark, chocolatey skin. Dimple in his chin.

"Yeah, we're talking about you," Xavier teased me.

And I wanted to cry. Xavier, my loyal friend. My pal. He'd always wanted something to happen for us. I pushed him away. Why? Why did I?

Again, the moron in me.

"You've always been there," I said. "And I wasn't. I'm so sorry." A tide of emotion swirled up and bowled me over.

"Aw, man, is she crying?" Trevor asked. "Is she crying? She's crying! Alana! What's the matter, girl?" He turned away. "Can't stand it when they cry."

"Come on, now." Xavier hoisted my left arm up over his shoulder and started walking me. The door opened and we were outside but he was still holding me up.

"Think you can stand?" he asked.

"Sure." And he released me and I turned and let myself fall against him, his lean, hard body, so solid and good.

I love you. I have always loved you, but I was too stubborn to let it show, too stupid to recognize the signs.

Had he heard me? He didn't answer, except for the deep sound of his breath.

"Oh, girl, we need to get you home," he said.

"Come home," I murmured.

"Yeah, yeah, don't worry." His arms pressed into my back. My support.

Something about a cab. And my bed . . . how I loved my bed.

48

Hailey

What a difference a reputation makes.

When I walked onto the set of *Days of Heartbreak*, everyone who saw me went out of their way to say hello, to give me directions, to make sure things were going smoothly. I passed a group of actors running lines, and they called out my name and burst into applause. I saluted them, feeling awkward but flattered. The security guard insisted on phoning Dante Ponce, the executive producer, who wanted to meet me immediately. Me! What a difference.

I just about danced up to his office, then remembered my new bad girl image and went for "pleasantly surly" as he brought the director, Piper Robinson, in to officially "greet" me. Me!

"We're pleased to have you with us." Dante spoke with his head listing toward the side, like my three-year-old nephew who preferred to see the world sideways. "I must say, your reputation as a hipster party girl and Deanna-basher precedes you."

"OK." I laughed. "Not sure if that's a good thing, but I'm looking forward to this role."

"I just have to ask you . . ." Piper paused, then said, "did you help push Deanna in the fountain last night? The occasion was your party, wasn't it?"

"Well . . ." I thought of Marcella's advice: let them think you're a girl behaving badly. "Let's just say, Deanna definitely made a splash at that event. And no, I didn't push her; I was too busy chasing Antonio Lopez with a butter knife."

They got a good laugh over that one.

"We're going to have a marvelous time working together," Dante said from his sideways pose. "Piper directs most of our episodes, and we're really a small, happy family. I'm sorry the writers have brought you in for only two weeks, but if things work out we'll get them to whomp something up for you."

"You can always return from the dead," Piper said. "I don't think they find your body when you die next week, do they?"

"No, no body," Dante assured us, "so we're good for the long-term. My assistant will show you your dressing room. Oh, and we've lined up a limo driver to bring you back and forth to the studio. Don't want our talent getting stuck in the subway."

"Sounds good," I said casually, restraining the urge to jump up and do a happy dance in Dante's office.

If this worked out . . . wasn't that what Dante had said?

Ooh, if I could get a regular role on a soap, wouldn't that burn Deanna's butt?

Success is always, always the best revenge.

49

Alana

Have you ever had a hangover that lasted the entire month of August?

In reality, I guess mine lasted only a day or two, but when I was finally feeling better, it was clear that the consequences of my wild night were going to last the rest of my summer. My parents had seen a photo of me in the newspaper. It showed me standing beside the Oscar fountain, where Deanna was railing, fists in the air. Not a bad shot. The smile on my face was a little smug, but then, I looked a hell of a lot better than the dripping Deanna.

"This is not the sort of publicity befitting a Marshall-Hughs!" my father had bellowed.

Like I didn't know that?

I wanted to ask him what a Marshall-Hughs was doing reading *Soap Opera Diaries*, since my incident didn't receive any coverage in the *Times*, but I had learned that the judge does not like to be cross-examined.

Then there was my final visit to LA Minute, where I

picked up my last paycheck and said good-bye to my coworkers. "You were the best!" Sage cried on my shoulder. "You made us these fabulous uniforms and got this place working like a Swiss clock. I'm so sorry about the Deanna incident. I keep feeling like I mishandled it."

"It's not your fault," I assured her. "You did the right thing. Who can figure out someone like Deanna?"

Minute Man seemed the most upset of all. "We're going to miss you around here," he said. "I wish I could keep you on, but after dumping a celebrity guest in the fountain, well . . ."

"I know." Add to that the fact that Deanna had threatened to sue the restaurant if I wasn't fired and it became clear that my days at LA Minute were over.

"But I'd like to keep you on as a seamstress for the staff," Minute Man offered. "The guys have been complaining about their shirts. I guess they're jealous of the girls' uniforms. And I really want them to have a new look by the time *Vanity Fair* does a piece on us in two weeks. Do you think you could swing it?"

"Actually, I'd like that," I told him. Before I left, I got measurements from a few of the guys—which, I must admit, was wicked fun—then I headed straight to the garment district in the West Twenties and Thirties. Most of the shops in the district don't sell to individuals, but when I'd worked on the women's uniforms I'd managed to barter my way in and strike up a few deals.

The men's uniform posed a new problem: men's fashion wasn't as wild, and short of putting them in tuxes, which would be expensive and uncomfortable, nothing immediately came to mind. The first day I explored various fabrics, chatted up the shop owners who spoke English, and window-shopped the men's garments they had on display. Then, since a decent breeze was blowing, I walked a block west, bought two hot egg rolls—gotta eat them while they're hot—and a copy of *GQ*, and sat among the students on the odd little plaza outside the Fashion Institute of Technology, where the rule seemed to be the more outlandish your attire, the higher your grade.

Two students sitting near me were talking about some sort of competition. I couldn't see their faces, but the girl wore a colorful turban on her head and the guy was extremely skinny from the back.

"Aren't you entering?" the girl whined. "You have to enter."

"Why? They never pick the best designs. It's all about who's blowing who."

"So? Then you should win."

"I don't care enough about it to pour myself into a design. For that prize?"

"Free tuition doesn't work for you?" the girl asked. "You want to be in debt the rest of your life?" She flipped open a notebook. "What do you think? Do I have a chance?"

I stole a peek over their shoulders. It was a sketch of a woman in a long India print gown. Interesting.

"You want a shot at winning?" the kid said. "Then start sleeping with Vera Nichols."

She slapped him on the shoulder and they headed off, but I lingered in the shade, wishing I could go with them. What did you learn in "fashion school"? Like any routine it became tedious, I was sure; still, I was intrigued enough to navigate my way around the school to the admissions department to pick up a catalogue. Fashion school. Daddy would get a good belly laugh out of that.

After two days spent struggling with the design for the men's uniforms, I proposed a simple gray T-shirt and sport jacket with black pants. "It may sound boring," I told Minute Man, "but the look is very Hollywood producer, and I found a cache of brushed cotton T-shirts that look very upscale, with darker jackets in a linen blend. Now, the jackets will need some alterations to the individual body type, but I'll do that myself." I handed him a sketch that I'd made. OK, I had traced the basic body shape, but the rest was my own work. "It's a clean, polished look, and it will come in on budget and on time if you approve."

I think the sketch won him over. It's amazing what colored pencils can do.

"OK, Alana," Danny said, handing me the sketch pad. "I'm going to trust you on this one. But make sure the uniforms are here on time. I don't want the guys looking like sad pirates when *Vanity Fair* comes."

Twelve days and counting . . . I had to start the alterations immediately.

Which made me miss the phone when Xavier called the first time. The whir of my sewing machine drowned out the chime of my cell. When I retrieved the message, I felt a little of that hangover nausea all over again.

"Hey, girl. Just calling to check up on you. You recovered yet? OK. Give me a call."

My heart thudded painfully in my chest as I thought of him. Not that the details of that night were clear, but I did have a hazy memory of throwing myself against him, falling into his arms. Please! I'd probably slobbered on the man.

Had I blabbered that I was falling for him?

I didn't remember. I thought of calling Trevor to pump him for information, but then he'd make an even bigger deal of it. And really, I couldn't be falling for a stand-up comic. Not Xavier. He wasn't my type at all, and pretty soon he'd be out in LA full-time, working on his new show.

The second time he called, he caught me coming out of the shower. I fell onto my bed and tried to think of the right words to say.

"I've been worried about you since the other night. Are you OK?"

"Fine! I mean, that night was a huge mistake, drinking the way I did. I was out of my mind."

"Yeah. Actually, you were kind of funny, but I could tell you'd lost control."

"Really? Did I say anything I should be taking back?" I probed.

"A few things that didn't make sense. Look, Alana, I know it's awkward, but we have something between us and I . . . I just don't think we should pretend it doesn't exist. You hear what I'm saying?"

"I hear you," I said. "But what's the point? You're headed out west, and . . . I don't know, X. We never did get along. Maybe it's just bad chemistry."

"So what do you suggest we do about it?"

"Keep a safe distance apart. The West Coast, that should be far enough."

"Yeah, but I'm still gonna call you."

"Don't torture yourself," I said. *Don't torture me,* I thought as he made a joke about my bad mood and hung up.

The third and fourth times Xavier called, I didn't pick up, but I saved the messages on my voice mail. For some sick reason, it made me smile to hear his voice. I kept thinking of the way he looked in that silly hat when he was the manager of McDonald's back in high school, and I smiled even more.

Oh, Lordy, I'd really stepped in it now.

50

Hailey

"Good afternoon, Ms. Starrett." Mr. Barnes tipped his hat as he held the door open for me.

"Thanks, Mr. Barnes." My heels clicked over the marble floor of the Manchester lobby, and I felt tempted to break into a tap dance. Good news does that to me.

"Ms. Marshall-Hughs had some visitors up there, but they just left. Three fine-looking gentlemen." He lowered his voice to add, "Mrs. Abraham in 8-F was complaining, but I told her she should enjoy those fellas while they're here."

I smiled. A few of the neighbors had expressed concern over the stream of men visiting our apartment lately, but Alana didn't think she needed to explain herself, and she had so little time to do the alterations for the entire male staff that she had stopped going back and forth to LA Minute and started calling the guys to stop by the Manchester instead.

Upstairs, I turned the key and pushed open the door. "Honey, I'm home!" I teased. "And I've got news."

Alana tipped her head back from the pool of light around her sewing machine. Her hair was pulled back in a ponytail atop her head, and she was dressed in skinny gray sweats with an oversize Harvard T. "Hey, there! What's the word from the outside world?"

"People like me!" I threw up my arms. "Cruella called me at work to let me know that I'm getting a Soap Opera Lovers Award. Can you believe it? Viewers voted me for it! But the ceremony is this Thursday and I need a dress. Dante let me tape early so I could leave and go shopping, and you have to come with me."

"Hailey, that's great!" She was already turning off her sewing machine and ducking into her bedroom to change. "That ceremony is televised, right?"

"Yup. I have to write a speech. Oh, God! Think of some pithy bad girl comments."

"For that you need to call Marcella."

"And you have to come with me to the ceremony. I can bring someone, and we'll have a blast. I mean, you should be finished with all your uniforms by then. So you need a gown, too." A few weeks ago, this would have been a disaster, but now that I'd earned some money on *Heartbreak*, I could afford a new gown. Even Marcella would agree, it was a business expense. "Where should we start? Bergdorf's? Saks?"

"The garment district." Alana emerged from her room in a smart red-and-white print sundress with a white duster. After an entire week in seclusion here, she still knew how to step out. "I know a place where we can get last year's designs for wholesale prices."

"Last year's?" I winced.

"Trust me. You'll save thousands of dollars, and with a few alterations, which I can do for you, no one will ever know the difference."

"But honey, you have no time. Those uniforms have

got you sewing round the clock, and I need my gown by this Thursday."

"I'll fit it in," Alana said. "Besides, I need a break. Those jacket alterations have me seeing pearl gray in my sleep. Do you know how complicated an alteration is when you have to cut into the lining? Please! Thank God the fabric is exquisite. Otherwise I'd be suicidal."

After we rode the subway downtown—I know, pee-yew, but it's one of Marcella's rules—Alana took me around to half a dozen places where she knew the vendors well enough to negotiate. We found a few possibilities but settled on a fabulous Dior—a bright red, off-the-shoulder gown that needed just a tiny bit of alteration in the waist. For Alana, we went with a Prada, a layered chiffon in various shades of brown from chocolate to russet to terra-cotta. Hers needed to be taken up, but Alana was up to the task, and the price was right. After Alana bartered with the vendor, the two gowns cost us less than five hundred dollars. Of course, we'd had to endure trying things on in tiny closets in the back of the shops, but it's all a trade-off.

On the subway ride home, I realized how much the tenor of our shopping trips had changed. And there was something else: Alana had changed. She was distant, a little too thoughtful.

"Are you OK?" I asked.

She frowned. "My head is all tied up in my work. And in Xavier."

"Uh-oh." I shook my head. "Men are always trouble, aren't they?"

"That's for damn sure. And I'm crazy about him. Can't stop thinking about him, though I'm hoping it's just a phase. That's possible, right?"

"If you feel that way, why do you keep pushing him away?" I asked. "Why not tell him exactly how you feel? I think he's got a thing for you, too."

"Nah." She waved me off. "It would never work."

"Why, Alana Marshall-Hughs, I think I've finally found something you're afraid of. You're afraid of falling in love."

She bumped into my shoulder as our train skidded to a stop. "That's a crock. I'm just overwhelmed with work right now. My perspective is all warped."

I just smiled. We both knew she was lying through her teeth.

51

Alana

Two more darts on Bear's jacket.

Heath needed to have the sleeves taken up, and I was almost finished pressing Robert's.

I was down to the wire, with *Vanity Fair* coming to LA Minute tomorrow afternoon, but things were under control. I could spend the rest of today altering Heath's sleeves and fixing up my gown for tonight's awards ceremony. Then, I'd have tomorrow morning to work on Bear's jacket, shower, and run these last jackets over to the restaurant. Piece of cake.

Just then there was the sound of a key in the door. "Hailey?" It was early for her to be home, but then with the awards ceremony, maybe they'd given her some time off.

"We have a slight problem," she said, staggering in the door, a sling strung over her purple silk blouse.

"Oh, my God, what happened to you? Sit down, honey."

"I'm OK. It was a really stupid accident on the set. I stood up into the open drawer of a file cabinet."

"What?"

"Don't ask. Everyone was all apologetic about it, but it was my own stupid fault. And now, my shoulder is all black and blue, just when I'm ready to slip into a shoulderless gown."

"That's right! Oh, you poor thing!"

"The doctor said I can forgo the sling tonight, but I need to keep the tape on." She shook her head. "I feel so stupid. And if I don't show at the ceremony, people will think I'm an ungrateful snob."

"You have to go. You must! We'll find something else for you to wear. There's got to be a gown with shoulder coverage in one of our closets, and if it doesn't fit properly I'll alter it right now." I got up from the sewing machine and marched Hailey into my room. "Come on, Cinderella. Time to whip up a gown."

Going through our closets, I was amazed at how many formal gowns revealed shoulder. All of my Veras, Oscars, Valentinos . . . such a waste!

A gold brocade Dolce & Gabbana jacket covered everything, but it was just too hot and heavy for August. But other than moving a beaded jacket onto another gown, we were running out of choices.

"Wait a second." I pulled out a Dior Homme skinny-legged tuxedo in a shimmering black fabric. "Remember when Nicole Kidman kept appearing around town in this? It's very chic."

"But still, so hot."

"So . . . leave off the blouse. We'll stitch it closed. That way, you can show a little cleavage, wear a stunning jeweled necklace that will sparkle on camera."

"And the man-style tux pokes a little fun at the bad-girl image." Gingerly, Hailey slid one arm into the jacket. "Let's see how it looks."

The seat of the pants needed a few tucks, as I had it let out for my buxom butt. "I'll take it in a little in the back, and you'll look killer cool."

"Thank you!" She gave me a one-armed hug, then slid off the jacket. "You're a lifesaver. I need to lie down now, before I pass out. I think those painkillers are kicking in."

"You rest! I'll wake you up in time to get ready," I said over the straight pins in my mouth.

I got to work, quickly realizing that the delicate fabric of the Dior pants would not survive my old sewing machine; every stitch would have to be sewn by hand. Working like a fiend, I sewed through the afternoon. By three o'clock, I was only halfway finished, and it occurred to me that there would be no time to alter my gown for tonight. I called Rory on his cell and arranged for him to play Hailey's escort.

Hours later, while Hailey finished her makeup, I smoothed out the last tuck. As she slipped on the pants and straightened out the jacket, I felt tears sting my eyes. She had endured so much this summer: her battles with Deanna, her heartbreak over Antonio, her public image, and her career struggles. But somehow, seeing her all sparkly and ready to accept a prominent award, it seemed that all those obstacles were part of the course to prepare her for this moment.

"You look so beautiful," I said, as if this were the payoff for my weeks bent over the sewing machine.

"Well, thank you, honey." And that was the moment she realized I wasn't dressed. "You're still in your sweats! Chop, chop! We don't want to be late."

"I called Rory. He's going to be your escort."

"Oh, no! You have to come! You deserve part of this award for yourself!"

"There's no time," I said, quickly trying to usher her down to the waiting limo. "I've got some more work to do for LA Minute. I'm exhausted and, stupid of me, but I forgot to do those alterations on my gown."

"Because of me!" Hailey's voice cracked as we stepped into the elevator. "You're always on top of that stuff, but you dropped everything to sew for me today."

"Honey, it's what I do," I said in a stern voice. "Listen, I've been stuck inside the apartment so long that those bright camera lights would probably blind me right now." The limo sparkled in the late-afternoon sun outside the Manchester lobby. As we approached the door, Rory climbed out, looking dapper in a navy tux.

"Hailey!" He waved. "They have cosmos and Caribbean martinis in here. What's your pleasure?"

She turned back to me. "I'm sorry for treating you like Cinderella."

"You'll have time to make it up to me. Now go and have a good time. A *great* time." I stepped into the sunshine and watched Hailey duck into the limo.

"Now I know it's difficult, Rory, but don't tie one on until after the ceremony."

"Right." He clapped his hands together. "Teetotal now, drink heavily later."

"And take good care of Hailey. Her shoulder looks nasty."

"Got it!" With a smile for the driver, he ducked into the limo.

I stood back to watch them pull away. That was when I saw him, watching me from across the street. He didn't wave or smile or anything, just waited until the traffic cleared, then crossed over.

"We need to talk," he said. "Where've you been? I've been calling you."

"I know." I couldn't admit that I'd been saving his

messages and listening to them when I felt lonely. It was a wimpy thing to do.

"Can I come up?"

"Sure," I said, trying to think of how to play this. Xavier knew me too well for me to lie. If I was going to deny my feelings for him, I needed some kind of diversion—a ruse to distract him, throw him off.

Once we got upstairs, he noticed the mess of fabric and scissors on my dining room table. "What, you running a sweatshop here?"

"It's my new job." I scraped the little wisps of hair off my forehead. "I'm making uniforms for the male staff at LA Minute, and actually, I've got a night of sewing ahead because it's all due tomorrow, so how about if we talk some other time?"

He straddled a dining room chair and loosened his tie. "Uh-uh. It's taken me this long to get through to you and I'm not going away now. You work. I'll watch."

"Come off it! You think I'm going to sit here sewing with you in my grill?"

"Well, you'd better get used to it, 'cause that's how it's going to be. I'm not giving up on you, Alana."

I felt the saltiness of tears forming in my throat, and I went to the window and looked out at the August haze of dying light. I wasn't in love with Xavier. This heightened emotional state was all about me being stuck in here for two weeks and sewing my heart out and sending my best friend off to the ball in a dress made out of rags like Cinderella. These tears had nothing to do with the man behind me. . . .

"When you gonna stop running, Alana?"

"I'm not running." I turned to face him. "But I've changed, Xavier. I've learned a lot about my limitations, my center of strength, my scope of control. And I don't think you can fit in there. We make each other crazy!"

"Good crazy, girl."

"I've worked so hard to get where I am now. I just can't give up that control."

He leaned on the chair and took a deep breath, obviously disappointed. "Tell me about the changes."

"Well, first, I don't want to rely on any man. I just learned a valuable lesson from my father, and I'm not going to toss it aside just because some hotshot comedian comes along throwing money on the bar. I'm earning my keep, and liking it."

"Ouch. But I hear you. Nobody's taking your independence away from you."

"And I'm not giving up my life here, my friends and family, to go out west and pursue someone else's dream."

"Yeah, I sort of got that message loud and clear. You drive a hard bargain, but I've made some changes of my own. I think I talked the cable network into letting me tape my show out here."

"Oh." That seemed to change a lot of things. "You did that for me?"

"For us."

I winced. "There is no us."

"Oh, yes there is. If you recognize that there are certain things in this world that we can't control. Sometimes somebody throws you a line, and you just got to catch it and hold on tight and enjoy the ride."

Dammit, I knew he was right.

I turned to him, those high, brown cheeks, dazzling white teeth. I put my finger in the dimple on his chin.

He scrunched up his face and pushed my hand away. "Can't stand that."

"Women love dimples."

"Yeah, all your aunts and your mother got their fingers all over my chin like I'm eight years old."

I laughed and put my finger back on it. "Like this?"

He grabbed my hand and pulled me into his lap. "You trying to drive me crazy, girl?"

"Damn straight."

"Well, it's working." He pressed his lips against mine in a soft kiss. I threw my arms around his neck and we both groaned and the pressure of his lips became more demanding.

I wanted him in the worst way, wanted him forever, and I knew that it was one of those things neither of us could fight anymore. We were meant to be together, raised together, fighting together, loving together. Sometimes those things just happen and people click, and pity the moron who doesn't figure out how to stop trying to stop the spinning wheel of destiny.

That night, we ordered Chinese, but I have to admit none of the food got eaten until it was cold. And you know what? For once, I really didn't care.

Part Six

**DON'T MISS THESE
LABOR DAY SAVINGS!**

52

Hailey

"Can you give your fans an overview of how your life has changed in the past few months?" Zoe Lemonda asked, holding a mike out to me.

We were on the set of *Days of Heartbreak*, and Zoe was doing her first on-camera interview for *Soap Opera Diaries—In Person*. The publication had decided to go multimedia and run a weekly show on a cable station, and Zoe had picked me to be the first featured interview.

"Let's see . . ." I smiled. "I have more money for shopping sprees, and no time to spend it. I spend most of my days and nights here on the set."

"All work and no play?"

"Oh, there's plenty of time to play, especially when you're surrounded by friends. It's just that we do it here in the studio and we get paid for it."

"And you've become a star in that time! How does that feel?"

"Wonderful! Exciting! Spectacular. Although my

friend Alana says there are no stars, just huge balls of burning gases. Took me more than two years in the industry to realize she's right."

"You wouldn't be referring to Deanna Childs, would you?"

"Did someone mention the Queen of Mean? I just have to say, I owe her a lot. If she hadn't falsely accused me of a crime, I would still be stuck on that show playing a fish-face. I mean a mermaid. Thanks, Deanna."

"And not to get personal, but how about your love life? Any truth to the rumor that you might be getting back together with Antonio Lopez?"

I shook my head. "Antonio and I . . . had a very special relationship," I said, trying to restrain myself from pointing out on camera that he was a lying, cheating pig. "But that's over now. And to be honest, I can't believe I was involved with an actor." I turned and looked right into the camera. "Girls, it's a mistake! Actors are crazy! Stay away from them!"

Zoe laughed. "Any new romances in the works?"

"How could I have time for that?" I teased. "I'm here twenty-four hours a day." But as I spoke, my gaze went beyond Zoe to the director, Sean Ryder, who had been hired over from *Tomorrows*. When Dante offered Sean a chance to direct, something he'd been working toward for years, Sean quit *Tomorrows* and never looked back.

And last week, we'd finally gone for that cup of coffee. Unassuming, articulate Sean . . . I enjoyed spending my days and nights with him when he was directing.

"One last question: what do you see in your future?" Zoe asked.

Watching Sean page through a script with a cameraman, I took a deep breath. "Possibilities," I said. "Some great possibilities."

53

Alana

"Alana, my dear, do you have Rory's shirt for the dream sequence?" Eden Barrio, the wardrobe director, peeked her head into the back room and smiled. "Not that it's a rush, but he's standing here half-naked."

"I'm just steaming it out now," I said, holding the steamer over a stubborn wrinkle near the collar.

"Truly, I don't mind doing the scene half-naked," Rory said, stepping into the sewing room where we repaired, altered, and prepped clothes for the actors. "It is a dream sequence, and as we all know many elements in our dreams don't make sense. Not to mention the fact that I always get more fan response when I go bare-chested."

"Wear the shirt," Eden called. "Our demographics are a little different from *Tomorrows*. Sometimes families watch."

"Oh, well." Rory smiled at me. "Worth a try. And truly, Eden has much better taste in clothing than that witch I left in the dust. If I had to wear one more golf shirt, I was going to scream. I think the country club look put ten years on me."

"You survived it well," I said.

"And look at you, slaving away, doing the drudge work. I don't know why you ever agreed to submit to such chaos."

"I love this job," I said. "The one drawback is pain-in-the-ass actors who want to appear on camera half-naked." I handed him the shirt.

"Doll, if I'm your worst problem, you'd better count your blessings."

I'd been doing a lot of that lately, grateful for my job as wardrobe assistant on *Days of Heartbreak*, grateful for my chance to attend the Fashion Institute of Technology, grateful for the special person in my life, the only one with the unique ability to please and torture me at the same time. Xavier had pushed our relationship on, and for once I was glad to be pushed. He'd managed to convince the cable network to let him shoot his show on the East Coast, and in the process, he'd hired on a new producer, his trusted friend Trevor. Since Trev took the job, he'd been working long hours, wheeling and dealing, but it was all good this time. He'd found a niche, and hell, I could relate.

Oh, and speaking of being grateful? There was one more biggy for me: peace with the parents.

I had appeared at a family council to plead my case, but this time, I'd come prepared with a plan, which included a financial statement and graphs that Marcella had helped me prepare.

"My spending is under control now," I said. "Pages three and four detail my monthly budget. The essentials like food and household items. With the money I'll be making on *Heartbreak*, I should have my credit-card debt paid off by February, when I plan to start making my own co-op payment. There's just one glitch."

Daddy had stared at me over his reading glasses.

"I need to ask you for a loan. Just a loan. I've enrolled at FIT. The Fashion Institute of Technology, in their design program. Marcella says I can work my schedule at *Heartbreak* around my classes, so I'll still be making money."

"FIT." Daddy let my proposal sail onto the table. "An appropriate name."

"Now Ernest," Mama warned him, "have some respect for Alana's goals. She's found something that will make her happy—right, dear?"

"I want to be a designer, Daddy. And I can do it. I know I can."

Tension rose when Daddy stood up and pushed away from the table. Mama and I exchanged a worried glance. Was he going to walk out?

Instead, he stepped forward, took my hand, and pulled me into his arms.

"I'm so proud, Alana. Finally, *finally*, you've found something to do with your life."

Mama beamed with pride and gave me a thumbs-up as I peered over Daddy's shoulder. "Children," she said, "you all grow up so fast."

"I have to ask you, though . . ." Daddy stepped back. "What was the catalyst for this? After all my years of lecturing on budgets and work ethics, what finally turned your view of the financial world around?"

I thought of the fiery redhead who'd once wrestled with me over a tube of lipstick. "The truth? I found a personal budget trainer."

Out on the set, they were getting ready to roll tape, so I went out to stand by for costume repairs. Balancing the job with school was going to be a challenge for me, but it would combine practical, hands-on work, like costume repairs, with design history and theory.

Hailey had used her clout with the producer of *Days* to get us all in the door—Rory, me, even Marcella, who had decided to take a job as a production associate, a position that utilized her managerial skills to the fullest. As I walked toward the lights, I passed her at the edge of a darkened set, negotiating with someone on her cell phone.

"What are you, crazy? I can't pay that much to rent a bunch of movie theater seats. Their sets look so fake, anyway. You tell him I said that. And tell him that he can cut his prices in half or we'll forget the movie theater scene. . . . Honey, I don't care! The writers will move it to the park or the pizza place or something. And did you get me that cat for the Tuesday taping? . . . Long hair, short hair, I don't know. Talk to the story editor."

I waved to Marcella, then noticed someone flagging me down from the exit. That gorgeous face and bright smile, my honey-lamb. X had convinced the network to shoot here in New York, and as luck would have it, his studio was on the same side of town. Sometimes we got together during lunch or dinner breaks.

"Alana!" he hissed, trying to keep quiet for the taping. "Your father called, said he's been trying to reach you."

I jogged over to him so we could keep our voices low. "Oops. I turned my cell phone off last night and forgot to turn it back on."

"You can't leave your cell phone off. The man was frantic."

"As I recall, we were a little busy, and you were the one who didn't want any interruptions."

"Well . . . anyway, he wants us to come out to the

Hamptons house. Thought maybe you could finish the redecoration you started at the beginning of the summer."

"Did you tell him there's no time? I start school next week, and the show has only one tape day off."

"He's your father, Alana. I can't tell him no. He told me to tell you he had to get rid of the green chairs. The fabric was splitting by July."

"Told him so."

"It was really strange to see his name on my cell. I mean, he's always been like an uncle to me. Uncle Ernest. And now, to think that he'll be my father-in-law . . ."

"Whoa, there, brother. Nobody said anything about getting married."

"Oh, come off it, Alana. You know you want to."

He was right, but I wasn't ready to concede yet. I loved giving him a hard time. "I'm just starting off on a new career. And we've just started officially dating. And you know what else? You're gonna have to work for me."

He put his hands on my hips. "You think so?"

"Absolutely. I want to be wooed, Mr. X-Man. Wined and dined."

He grinned. "You planning to spend all my money on expensive shoes and dresses, right?"

"Please!" I shook my head. "When it comes to shoes, I'll spend my own money."

54

Hailey

"Oh, look at these! They're so cute I can barely stand it." I held up a little wooden shadow box painted in pastel teal, blue, and summer white. Inside the glass, the frame contained white sand and a few tiny shells that shifted gracefully when the picture was moved. "Don't you love it?"

"That would work in the new pool house bathroom," Alana said thoughtfully. "You know that tiny alcove between the shower and the vanity? And it goes well with the decorating theme. The question is, which one works best?"

Marcella waved her hand at us. "I say get two. At that price, they're a steal."

"Really?" I gaped. "Now you're talking crazy talk."

"And we should all get some of these little plastic caddies," Marcella said. "They're really handy for organizing drawers and cupboard space. You know? So your lipstick doesn't keep rolling to the back of the drawer. Pens and pencils stay where you want them. You could even use them to organize your sock drawer."

"Like any of us has time for that?" Alana carped.

"You'd be surprised." Alana adjusted her fabulous Fendi sunglasses on her head. "When you get organized, you have time for these things. And look at these brandy snifters, ladies. You know, winter is coming. Wouldn't these come in handy when you want a little something to warm up you and your honey?"

"I'll take two," I said, placing the brandy snifters in my basket, which was filling up. "Or maybe not. Should I put the organizers back? Or . . . I don't know. I've got an awful lot of merchandise here."

It had been a long time since I'd shopped with such abandon, and I worried about undoing the progress I'd made with Marcella.

"What did I tell you about shopping with purpose, honey?" Marcella asked. "If there's need, if there's a purpose, and if the price is right, you can go for it."

I let out a sigh of relief. "I can buy all this?" That tiny thrill was rising again—the adrenaline rush of a worthy purchase.

"I know," Alana said, turning a statue upside down to eye the manufacturer. "It's nice to be back in the game again. Tap that wild huntress within us."

"Honey, this is one place you can let the huntress go wild," Marcella said. "Thank God for the dollar store."

Smart, perceptive, and deliciously funny, Roz Bailey's novels are impossible to put down. In *Postcards From Last Summer,* she follows the lives and loves of three girlfriends as they reconnect in the Hamptons each summer for cold margaritas, hot hookups, and plenty of drama . . .

WISH YOU WERE HERE . . .

Darcy Love is a lot like her lipstick-red convertible: fast, pampered . . . and sometimes off the road. Though she's still cruising guys and playing it loose enough to worry her friends, she knows that this will be the summer when Kevin, the love of her life, finally falls for her. This summer is supposed to be a hot one, and she's planning to make it even hotter . . .

Every summer Tara Washington regrets leaving her quiet and sane friends in Manhattan for the Hamptons—until she gets there. It's such sweet relief to cut loose and be away from the unending pressures to meet a man who's also African-American. She loves the craziness of the Hampton girls, especially her friends, and before long she's getting crazy right along with them . . .

Lindsay McCorkle just *knows* she's the only woman on the beach who shouldn't be wearing a swimsuit. Spending the winter indulging her passion for ice cream and chocolate hasn't helped her figure—or her confidence. For once she'd like to meet a guy with a brain, but that doesn't mean she can't occasionally give in to the temptation of a hunky lifeguard's kiss . . . or *more* . . .

From friendship to freedom to sex—and everything in between—Darcy, Tara, and Lindsay will make this and every summer unforgettable as they pick up the right guys, the wrong guys, the tab, and, always, each other . . .

Please turn the page for an exciting sneak peek of
Postcards From Last Summer
coming next month in trade paperback!

May, 1997
Southampton, New York

"**A**nybody here?" Darcy hugged the container of take-out sushi to her chest, hoping that one of the cleaning ladies or the day maid, Nessie, might still be around.

She hated coming home alone. Next time she was going to drive Kevin straight over and dump him on the overstuffed sofa. Even passed out, he'd be more reassuring than the hollow darkness.

Damn Kevin. Damn Nessie, too.

When there was no answer she braced herself and stepped into the grand foyer, hardwood floors gleaming up at her, the new tapestry-print runner zigzagging up the stairs looking more welcoming than last year's cream burber carpeting. Mother had swept through here with Miguel, her design consultant, last month and ordered a few decorating changes, but no amount of renovation or redesign could bring the life that was lacking to this house—people.

Darcy hated being alone in the house. She was often the only one living here, and some nights, when she was alone in bed and listening to the scrape of tree branches against the side of the house, she felt like the last person on earth.

Lowering the thermostat, she wished Kevin had come home with her. Even if he wanted to sleep, it would have been better just having him in the house, but somehow he didn't get that. No one understood how lonely Darcy's perfect life was inside this architectural gem.

The Love Mansion was the envy of anyone who dared to trespass down the private Mockingbird Lane. Darcy saw them sometimes from her bedroom window—faces looming in the open windows of Mercedes and Audis, twenty-somethings in big, bruising SUVs soaking up eyefuls of the lush, luxurious estate. But Darcy wanted to yell at them that it wasn't all it seemed. Despite the family name, this gorgeous house had never become the warm, familial home she'd dreamed of when her parents had purchased it from a famous actress. Dad had rarely spent more than a weekend here. As CEO of a giant corporation, his job had always demanded his presence in the office, in the boardroom, in the convention center. On the rare weekend when he did make it out to the Hamptons, Bud Love spent his time barking on the phone by the pool or golfing with business associates. And while Darcy's mother, Melanie Love, had plenty of time on her hands, she'd always found it difficult to extract herself from the social whirl of their home in Great Neck, the Garden Society, and the girls at the country club and, of late, the young tennis pro at the club who Darcy suspected was fooling around with her mother. Disgusting. Not that Mother hadn't kept herself in good shape, but really, what did a young, okay guy like Jean-Michelle see in her mother, a woman as regal as a cathedral statue and cool as cucumber gazpacho?

No, the Love Mansion had never fulfilled its name. Couldn't feel the love in this place. "It's all crap!" she once shouted down from her window to a bald man with the nerve to drive by in a Porsche convertible. "It's *crap!*" He'd turned that dick-mobile around pretty fast.

"Hello?" Darcy called out again, but Nessie was long gone. Damn. Although Ness had done a good job cooking and corralling Darcy and her friends for many years, Darcy didn't really need her anymore. Twenty-one and going into her last year of college, she didn't need a nanny. And now, each afternoon, Nessie seemed eager to get back to her own family in Riverhead, Long Island, much to Darcy's regret. She didn't blame Nessie, and she didn't know how to ask her if she could occasionally stick around to keep her company, to make some normal household noises and ward off the evening shadows.

If only she could have a big, noisy houseful of people, the way it was at the McCorkle house. Darcy loved staying over with Lindsay, listening to Granny McCorkle's stories and sitting at the dinner table with all the cousins. She'd have to work on Lindsay and wangle an invitation for tomorrow night. Though Lindsay had seemed a little testy on the beach. Ach! Poor Lindsay had blimped out and wearing those boy swim trunks only made it worse. Darcy couldn't understand how her friend could let herself go that way. For chrissakes, why didn't she just stop eating? And then, when Darcy tried to help with a little joke, Lindsay and Tara just weirded out. Whatever. But they'd get over it if they wanted to hang out with Darcy. And they always did.

Darcy hopscotched down the hall, stopping to stare into the darkness that loomed there. The living room, or parlor, as Mother called it, was way too grand for anyone to ever relax or want to spend any amount of time there. A large stained glass piece set into the center window always reminded Darcy of a medieval chapel, and the silk upholstered furniture, including authenticated pieces from one of those King Poopypants dynasties, made the room feel like a museum. Darcy paused in the doorway, wondering for a moment if she'd ever, in fact sat in that room.

She padded barefoot over the Chinese rug and chose the red silk chair, sitting like a queen on her throne. The chair creaked, and a faintly musty scent mixed with the mango-coconut smell of her suntan lotion. Wouldn't Mother freak to know she was getting Coppertone on the antiques.

Whatever.

Popping open the container, she bit into a slice of California roll, not worrying about the grains of rice that fell to the floor. That's what the cleaning people were for, right? Gotta give Nessie and the girls something to do.

The cozier den in the back of the house, with its brown suede chairs, entertainment center, and gray stone fireplace was more her style. She snapped open a diet Pepsi, turned on the VCR, and sank into a chair to devour sushi and catch up on the soaps she'd missed that day. The characters of daytime dramas were Darcy's year-round friends, and they never failed to appear with a new scandal or heartbreak, a thorny, submerged problem that made the issues swirling beneath the surface of Darcy's life seem simple and harmless. Soaps broke through the hollow aloneness. So what if her mother was sleeping with a tennis pro? Affairs were a daily occurrence in soaps. And all the accusations swirling around Dad's investment firm were petty grievances compared to the serial murderer, switched-at-birth babies and vindictive lovers of the daytimes soaps.

Watching as two lovers shared a kiss on a moonlit balcony, Darcy glimpsed her own future, and it was good. No more putting up a happy front and knocking around in empty houses. No more being alone. No more just Darcy . . . but Darcy and Kevin. The McGowans. Mrs. Kevin McGowan . . . God, that sounded good. Together, Darcy and Kevin were going to make a life right here on America's Riviera, where Kevin's father already owned a small gold mine. She and Kevin would have money, houses and cars, great bodies, and lots of good sex.

Really, when you got down to it, what more could a person want?